The Race for the Lost Keystone

Val Rutt is a teacher and lives in North London with her husband, two children and a spaniel called Dave. She would like her readers to know that they must never give chocolate to dogs – in spite of their keen interest in the stuff, it is extremely bad for them.

PUFFIN BOOKS

Published by the Penguin Group
Penguin Books Ltd, 80 Strand, London WC2R ORL, England
Penguin Group (USA), Inc., 375 Hudson Street, New York, New York 10014, USA
Penguin Books Australia Ltd, 250 Camberwell Road, Camberwell, Victoria 3124, Australia
Penguin Books Canada Ltd, 10 Alcorn Avenue, Toronto, Ontario, Canada M4V 3B2
Penguin Books India (P) Ltd, 11 Community Centre, Panchsheel Park, New Delhi – 110 017, India
Penguin Group (NZ), cnr Airborne and Rosedale Roads, Albany, Auckland 1310, New Zealand
Penguin Books (South Africa) (Pty) Ltd, 24 Sturdee Avenue, Rosebank 2196, South Africa

Penguin Books Ltd, Registered Offices: 80 Strand, London WC2R ORL, England

www.penguin.com

First published 2004
3

Copyright © Val Rutt, 2004
All rights reserved

The moral right of the author has been asserted

Set in Monotype Baskerville
Typeset by Rowland Phototypesetting Ltd, Bury St Edmunds, Suffolk

Made and printed in England by Clays Ltd, St Ives plc

British Library Cataloguing in Publication Data
A CIP catalogue record for this book is available from the British Library

ISBN 0-141-31747-7

The Race for the Lost Keystone

VAL RUTT

To, Edward,
Best wishes
Val Rutt

PUFFIN

*This story is dedicated to the memory
of my father, Norman Rutt*

*And with love to
Richard, Alice and Dan*

*I am eternally grateful to Annie Graham
for the generous loan of her eccentric family
(including Fearless) and for inspiring and
motivating me to write this book*

A Secret Revealed

Everyone has heard of ordinary families living ordinary lives, and everyone thinks they know one. Everyone who knew the Reynolds family believed them to be perfectly ordinary. And perhaps to a point they were. At least from the outside.

Kate, and her younger brother, Philip, lived in an unremarkable part of England in an ordinary house. They went to school, where Kate did rather well, and both were ordinarily happy. They had ordinary, caring parents.

Like countless other families they had goldfish and a cat. One of the fish had once leapt from its tank and survived overnight in a toy box, while the cat was surprisingly sprightly for its age – but then, pets often have their quirks.

Kate had straight, thick brown hair and interesting eyes; unusual perhaps, but not extraordinary. Phil, freckled and untidy, had a chipped front tooth – not uncommon in nine-year-old boys who would as soon climb a tree as look at one.

Kate looked at Phil and she saw an irritating little

brother, much like the ones her friends had, although in fact (and she kept this thought very much to herself) he was not as annoying as most of them. Phil looked at Kate and saw a smart and clever goody-two-shoes who could fight like a terrier when roused.

So, an ordinary brother and sister then. It is true that their dad was English and that a childhood accident had nearly killed him and that their mother was American and had travelled the world; but then, every ordinary family has its share of drama and intrigue to be recalled at wider family gatherings.

Yet Kate and Phil both had a feeling about themselves that suggested they were not as ordinary as people might suppose. This feeling did not preoccupy them unduly: it was a faint tug in their hearts that became a little more vital each summer of their lives. As July warmed up, most people relaxed into the longer, warmer days and looked forward to the summer holidays. It was at this time that the tug in their hearts became more of a rolling wave in their stomachs, and Kate and Phil had a feeling that something out of the ordinary was going to happen. This was not just fancy on their part (perhaps an outsider would see nothing amiss or suspicious) but for the children there were definite signs that things were not quite right.

One Saturday morning, as he was about to walk past the kitchen, Phil overheard his mum and dad talking together in such serious tones that he hesitated at the door. His mother's earnest voice caught his attention;

what did she mean about 'duty' and 'keeping a promise'?

And then his father replied: 'I just don't understand you, Charlotte. You've always agreed with me before. We were going to wait until the children were much older. There's no way that they're ready for –' Then, sensing Phil's presence perhaps, he stopped, and both parents turned to look at the doorway, while Phil, trying to appear nonchalant, continued on his way. He heard them discussing the earthquakes, volcanic eruptions and other disasters that were being reported on the news as if they were resuming a conversation about the terrible state of the world. But Phil knew what he had heard even if he did not understand what it meant. He decided to talk to Kate about it.

On his way to her room Phil glanced out into the garden and saw Kate's feet sticking out of the tree-house window. Their dad had made the house nine years ago for Kate's third birthday, and now she had to double herself up or spill out of it to use it. Still, she liked to read in there.

Phil, who at nine and a half was not much shorter than Kate, abandoned the idea of using the rope-ladder to get to the door of the tree house and instead climbed into the plum tree. This was Phil's preferred way up – not least because he knew Kate couldn't do it. Not that Kate admitted anything; she always made out that it was just plain silly to climb up the tree and scramble in through the window when there was a perfectly good ladder and door, but Phil knew the truth: Kate couldn't stand heights. Phil was not a particularly mean-spirited boy, he had never teased Kate about this phobia, but when you are nine and your sister is twelve, such things are useful to know.

Phil swung himself up and over a branch and stuck his head through the window so that he was peering, upside down, directly into Kate's face.

Her response was immediate: 'Go away.'

'Something's up with Mum and Dad,' said Phil. 'They've gone all whispery and weird.'

Kate sighed, pulled her legs in, and wriggled sideways on her bottom to make room. Phil swung himself over and upright, tucked his feet neatly through the window and slid into the space Kate had just left. He settled himself, cross-legged, beside his sister and both leant their backs against the ship-lapped wall.

Kate sighed again. 'It's to do with those phone calls. Did you see the way Dad jumped out of his skin when Gran phoned last night?'

'It's got something to do with Gran then?' a puzzled Phil asked.

'No, twerp ... Dad didn't know it was going to be Gran, and it was before he answered that he looked really nervous. It's like they're expecting bad news.'

Phil said, 'They've got to keep a promise. I heard Mum say so. Maybe someone phones up and says, "Hey, you better keep that promise you promised me." I think it's happened before you know: them being weird about the phone ringing.'

It had, in fact, been happening for as long as Kate could remember.

Her earliest memory that things were not quite right was when she was five years old. She and her mum had walked home from school together. They had held hands and some of the time they had skipped and then Kate had run ahead and jumped out of gateways and her mum had screamed with mock fright. That day was especially memorable because Phil was ill and not at nursery school. The walk home without him and without Mum being constantly distracted in case he shot off the pavement or fell over was wonderful. They reached home and Dad had been there at the gate waiting for them, with Phil in his arms. Kate could remember feeling cross at seeing them; she was enjoying having her mum to herself. She could also remember her dad's face, pale and worried, beside Phil's, flushed deep red from his virus, his puffy eyes half closed. As they had come up the garden path, the phone had begun to ring and Kate's annoyance had turned to unease as her mother dropped her hand and rushed inside to answer it.

Over the years there had been other occasions, and though they were too infrequent to be terribly disturbing, each event had been upsetting in its own way. And with each incident Kate had put her imagination (which was just as vivid, though more practical than Phil's) to work on a theory to explain these mysterious phone calls that set her parents all of a jitter.

She decided to tell her brother what she secretly thought. For the last three years Kate had made a note of the phone calls in her diary, and she had recently seen a connection. The call always came during the last week of July.

'Actually, Phil, I think it's about me. I think someone phones each year to ask if they can see me, and I think Mum and Dad don't want them to.' She hesitated, took her finger from the book she had half closed and turned to look directly at her brother. 'I think I'm adopted, and my real parents want to meet me. I reckon they must call up on the anniversary of the day they gave me up for adoption. I think Mum and Dad are scared in case I like my real parents better.'

Phil thought about this for a moment while staring doubtfully at his sister's face, then he said: 'You can't be adopted, Kate, you've got a green bit in your left eye just like Dad.'

Kate was quick to answer and she spoke enthusiastically: 'Yes, I know, I've thought about that. That's exactly why they chose me when they saw me. They decided it was fate and they had to have me.' Then, as an afterthought, Kate added emphatically: 'You're not adopted; I remember you being born.'

Phil sat for a moment, taking in his sister's news. He had an itch on the sole of his left foot and he was trying to wiggle his finger down inside his sock without taking his trainer off.

'My feet itch,' he announced. 'Gran says that when

your feet itch, it means you're going to visit some place you've never been before.'

'Don't count on it,' said Kate, then she added thoughtfully, 'although I suppose my real parents might live somewhere amazing and you might get to visit me there.'

Kate smiled to herself as they sat quietly for some moments, both imagining a succession of exciting locations where Kate's real parents might live.

'What are you going to do about it?' Phil asked at last, banging his itchy foot against the side of his other shoe. 'About being adopted, I mean.'

'Well,' Kate said, frowning and inching herself away from her fidgety brother, 'I've decided to meet them. I reckon, even if they're really nice I'd probably stay living with you guys and just visit them for holidays and stuff.'

Phil and Kate spent the next few days rapt in thought. Their speculations were fuelled by any contact they had with their parents, who were definitely behaving oddly. At mealtimes Kate noticed the way her father's gaze darted away from her face every time she lifted her eyes from her plate. And Phil overheard his mother talking to the cat, not in the usual 'good puss', sweet-talk kind of way, but as if she were actually asking the cat his opinion about something. She was cooking dinner and the gleaming knife in her hand hovered over a board of partially chopped onions. Phil, of course, knew what onion-chopping did to a person, but it troubled him to see

7

his mother's eyes full of tears, and it bothered him more to hear her asking the cat what he thought the right thing to do might be. Then, just as Phil turned away, he thought he saw the cat shrug. It was the smallest and least perceptible of movements, but his mother seemed to nod in response as she brought the knife down sharply and resumed chopping. As Phil climbed the stairs back to his room, his mind echoed with the thought of one word and he muttered softly, 'Weird . . . weird . . . weird . . . weird,' with every step he took.

And so the days passed, with Kate and Phil continuing to do all the ordinary, everyday things like going to school, eating meals and watching television, while their hearts were quietly troubled and their minds were preoccupied. For Kate, the possibilities concerning her biological parents' wealth, physical beauty and exotic occupations afforded much pleasurable mulling over. Phil's day-dreaming, however, took a more sinister turn. He had a horrible, hollow feeling in his tummy that wouldn't go away, despite the prospect of the summer holidays.

As he arrived home on the afternoon of the last day of term, an alarming notion sprang into his mind. It shocked him, both by its suddenness and by the accompanying tidal wave of nausea that hit his stomach. Kate was wrong – Mum and Dad weren't keeping some terrible secret about her at all.

The whispered discussions whenever they thought he was out of the way, the anxiety every time the phone rang – it all added up, Phil realized at last, to his parents' deliberating about whether or not to send him to boarding school.

The truth, having come to him in a flash, now played itself out effortlessly in his mind. Each year they waited for this fabulously strict and stern headmaster (called something like Dr Theodore Sprake) to phone and offer them a place for Phil at his remote boarding school.

As if he were in a darkened cinema watching a film, the world around Phil became lost to him and a vivid scene unfolded in his head. A broad gravel drive disappeared between two vast wrought-iron gates, above which, swinging in the wind, hung a sign.

MURKYGORE TOWERS

Centre of academic excellence where home comforts, along with visits from parents, are not allowed.

Recoiling from this dark and gloomy image, a new scene began to play itself out in Phil's mind.

It is a grim winter's day and icy rain sweeps across London. Hurrying home to his loving family, Michael Reynolds hears a most peculiar sound: a combination of screams and gurgles. He turns and follows the sound to some steps which lead down to a canal. There, thrashing about in the oily water, his thin, beaked nose pointing skyward, is the drowning Dr Theodore Sprake. Without the slightest hesitation and with utter disregard for his own safety, Michael Reynolds dives to the aid of the previously doomed man.

Duly rescued, Dr Sprake expresses his eternal gratitude to Michael Reynolds with an annual telephone call offering his son, 'Master Philip', a free place at Murkygore Towers. Michael Reynolds promises that one day, when the time is right, he will accept this kind offer. After all, he has a duty to educate his son to the highest possible standards. And, of course, the telephone call would come at the end of the summer term so that everything would be settled in time to pack Phil off the following September.

The canal scene, as vivid as an action replay, returned to Phil's mind. There was the struggling man and there was his father dashing down the steps and racing to the water's edge.

The clarity of the image startled Phil and he cried out suddenly: 'Dad! Leave him, leave him – push him under, Dad!'

Hot-faced and shaken, Phil sat down on his bed. He looked around at the posters of Premier League players, his books and his miniature pool table. He reached a hand across his bed and found the squashed and tatty bear that had been new when he was a week old. He saw the papier-mâché puppet he had made in Year Two and the incomplete and dusty cut-out cardboard model of a Roman amphitheatre he had been given for Christmas. He felt homesick in his own bedroom.

Kate, meanwhile, had pondered and wondered about the identities of her birth parents until she could no longer bear the suspense. The peak of Phil's anxiety coincided with Kate's resolve to demand that Mum and Dad could no longer keep her from her destiny. The two children met on the landing and hurtled downstairs, shoulder to shoulder. Looking wild-eyed and determined, they arrived at the kitchen together and spoke simultaneously.

'I know I'm adopted,' Kate cried defiantly. 'You can't keep it from me any longer. I know – I've always known!'

With a more desperate edge to his voice, Phil berated them: 'You can't send me to that terrible school. I'll starve! They'll beat me, I'll grow up weird like the man outside the library who thinks he's Napoleon – I bet he went to boarding school!'

Now, Charlotte and Michael Reynolds were affection-ate and caring parents who thought they knew their children well. However, they had absolutely no idea how great an effect their own worries were having on them. They stared at them in astonishment.

At last Michael Reynolds looked at his wife, who nodded her agreement.

'Well,' said their father, 'I think it's time we told you two what's going on.'

*

The family sat together at the kitchen table. Barking, the cat, walked in at that moment and stopped dead in his tracks to see them all sitting there, it not being a meal-time. Then, with a flick of his tail he sauntered off as if to say he did not much care what they did anyway.

Michael Reynolds cleared his throat and looked at Kate, which made her stomach lurch, and she was suddenly not sure that she wanted to hear what was coming next. She scraped her chair forwards and shuffled her feet closer to the table so that the wings of the chair almost touched the table's edge and her small frame was nestled in a shell of wooden armour. She glanced at her brother who, for once, had nothing to say.

'Each year, since you were a baby, Kate,' Michael began, gazing at her small face, 'we have been asked by your mother's Aunt Elizabeth if she can take you . . .' he paused, 'on holiday.'

For the children, who had been considering strange and wonderful explanations, this was totally unexpected and completely . . . dull.

'Who is Aunt Elizabeth?' Phil asked.

Charlotte Reynolds took a deep breath and sighed. 'Your Great-Aunt Elizabeth,' she said slowly, 'is a very unusual person.'

'Why haven't you told us about her before?' Kate wanted to know.

'It's a little difficult,' Charlotte began, glancing at her husband as she spoke. 'She really is . . . um . . . extra-ordinary.' Both Kate and Phil were now giving their mother their full attention. She continued: 'When I was a little girl growing up in America, I spent most of my time with Aunt Elizabeth – it was wonderful and, quite simply, extraordinary. Aunt Elizabeth taught me so much, it was amazing.'

'What sort of things did she teach you, Mum?' Phil asked as relief and curiosity finally snuffed out any trace of the boarding school.

Charlotte stole a quick look at her husband.

'Well, she taught me to read . . . and to swim . . . and to play the drums . . . and, well, once she taught me to fly a helicopter.'

It was their dad's turn to sigh, while Kate and Phil sat, wide-eyed and gaping.

'What your mother should also tell you,' said their dad, 'is that while teaching your mother to read, your Great-Aunt Elizabeth managed to lose her for three days and nights in the Vatican library in Rome. That her ability to swim was learnt with great urgency 750 kilometres from shore in the shark-infested Pacific Ocean.' He stood up and began pacing the kitchen floor. 'That she learnt to play the drums while being held prisoner by jewel thieves in Central America and,' he spluttered, 'the helicopter incident is a United States Federal secret.'

Phil looked at his mother as if he was seeing her for the first time. 'Wow!' he said. 'You can fly a helicopter! Do you think Aunt Elizabeth would teach me?'

'Most certainly and definitely not,' his father cried.

Kate's mind was a jumble of thoughts. Suddenly

her daydream about being adopted seemed silly and commonplace. She tried to make sense of her parents' secrecy and worry.

'So,' she said, 'every year, on the same date, Great-Aunt Elizabeth phones and asks if she can take me and Phil with her on holiday, and you don't want us to go?'

'Every year,' said her dad, 'I think of an excuse so that you won't have to. It was easier when you were younger, and then last year Phil was getting over chicken-pox, and, the year before, your asthma was bad.'

'But I want to go,' Phil interrupted him. 'Why can't we go?'

'We really think,' said Michael, glancing at his wife for support, 'that it is just too dangerous. It's twenty years since your mother's last *vacation* with her aunt, she is a pretty old lady now and she wasn't very, well, responsible then.'

Charlotte reacted angrily. 'Mike, that is unfair and untrue!'

The Reynolds children were very interested and not a little uncomfortable at this outburst. Barking, who had been washing himself in a triangle of sunshine on the kitchen floor, sprang across as if he had been called and jumped up on to Charlotte's lap. As Charlotte stared steadily at her husband, Barking stood on her lap and glared at him, his fat tail vertical and swishing across Charlotte's face like a windscreen wiper.

After a moment Charlotte spoke, quietly but firmly.

'There are lots of things about Aunt Elizabeth that I can't explain, but I know the children will be all right.'

Kate and Phil looked at their dad.

'OK,' he said slowly. 'Why don't you tell them about your last trip with Aunt Elizabeth?'

With a deep sigh, Charlotte slowly nodded her consent. 'My Aunt Elizabeth has always been involved in – well, I suppose you could say she solves crimes.'

'She's a detective?' Phil asked with joyous incredulity.

'Not exactly. She is just, well, she kind of gets involved in things – a good citizen, I suppose you could call her.' Charlotte continued her story. 'When I was about your age, Kate, Aunt Elizabeth and I were in Zanzibar, where your great-aunt had stumbled across an appalling trade trapping wild animals and sending them to America and Europe as pets. The organization behind the trade was run by a terrible, evil person. I am afraid that on that occasion Aunt Elizabeth did ...' Charlotte's voice lowered slightly and she glanced carefully at her husband, 'make a mistake. Unfortunately, while buying fruit in a market, I was kidnapped.'

For the spellbound children this was shocking indeed, but their mother was sitting in front of them, their pet cat in her arms – living proof that her story would have a happy ending. Along with all the other extraordinary confessions they had just heard, neither Kate nor Phil could see why a kidnapping should be worse than being lost in the Vatican or held prisoner in a cave.

Charlotte looked at her son and daughter's expectant

faces and continued: 'Aunt Elizabeth rescued me, of course, but my kidnapper vowed to strike again one day, and warned that next time there would be no escape. The kidnapper was someone Aunt Elizabeth had crossed paths with before – it was a threat we had to take seriously.' Charlotte paused, then continued in a lighter tone of voice. 'So I changed my name from Gina to Charlotte and came to England where I was adopted by George and Martha – Grandpa and Gran, to you.'

'*You* were adopted!' gasped Kate.

'Yes,' Charlotte smiled, 'and before I was adopted I went to boarding school,' she added, lifting an eyebrow in Phil's direction.

For a moment everyone was frozen in the silence of the kitchen: Charlotte with a small smile on her lips, Kate with her fingers over her mouth, Michael with a hand over his eyes and Phil with a wide and slightly inane, open-mouthed grin on his face.

And then the phone rang.

Lampton Laboratory

Many thousands of miles from the Reynolds home in England, Emily Carter neatly sidestepped an elderly man who had stopped dead in front of her, and she continued to glide effortlessly past her fellow passengers. Unencumbered by luggage or companions, she trailed her compact-wheeled suitcase behind her where it kept a constant distance from her heels like an obedient dog. She had always been able to fit her possessions into one bag. She had always travelled like this, even as a child, when she had endured the company of one unknown chaperone after another. The arrivals lounge at Reno airport echoed with the tannoyed announcement of flight details. It was crowded with people who were trying to keep together, in couples and family groups, and establish who was responsible for the masses of shared baggage. A harassed woman stood beside a pile of luggage, trying to hold on to two small children who scrabbled and slid a frantic game of tag round and round her legs. Her eyes kept returning anxiously to the spot where her husband had disappeared into the crowd to look for a trolley, some moments before. Emily slipped through the chaos and was the first to pass between the automatic doors and be greeted by the line of expectant faces gathered to meet the passengers of Flight 934.

She saw her chaperone immediately; he stood to one side and held up a card in front of his chest with her name on it. It reminded her instantly of her earliest memory. As a crawling infant of nine months old she had sat straight-backed before a faceless person who held flash cards in front of her for hours at a time. Emily Carter was the product of a social experiment called hot-housing. An orphan, she had been raised by an educational trust. Over the years, a succession of carers and tutors had been responsible for her, but there had been no long-term relationships; she had no family. The face behind the flash cards was blurred and unmemorable, but twenty-three years later she could still see the writing on the cards as if it were yesterday. When baby Emily had spoken her first words at the precocious age of ten months it was not 'mama' or 'dada' that issued from her lips but 'hydrogen, lithium, sodium, potassium' and the rest of the elements in the periodic table.

Emily stopped for a moment to study the young man who had been sent to meet her. She estimated that he was about her own age. He was tall and stocky and his hair had been cut, almost shaved, into a scalp-hugging crop. He looked like a bodyguard or one of the bouncers who stand outside nightclubs and vet people on the way in. Emily smiled to herself; he had glanced at her as she appeared in the arrivals lounge but had then looked away. He was expecting Professor Carter to look different. A man, most probably, a middle-aged one with dishevelled, greying hair, not a fair-haired, slightly built young woman.

Emily Carter walked purposefully towards the man and he looked straight at her but still did not understand. As the automatic doors opened again, he leant to one side in order to look past her at the new arrivals.

She stood in front of him and held out her hand. 'I'm Professor Carter, pleased to meet you,' she said.

The card with her name on fluttered to the floor as he jumped into action, taking her hand and reaching with his other to take her suitcase from her.

'And my name's Eddie – Eddie Bardolph.' He looked her up and down and began to chortle. 'I thought you'd be ...' he began, but his voice trailed away as Emily raised her eyebrows above her large, round spectacles. 'Right then, let's go to the car and get you delivered to Mrs Lampton.'

He turned to go, but Emily remained where she was, startled by his words. She had discovered only a few weeks previously that it had been Lorabeth Lampton who had overseen her education and kept her living in complete, if lonely, luxury her entire life. Emily had written to thank Lorabeth Lampton for her patronage but had received no personal reply, merely an official letter telling her to report for work at a location in Nevada, and enclosing a plane ticket. She had not anticipated actually meeting her mysterious benefactor on this trip.

Emily caught up with Eddie as he was dropping her small case into the boot of the car. He moved forwards swiftly and opened the door for her.

'So,' he said, as he swung himself into the driver's seat and turned the key in the ignition, 'you're coming to work for Mrs Lampton?'

Eddie checked the rear-view mirror and had to angle it down in order to see the small woman in the back of the car. She was looking out of the window and seemed determined to ignore him.

Eddie smiled broadly and continued, unabashed. 'I'm new myself. Following my dad into the firm. He's been with Mrs Lampton for donkey's years; they go way back, him and Mrs Lampton. What about you? You following in your dad's footsteps? A scientist, was he?'

Emily turned her head away from the stunted scrubby vegetation outside and sighed. 'I don't know. I never knew my parents.'

'You didn't?' He was interested now and studied her closely in his mirror. 'What made you come then?'

Emily felt irritated, but she saw no option but to answer him. 'Well, Mrs Lampton has been very kind to me. She paid for my education, my keep, lodgings – everything.'

Eddie gave a low whistle. 'Are we talking about the same Mrs Lampton?' he asked.

'I wouldn't know,' Emily snapped. 'This will be the first time I have met her. In fact, until two weeks ago the identity of my benefactor was entirely unknown to me.'

Eddie turned his head and looked directly at her. 'You're kidding me, right?'

'I assure you I am not.'

Eddie drove on silently for a full minute, his broad shoulders shaking slightly.

Suddenly he threw back his large head and roared with laughter. 'Man, oh man, are you in for a surprise!' was all he managed to say before great blasts of Ho! Hoo! and Ha! racked his body again.

They had been speeding along what was little more than a desert track and he continued howling with laughter as he turned the car through a gateway set in a large perimeter fence. Ahead of them a vast metallic building shimmered in the blazing sun of the red desert.

'Here you are,' he snorted as he wiped tears from his eyes with the sleeve of his black suit. 'Home sweet home – Lampton Laboratory!'

A Heartstone for Kate

Phil was delirious with excitement. His normally busy mind was on overdrive and, as thoughts went rushing through his head, he was compelled to keep his body moving. That joyous end-of-term feeling was now exaggerated by the prospect of adventure, and the first Saturday morning of the holiday found him running furiously round the garden, whooping and jumping. Every so often he would dash in to his mother with a question.

'About how many snakes were there in the rebel's cave exactly?'

'Did you meet the president of the United States?'

'Does Great-Aunt Elizabeth really eat chocolate all the time?'

'What does she look like?'

While Charlotte attempted to answer this barrage of questions, Phil remained still barely long enough to hear her before resuming a loud and hectic circuit of the lawn.

Kate, too, was excited in her own quiet way. Everything had suddenly and dramatically altered, and she noticed the difference everywhere she looked. Her home, her bedroom, her very life itself, familiar as it was, had somehow taken on a new quality in the light of her parents' revelation. She even felt physically different, and it was a delicious sensation, as if she were conscious of each individual cell in her body.

Late in the afternoon, Kate found her mother in her bedroom, sitting among a pile of old papers and letters.

Charlotte smiled at her daughter as she slipped quietly into the room. 'Hello, sweetheart.'

Kate sat on the edge of the bed, one foot tucked under her while the other dangled free. 'Mum, how come Great-Aunt Elizabeth chases criminals and stuff? I mean, it's not what old ladies do, is it?'

Charlotte nodded in agreement. 'No, it isn't what you would expect at all, but then your Great-Aunt Elizabeth isn't your common or garden old lady.'

Kate waited for her mum to say more, but she fell silent and continued to leaf through a closely written notebook.

'What's that you're reading?' Kate asked eventually.

Charlotte looked up and studied Kate's face for a moment.

'I'm looking through some things I wrote when I was a girl.'

'Did you keep a diary?' Kate asked. 'Can I read it?'

'I've been wondering whether to let you read it. I know your head will be teeming with questions about Great-Aunt Elizabeth and why I've kept so much a secret from you.'

'Shall I just read it . . . I can ask you if I don't understand.'

Charlotte frowned, 'I think it will be better if you wait until you meet Great-Aunt Elizabeth and start finding things out for yourself.'

Kate felt a sudden rush of irritation. Why on earth did adults think it was all right for them to withhold information but it was sneaky when children did it? But she knew better than to take her mother on in an argument down *that* road. If she was going to get her mother to tell her stuff, then she was going to have to ask the right questions.

'Mum, when you got cross with Daddy, you said that we would be safe with Great-Aunt Elizabeth . . . well, how can you be sure? . . . I mean, Phil will probably fall out of a tree at least . . . he does, most summers.'

Charlotte smiled at her daughter and, moving aside some papers and letters that obscured it, lifted an old-fashioned book on to her lap. It was thick and the pages were edged with gold. A small ornate clasp held the book closed. As Kate watched, fascinated, her mother unlocked it with the small key that she always wore on the chain round her neck. She turned the book over and lifted the back cover to reveal a cut-out hiding place in the middle of the page. Wedged into the hole was a small black box. Charlotte pulled the box out and held it out to Kate.

'This is for you.'

Kate nodded, but she just looked at the box in her mother's proffered hand and did not take it.

Charlotte sighed. 'It does seem totally bizarre for an elderly woman to be a crime fighter. When you meet her you'll hardly believe she is real.' Charlotte examined Kate's face closely. 'You have a lot to learn and you will have to learn from your own experiences – not mine.'

Kate took the box at last and opened it. Inside was a necklace, a small black stone on a dark-gold rope chain. Kate had seen the curiously shaped stone before; it was similar to one that Barking wore on his collar.

She looked up at her mother quizzically. 'A necklace?'

Charlotte shook her head. 'No, darling, it is much more than that. It is a heartstone and it will protect you; it has a special sort of energy – a power.' Charlotte frowned as she struggled to explain. 'Remember what I said earlier, about Great-Aunt Elizabeth making a mistake in Zanzibar? Well, it was my mistake – I removed my heartstone. I had been wearing it for so long, I just wanted to see how I would be without it. I soon found out. I thought I could just slip off to the market like an ordinary, normal girl. One moment I was in a bustle of people queuing for mango, then suddenly I was yanked backwards into darkness. I had been taken completely unawares, with no sense of any danger at all. Had I been wearing the heartstone, that would never have happened.' Charlotte smiled into her daughter's bewildered face. 'Which is how I know that you will be safe. Perfectly safe,' she added, 'just so long as you always wear the heartstone.'

'Why don't you wear it? Why have you kept it in a box?'

Charlotte glanced into the box then back into Kate's

eyes. 'I made the decision to live an ordinary life, marry Daddy and have a family . . . Aunt Elizabeth didn't need me, after . . .'

She broke off and gently touched Kate's arm.

'But now Aunt Elizabeth needs you, Kate. It is your turn to wear the heartstone.'

Kate took the necklace from the box and, holding the stone in the palm of her hand, she studied it. It felt surprisingly warm; it was deep black and had a curious kind of fogginess to it. She turned it over, and there, on the other side, was a faint red glow. Her mother saw it too and exclaimed, 'Oh my goodness!' And then, 'I might have guessed! Such a strong reaction!'

'What is it?' Kate asked, alarmed, dropping the necklace into her mother's hand, where the red glow intensified.

Charlotte quickly picked it up by the gold chain, allowing the heartstone to dangle. 'Kate – you are meant to wear a heartstone, and you will soon learn what it and you are capable of. Now we had better get ready because that old aunt of mine is on her way.'

'But how . . .?' Kate's voice trailed away. She did not know what question she wanted to ask.

Charlotte unclasped the necklace and reached out to put it round Kate's neck. Her deft fingers snapped the clasp in place and she took Kate's face in her hands. Charlotte smoothed back her daughter's thick, dark hair and looked carefully into Kate's flecked eyes.

'There. Great-Aunt Elizabeth will seal it for you and

then there'll be nothing to worry about. The things you will be capable of, now that you have the heartstone, will exceed your wildest dreams.'

Kate's brow furrowed in confusion.

Charlotte sighed, looked skyward and thought carefully. At last she said, 'I know you must have loads of questions, but you must be patient. You'll start to understand as soon as you meet her.'

'But why didn't you tell me about Great-Aunt Elizabeth before?' Kate asked.

Her mother smiled at her and spoke gently. 'Helicopters, kidnappers and jewel thieves? I don't think you would have believed me, do you?'

Charlotte stood up purposefully and began gathering up the papers and notebooks strewn across the bed. Kate stayed sitting where she was, touching the stone with her fingers and feeling its warmth against her skin. As her mother moved away to lock her things into her desk, Kate caught her sleeve.

'Mum, this little heart-shaped stone is just like the one on Barking's collar.'

'Yes, that's right.'

'Well, if it's so special, why has the cat got one?'

Before Charlotte could answer, Barking appeared in the doorway, his thick tail flicking and swishing, and the small heartstone at his neck, which was normally barely visible against his black fur, glowed ruby red. He jumped up on the bed beside Kate, opened his mouth and . . . spoke.

'Well, I like that! So, I'm not special, eh? – You're in for a few surprises, I can tell you.' He leant close to Kate and licked her nose with his small, barbed tongue.

Kate was too shocked to speak or move, and her mother merely said in a calm and steady voice, 'You see, my darling – there are certain things you just have to experience for yourself in order to believe them.' And then, while her heart raced inside her immobilized body, Kate watched as her mother spoke to the cat. 'So, Barking! Aunt Elizabeth is on her way. I must go and talk to Phil, and he will have to listen very carefully for once.'

Charlotte left the room and, as Barking shot after her, Kate heard him say, 'Maybe I should tell him . . .' before his thin, reedy voice went out of earshot and the tip of his tail disappeared round the door.

Whereas Kate had been struck dumb, the amazing revelation about Barking unleashed a babble of exclamations and questions from Phil, many of which were not complete sentences. Eventually he said, 'But how? . . . Does Kate know?' And he paused for an answer.

Charlotte took her chance and answered him while holding his chin gently in her hand so that she could keep his attention on her. 'Kate knows, but Dad doesn't, and we have to keep the fact that Barking can talk a secret from him . . . OK? I'll explain it to Daddy later, but I don't want him worrying just for now.'

Barking looked up from the paw he'd been licking and said, 'I shouldn't worry too much, Lottie. I'll be careful and Michael will put it down to Phil's wild imagination if he lets anything slip.'

Kate, having at last recovered her wits sufficiently to move, appeared in the doorway.

Phil rushed to her. 'Barking talks, Kate! He does, he can speak, he can say anything really properly. Not like that dog on TV who kind of woofs "sausages", but like you can have a conversation with him.' Phil turned to where Barking was washing on the bed. 'Can't you? Tell Kate you can talk, tell her something. Can you sing? How about a song?'

'Certainly not,' Barking replied emphatically.

Meanwhile, Charlotte was pulling clothes from Phil's chest of drawers and folding them into a bag. 'I know this seems sudden, but Great-Aunt Elizabeth is going to come for you soon,' she said, holding up and frowning at a pair of new jeans with ruined, shredded knees. 'You'll need to pack some things too, Kate,' she said, glancing around to smile at where Kate still stood in the doorway to Phil's bedroom. Kate did not return the smile but stared, steadily and stony-faced, at the cat.

Charlotte recognized Kate's mood. 'Come in, Kate, and shut the door – there's a couple of things I need to say to both of you.'

Kate came in but kept close to the door.

'I know that you're going to have a wonderful time with Great-Aunt Elizabeth. But Daddy isn't so sure – he doesn't know her like I do. You are going to have to trust me ... and you mustn't worry your dad with this.

Your Great-Aunt Elizabeth has an enemy and may, in the future, need your help.'

Kate found her voice at last. 'So Dad's right, it isn't safe. And anyhow, how are we supposed to help?'

Charlotte looked quickly at Kate and hesitated for a brief moment before speaking carefully in a low voice. 'If Great-Aunt Elizabeth's old enemy does come back, then yes, you could be in danger.' She sighed deeply. 'But that's why you must go with her, because she can teach you how to look after yourselves. And as long as you always wear the heartstone, Kate, you will be protected.'

Charlotte turned to Phil and placed her hands on his shoulders.

'I've given Kate my old heartstone, but I'm afraid there isn't one for you.' Charlotte spoke carefully and Phil sensed that she expected him to be disappointed.

He swivelled his eyes to look at Kate and saw a strange red gemstone shaped like a lop-sided heart glowing round her neck. An initial surge of jealousy sank through his body and became relief by the time it reached his stomach. He would not want be seen dead in a necklace like that.

He looked back at his mum. 'Do I need one?' he asked.

Charlotte smiled. 'Stay close to Barking,' she said, as the cat wove himself round her legs. 'It's the same thing.'

'Just think of me as your feline bodyguard,' said Barking as he curled his sleek black body round and wound himself through Phil's legs.

Suddenly, Barking sprang into Charlotte's arms.

'I've got a strong feeling that Aunt E. is close,' he said. 'My whiskers are tingling and I'm feeling decidedly hot around the collar.'

'Yes, I'm getting a strong sense of their presence too,' said Charlotte, beginning to laugh. 'That explains why Kate's stone was so bright!'

'What?' queried Phil. 'Great-Aunt Elizabeth? Is she here? . . . And what do you mean by *their* presence? Who else is with her?'

'You'll see soon enough!' Charlotte laughed, turning towards the door where Kate still stood looking around with troubled eyes. Charlotte paused to whisper in Kate's ear as she reached for the door handle and passed on to the landing.

'Trust me,' was all she said.

Pushing past his sister, Phil clattered downstairs and yelled in through the door of the small room where his father worked: 'Hey, Dad, Dad! Great-Aunt Elizabeth's coming!'

Michael looked up in surprise from a page of closely written mathematical formulae and he frowned. 'What? Here already?' he asked.

'I think,' Charlotte announced, appearing at Phil's side, 'you are going to have to resign yourself to the fact that this time there are no excuses.' Charlotte beamed. 'The children are off for an adventure with Great-Aunt Elizabeth!'

'But she only phoned yesterday. How on earth did

she get here so quickly?' Michael spluttered, then, as a more urgent question sprang to mind, he rose from his desk and blurted, 'They can't just pack and go! These things have to be discussed and considered –'

Charlotte shrugged. 'I don't know, maybe she was already in England when she phoned.' Michael looked incredulously at his wife as she continued, 'Look, darling, I've been thinking, we've had all those estimates for the roof repairs. Maybe we should take this opportunity to get the builders in this summer. It'll be much easier if the kids are out of the way.'

'Now, hang on a minute …' Michael began but was cut short by a deep rumbling noise and vibration underfoot. 'Good heavens, what the devil's that?' he murmured.

'That,' Charlotte sang cheerfully, 'will be Great-Aunt Elizabeth.'

Great-Aunt Elizabeth

A s the Reynolds family came out of their front door, they witnessed the arrival of Great-Aunt Elizabeth on her gleaming black-and-silver Harley-Davidson. All around, their neighbours stopped what they were doing and turned towards the thunderous roar of the engine. Mrs Parker, always a vigilant neighbour, slowly straightened up beside her hedge and let her trowel fall to the ground. Children skidded to a halt on bikes and skates. Those people who had been inside their houses came out of doors, amazement quickly replacing any look of curiosity.

The Harley with its impressive sidecar pulled into the drive and stopped. Sitting astride the machine and slowly unbuckling her helmet was an enormous leather-clad woman and beside her, behind the glass dome of the sidecar, sat a large, grinning golden retriever. The enormous woman dismounted and strode towards the house, pulling off her helmet as she advanced and shaking loose a mass of dark grey-streaked curls.

'My darling child!' she cried as she reached Charlotte

and pulled her into her arms for a smothering embrace. Behind her, the dome of the sidecar rolled back and the large golden retriever bounded out.

Barking ran forwards, and the cat and dog chased each other playfully round the garden.

Aware that all eyes in the street were upon them, Michael Reynolds ushered the newcomers inside the house. There was a snag in the doorway as Phil got caught between the door-jamb and Great-Aunt Elizabeth's expansive left thigh. Eventually they were all inside, closely followed by the galloping animals.

'Steady on there!' cried Michael as the retriever leapt up at him in an enthusiastic greeting. Placing two huge splayed paws on his chest, the massive dog lathered Michael's scrunched-up face with lavish licks from an enormous pink tongue. At the back end his gigantic tail swept vigorously from side to side in joyous wagging.

Great-Aunt Elizabeth raised a portly arm, 'Fearless!' she commanded. 'Lie down!' Kate noticed that she gave the dog a kindly wink before adding, 'I think someone has left his manners at home!'

The dog immediately retreated and flopped flat on the kitchen floor, his nose resting on his paws. Barking sat down neatly beside him.

'We weren't expecting you, I'm afraid,' said Michael, wiping his face on his sleeve and frowning down to where the dog appeared to be smiling up at him.

'But we're so pleased to see you,' added Charlotte quickly, 'it's been far too long.'

'Now, let me see these wonderful children,' beamed Great-Aunt Elizabeth.

Everyone turned towards Kate and Phil, who stood, side by side, just inside the doorway. Phil fidgeted nervously from foot to foot.

'Goodness me, Charlotte, they look just like you – I would have known them anywhere!'

Kate noticed that Great-Aunt Elizabeth's gaze dropped from her face to the necklace at her throat and then returned once more to her mother.

'So, Charlotte, do you remember the wonderful times we had?' she asked.

'How could I forget?' Charlotte replied.

Michael cleared his throat and shuffled a little in order to bring himself up to his full height. Though a tall man, exceeding six foot, Great-Aunt Elizabeth towered over him.

'Actually,' he said, 'we've been trying to explain to the children about some of your adventures. Though I suppose you're past all that now, are you?' he added hopefully.

'Life has been rather quiet for many years,' Great-Aunt Elizabeth mused, 'although one can never tell what is round the corner.' She hesitated a moment before continuing: 'These days the power-mad are more likely to take over the world by opening a chain of fast-food restaurants!' and she laughed loudly.

'The thing is,' Michael interrupted her, 'I want to be sure that the children . . . well, I don't want them to get . . .

er . . . they are very young and, well . . . I don't want them mixed up in anything risky!' he blurted out finally.

Great-Aunt Elizabeth put a hand on his shoulder and nodded. 'I understand, Michael. You mustn't worry. I'll take good care of them.' She smiled and patted his shoulder reassuringly, but Michael did not look convinced.

'And how are you, Michael?' Great-Aunt Elizabeth suddenly enquired, continuing to scrutinize him with her intense gaze. 'Have you been able to remember any more of your childhood? Any flashbacks to the accident? Dreams perhaps?'

Michael's face darkened, he frowned and shook his head. 'No, no, still an empty box I'm afraid,' he murmured.

'Oh, hardly what I'd call an empty box,' Great-Aunt Elizabeth interjected. 'I read the lecture you gave in Vienna last year on Quantum Gravity – marvellous stuff!'

Kate threw a worried look at her dad. He never talked about the accident that had nearly killed him when he was thirteen years old. Kate was shocked at the way Great-Aunt Elizabeth had just brought it up out of the blue, knocking her dad off balance.

Noticing the concern in his daughter's eyes, Michael grinned at Kate and ruffled her hair. 'Come on,' he said cheerfully, 'let's make your grand old Great-Aunt a cup of tea after her long journey.'

While the kettle was being boiled and biscuits were tipped on a plate, Phil knelt down beside Fearless.

Sprawled across the kitchen floor, the dog stretched almost from one wall to the other. Phil examined the soft, grey-pink curl of the dog's lip and noted how the strong white hairs of his whiskers and brow stood out against his yellow fur. The glossy sheen of his coat was splendid as Phil stroked him in long sweeps from his neck to his flank. Kate was crouching on the other side, beside Barking. She kept a watchful eye on the cat for more signs that he might be about to speak, but he just sat, washing in a fastidiously feline way. The adults stepped over and round them until Charlotte at last picked up a tray and ushered everyone into the living room. Great-Aunt Elizabeth settled herself on the sofa, which looked doll-size beneath her, and began to reminisce with Charlotte about her childhood holidays.

Although their mother had often told them about the exotic places she had visited as bedtime stories or when something happened to remind her of her past, she had neglected to mention any of the thrilling details of her adventures with Great-Aunt Elizabeth. Listening eagerly to the conversation, what they now heard was wonderful, as it suggested the exciting times that might well be in store for them this summer. Fantastic tales of a tall ship sailing through the Barents Sea accompanied by a pod of whales; living in a canopy tree house in the rainforest; making goat's cheese in an Alpine cottage.

From the corner of the room where she quietly perched on a cushion on the floor, Kate began to lose her feeling of foreboding. And as she warmed to the idea of travelling with her great-aunt, she became conscious of the heart-stone warming her skin.

Sitting on his father's lap in an armchair directly opposite the imposing visitor, Phil listened without interrupting, but he fidgeted mercilessly, unable to get comfortable on his father's bony knees. As he wriggled, Great-Aunt Elizabeth paused in her narrative and gazed at him with her large dark eyes. Her grey-streaked hair had once been black and it curled wildly about her face and shoulders.

'Your boy has spirit,' she said at last, 'and plenty of energy and imagination too, I see.'

Squirming all the more from this attention, Phil racked his brains for a reason to leave the room. Earlier he had put a few things in his rucksack and he now remembered that he had not packed his binoculars. With a mumbled explanation he shot off to search for them, relieved to remove himself from his great-aunt's inquisitive stare. Michael went to help him look.

When Michael had left the room, Great-Aunt Elizabeth leant towards Charlotte and spoke more quietly than before. 'I need the children, Charlotte, you understand that, don't you? I promise I shall keep them safe.'

Charlotte gazed anxiously at her aunt. 'Something's happened?' she asked in a whisper.

'I have had signs: dreams, sudden feelings of dread. Nothing specific, but I am afraid, my dear, we do have cause for concern. I learnt something this last week that changes everything.'

Charlotte's face paled and Barking jumped on to her lap. Kate thought at first that she had been forgotten, but her great-aunt's words were accompanied by a piercing glance in her direction.

Great-Aunt Elizabeth took a chocolate from her pocket, unwrapped it and popped it into her mouth.

She looked over at Kate once again and added in a more forthright and cheerful voice, 'Look how well this daughter of yours wears the heartstone. Charlotte, you must not worry.'

'Barking and I will take care of the children,' said Fearless, getting up from the rug and gently pawing Charlotte's knee.

Startled, Kate noticed that he too had a small stone glinting at his collar.

Charlotte looked over at Kate's bewildered face and stood up quickly, causing Barking to spill gracefully on to the floor.

'Don't worry, darling,' she said, reaching for Kate's hand and pulling her to her feet, 'everything is going to be all right, I promise.'

It occurred to Kate that her mother's words were as much to reassure herself as to allay any fears Kate might have. Yet somehow, despite everything she had just heard, Kate wanted to believe her.

Her mother gently touched her on the cheek and added, 'And you will have a wonderful time – please trust me.'

At last, Kate smiled back at her mother, 'I do trust

you,' she said, and as the words left her mouth she felt a sudden conviction that everything would be fine. The heartstone felt reassuringly warm at her throat.

It was a less than ordinary evening and a most extraordinary supper. Great-Aunt Elizabeth announced that she had no desire to impose upon them and, from beneath a seat in her sidecar, produced an enormous casserole dish which was as hot as if she'd lifted it straight from the oven. Kate watched her father stand at the front door, surveying the Harley with a puzzled look as Great-Aunt Elizabeth strode towards him with the steaming pot balanced on one leather-gloved hand as if it were a tray of drinks. Turning to follow her, Michael declared, 'Now that's amazing. How do you . . .?' But he was stopped short by a dismissive wave of black leather as Great-Aunt Elizabeth marched to the kitchen. Michael looked at Kate and shrugged.

'She's amazing, isn't she?' said Kate.

'You can say that again,' said Michael, closing the door. 'You will take care of yourself, won't you?'

'Of course I will, Dad,' Kate answered, and she felt a small surge of warmth from the heartstone.

'You do want to go? asked Michael. 'You know, if you don't want to, I'm sure we can –'

'No, Dad,' Kate interrupted him, 'it's fine. I do want to go – I can't explain, it's like I've always been expecting . . . something.' She gave a small smile.

Michael placed his arm across his daughter's shoulders

and they entered the kitchen, where they found Phil setting the table.

'Now that,' laughed Kate, 'is a truly amazing sight.'

Although he still harboured private reservations, Michael seemed to have resigned himself to the fact that the children were off on an adventure with his wife's barmy old aunt. He could see the sense in getting the roof done before next winter and he agreed with Charlotte to call the builders first thing on Monday morning. Secretly, however, he resolved that, should anything give him the slightest doubt about his children's safety, then he would simply get on a plane and follow them.

During the meal, the conversation turned, ordinarily enough, to the weather – except, the weather hadn't been too ordinary of late: there were floods and storms and all sorts of unusual conditions all over the world, including hailstones the size of walnuts in Scotland. 'I hope the weather doesn't prevent you from travelling,' Michael said a little too cheerfully.

Great-Aunt Elizabeth positively beamed with glee and professed to enjoying dramatic weather. She told them how she had once ridden her motorbike in the eye of a tornado. 'I was driving fast, of course, steering carefully to keep myself within the eye where all was calm, while these great towering walls of wind swirled around me. It was utterly thrilling,' she announced.

'How did you get out?' Phil asked.

'Ah, very fortunate,' replied Great-Aunt Elizabeth.

'As the storm passed over a tunnel I simply drove down into it.'

'Well,' said Michael 'no tornado-riding with my children in tow, OK?'

'I wouldn't dream of it!' said Great-Aunt Elizabeth; but she winked at Phil as his face dropped, and he grinned happily back.

That night a ferocious storm broke, sending torrents of rain drumming against the windows with a violence that woke Charlotte and caused everyone to stir. Going down to the living room, where Great-Aunt Elizabeth had stated a preference to camp out, Charlotte found her awake, her impressive silhouette before the French windows.

'Do you sense anything, Charlotte?' she asked without turning round.

'I think the storm woke me,' replied Charlotte. 'What is it? You don't think you've been followed, do you?' A small edge of fear thinned her voice as she remembered their earlier conversation. 'Tell me everything. Have you seen her?'

Great-Aunt Elizabeth turned from the window and faced Charlotte. 'Every year, on the third Monday in July, the Parole Board has met to consider giving her time off for good behaviour and up until now the Board has listened to my recommendations and refused her release. I have been able to call you and tell you not to worry, that we were safe for another year.'

'Yes, I know that,' Charlotte answered in a small whisper.

'This year it was unanimously decided by the panel that they had to release her. There was nothing I could do to dissuade them. Apparently she has been a model prisoner and the persistent denial of permission for early release was affecting the morale of the other inmates.'

'Yes, but if she's only just got out, then we have time; you can train the children and they'll be ready before she has a chance to do anything.'

Great-Aunt Elizabeth placed her large hand beneath Charlotte's elbow as if to guide her. 'I went to the prison to see her come out.'

'And ...?' Charlotte's voice was a barely audible whisper.

'It wasn't her.'

'No, no, you must have made a mistake!' Charlotte's words tumbled out and she shook her head frantically.

Great-Aunt Elizabeth clasped Charlotte's shoulders and held her still. 'The woman who walked free from prison two days ago had her name, resembled her physically, but it wasn't her. She didn't keep up the pretence long, not once she realized that I had rumbled her. She told me her name was Hildy Martin and that she had served fifty years of a life sentence. She was a gentle old thing who had earned her own parole and had not wanted it. Prison life was all she knew, she had no family, no home, she was terrified of life on the outside, and so she had agreed to swap identities. I'm afraid, my dear, our old enemy walked free in her place.'

'When?' asked Charlotte. 'How long ago?'

'Ten years.'

'Ten years! She's been out for ten years! That's before Phil was even born!'

'It was ten years ago that I sent Barking to live with you – you remember, I had a strong feeling then that something was wrong. But there has been nothing since . . . not until now, that is.'

'But I've just given Kate my heartstone – it's active again and she might sense it!' Charlotte wailed miserably.

'Now, don't take on so, my dear. It's going to be all right. I'll take the children with me. I've got Harold doing everything he can to trace her, and she knows she's no match for me.'

Charlotte shivered. 'When you find her, you have to stop her for good this time, Aunt E.'

'I will try, my dear, I will try,' came the weary reply.

While the night's rain lashed at the fields and towns of southern Britain, in Nevada, USA, a scorched and hazy desert cowered beneath a fierce sun. Roads through deserts are designed to cut the quickest route to the other side; junctions and turnings are rare and lead nowhere, so most are ignored. Few, then, would stumble accidentally upon the shimmering steel building miles from anywhere and invisible from the main road. Fewer still would guess at the sophisticated laboratory technology and luxury within the harsh metallic walls.

In this secret location a woman sat at a large, uncluttered desk. There was no external window to the room and so the glare from outside had no effect upon the dimly lit air-conditioned office. The woman was thin and elegantly dressed in a style from a bygone era. She had high, arched eyebrows and the expression on her beautiful but cold face was one of haughty arrogance.

Lorabeth Lampton tapped slowly and rhythmically on her desk with the fingers of her right hand; her left hand she held in a loose fist. With slow-blinking eyes she watched the second hand rotate round the gilded face of a large and ornamental carriage clock that rested in front of her. She was waiting for her most recent employee, whom she had summoned moments before over the tannoy. She knew that Carter was an outstandingly accomplished scientist and physicist, for she had invested twenty-three years and a small fortune in the careful education and development of that extraordinary brain. However, for each second she was kept waiting Lorabeth Lampton's opinion of Carter lessened and her irritation grew.

A brief tap at the door and Carter stood before her, squinting in the gloom.

'You wanted to see me?' Carter asked breathlessly.

Detecting disrespect in her employee's voice, Lorabeth Lampton's cruel, reptilian eyes narrowed. She studied Carter carefully. Carter looked, in the white lab coat, like a child dressing up. A few wisps of fair hair had escaped from her untidy ponytail, which she had scraped roughly behind her ears and under the arms of her thick-rimmed glasses.

'I'm very busy,' Carter added boldly.

'You have had two days. You should have familiarized yourself with the laboratories by now. I have an important job for you,' snapped Lorabeth Lampton. Carter began to protest but Lorabeth Lampton raised a languid hand, saying, 'I want you to investigate this.' She held out her fist, palm down, slowly turned it over and uncurled her fingers.

Although her slender face was tense with anger and her mind was flying to thoughts of resigning, Carter could not resist her professional curiosity and the sense of wonder that overcame her when she saw what lay in her employer's long and bony hand.

She glanced at the beautiful, cruel face of Lorabeth Lampton, who signalled her permission for her to take it with a slow blink of her eyes. Gently, Carter took the curious object into her own hand. It was a small lumpy stone, dark and foggy and quite unlike anything she had ever seen before.

Carter's face registered the shock of surprise as she touched the stone and felt the warmth coming from it, not the heat from being held in a fist, but as if the stone were generating some kind of energy of its own.

'So, you will accept the assignment?'

'Just tell me what you want me to do,' Carter replied in a hushed voice.

5

Hold-up in Manhattan

The night's rainfall left the Reynolds' house glistening in the early morning sun and everywhere smelt sweet and refreshed. After lengthy hugs and goodbyes and promises to write and phone, Kate and Phil, their luggage and the two animals were bundled into Great-Aunt Elizabeth's surprisingly spacious sidecar.

'How come there's so much room?' Phil clambered about in restless excitement.

Barking swished his tail and opened one eye. 'Please stop fidgeting! Fearless, will you explain the dimension expansion technique incorporated in the design, please.'

Fearless tossed his great head and sparkled a grin at Phil. He had a surprising voice, a bit like the thick warm tones that announce the new films at the cinema.

'Aunt Elizabeth needed a vehicle which was convenient but which could carry as much luggage and as many passengers as she required. Harold customized the Harley and built this sidecar with an Interior Expansion Device. It looks the same on the outside, so there's no worrying about getting through tunnels or barriers into supermarket car parks. Very clever, really.'

'Can you sing?' Phil asked Fearless the same question he had asked Barking, but he was not, this time, treated with disdain.

'Sing?' cried the dog gleefully, and immediately launched into a popular folk song.

'Who is Harold?' asked Kate, who had been quietly thinking over the events of the last few days.

'Harold Baker,' announced Barking, stirring himself with a sigh, 'inventor and fruit-loop of the highest order. Finest scientific mind of his generation – graduated from university in Cape Town when he was ten years of age. He is Aunt Elizabeth's right-hand man. You'll meet Harold when we get there.' Barking stifled a yawn while smacking his tongue against the roof of his mouth. 'Now, you do realize that cats customarily sleep for seventeen hours in twenty-four? Are you aware how little sleep I've had these last few days?' And, frowning in the direction of the singers, Barking closed his eyes and settled his chin on his paws.

They had left the motorway, where Phil had enjoyed looking out at the rest of the traffic, catching glimpse after glimpse of surprised faces, heads jerking to get another look. The Harley was now heading west towards a small village on the Atlantic coast from where the strange party would travel to America. Kate's attention was caught elsewhere. She looked up at Great-Aunt Elizabeth's powerful profile. With her open-face crash helmet and old-fashioned pilot's goggles, her strong features thrust forwards into the wind, it was a face to be carved on the prow of a warship. All of a sudden Great-Aunt Elizabeth glanced into the sidecar and beamed at Kate. As they wound their way through the countryside, Kate watched and wondered. She wondered about Great-Aunt Elizabeth and she wondered about herself. She could barely describe her own feelings, they were so mixed up into impossible combinations. Kate suddenly remembered learning about 'oxymorons' at school. Her teacher, Miss Candle, had said that putting contrasting words together added dramatic effect. Well, at least Kate could agree with that. She felt thrilled and fearful, keen and wary. Her previous life had not equipped her for such surprising relatives, talking cats, singing dogs and impossible motorbikes. She returned her attention to Phil and Fearless, who were singing a loud rendition of 'She'll Be Coming Round the Mountain'. When people list the pleasures in life – log fires in winter, cool lemonade on a summer's day – then the sight and sound of a large golden retriever singing with gusto ought to top the list. Kate joined in at the next chorus, which earned her a brief, one-eyed glare from Barking.

Soon the motorbike stopped at a deserted harbour. As Great-Aunt Elizabeth dismounted, she rapped sharply on the glass dome of the sidecar.

'Out you get and stretch your legs!' she ordered cheerfully.

Although strong sunshine warmed their faces, it was a blowy day and the sea looked choppy and wild. The grey-green water swelled and rolled, and Kate felt queasy at the thought of a rough crossing as she looked around nervously for a boat. And goodness knows how long it would take.

'Why so worried?' Barking asked, rubbing against her legs.

'I think I'm going to be seasick . . . sorry.'

'Nonsense!' cried Great-Aunt Elizabeth, overhearing though some distance away. 'You'll be fine. We shall be gliding along as smooth as custard, and there in no time.'

Great-Aunt Elizabeth had parked the Harley in front of two large steel doors set on the ground. Just like the delivery hatches on the pavement outside public houses and hotels, Kate thought, eyeing them nervously. She had always been afraid to step on such doors in case they fell open and she plummeted into a dark, beery cellar. More worrying even than that, these doors were rather close to the harbour wall. Phil stood nonchalantly on them and peered over the edge. The water level was high, rolling just a few feet beneath him.

'Mind yourself, young man!' Great-Aunt Elizabeth ordered, and Phil stepped aside and watched as she unlocked and lifted the doors to reveal the entrance to a shallow, brick-lined pit.

Great-Aunt Elizabeth smiled at Phil as he peered inside. 'A cunning deception to put off any curious intruders!' she announced.

She pulled what looked like a small TV remote control

from her pocket and aimed it into the pit. Phil blinked once and suddenly found himself looking into the clean, brightly lit entrance to a tunnel. That in itself was surprising, but the tunnel appeared to descend into the sea. On Great-Aunt Elizabeth's instructions they all got back into the sidecar although there was, she said, no need to close the roof since they would be going quite slowly. The motorbike purred gently down the slope and the doors closed behind them. There was less light now, and as their eyes adjusted Kate and Phil saw seaweed, tall swathes of bladderwrack swaying above the rocks and even the odd fish darting about. The Harley was gently cruising through a glass tunnel under the sea. As they went further and deeper into the tunnel, they noticed dark shapes moving sedately past, and Kate recognized a dogfish by its whiskers as it turned suddenly away from the glass wall of the tunnel.

'Make sure you take in the view, you never know what you might spot!' cried Great-Aunt Elizabeth, adding hurriedly, 'Look! Octopus!'

The yellow-white suckers of a large octopus disappeared overhead. The decline, though not steep, was steady, and soon there was too little light to see much in the water. Phil squinted into the murky shadows, his mind conjuring up images of mighty narwhals and conger eels as swirling patches of darker water caught his attention.

All of a sudden, they came to another door. Great-Aunt Elizabeth stopped the Harley and the door opened automatically. She drove the bike on to a metal stand, which rumbled slightly and clamped the Harley's wheels. The door closed behind them. They were in a large, brightly lit room, which reminded Kate of the departure lounge at an airport, except that the seats looked luxuriously comfortable and each had a sturdy padded seat belt designed to come down over the occupant's head. Phil climbed out of the sidecar and gazed around, opened-mouthed. Fearless jumped up into one of the seats and the padded belt automatically closed round him, adjusting itself to fit perfectly across his shoulders and chest.

'Superb design, isn't it?' said Fearless. 'Come and sit next to me, Phil.'

While Phil chattered away enthusiastically to Fearless, Kate moved slowly towards the remaining empty seat. The seat responded immediately she lowered her body into it; the seat belt slipped over her head and tightened gently but snugly against her body. She was disconcerted and her body tensed.

'I know it feels a bit odd,' Barking whispered beside her, 'but you will be glad of it when we set off.'

Great-Aunt Elizabeth sat in front of them in a seat that had a panel of buttons, sensors and flashing lights on the armrest.

'Everyone ready?' she asked in her stentorian sing-song voice and, without waiting for an answer, she began tapping the buttons.

There was a low rumbling sound and Kate felt herself

being pressed back into her seat. Suddenly she had the sensation of hurtling along at great speed. It was a bit like falling, Kate decided, unhappy to be reminded of the unpleasant sensation she felt when looking down from any height. She closed her eyes and immediately felt sick. Taking in a gulping deep breath, she tried to stop thinking about herself and focused her attention on Phil, who was whooping with excitement. Kate thought it was just as well that he was strapped in or he would be bouncing off the walls. And then, quite suddenly, it was all over. The rumbling sound slowed and became fainter and the seat harness rolled back.

'What's wrong?' Kate asked, alarmed. 'Have we broken down?'

'Nothing's wrong –' said Barking, licking his paw – 'we've arrived in New York.'

Kate and Phil were astounded.

'It takes longer than that to get to Granny's,' said Phil, grinning widely at the excitement of it all.

Kate frowned and looked with irritation at Phil's smiling profile. Her long dark hair fell across her face and she pushed it away roughly. 'It's not possible,' she said. 'We were in England less than ten minutes ago.'

Great-Aunt Elizabeth studied both children for a moment and then she said, 'You two are going to have lots of surprises. You must be very careful to behave normally. A lot of what I do is undercover work and I don't want you giving anything away. The Interior Expansion Device and the Sub-Atlantic Transfer System you've just travelled on must not be divulged to anyone. You mustn't expect the animals to answer questions when there are people about. Do not draw attention to yourselves and, most importantly, don't leave the inexplicable lying around where members of the general public might find it.'

This speech was given very formally and Phil stood to attention, his freckled face upturned and earnest as if he was being briefed by a senior officer. Kate, however, was somewhat affronted and her mouth dropped open wide and stayed open as she waited, poised to make her reply, as soon as Great-Aunt Elizabeth had finished.

'But we don't draw attention to ourselves!' she cried at last. 'People are looking at *you*, Great-Aunt Elizabeth – at what you wear, at the motorbike, even the animals. You don't see a dog and a cat together – it's unusual, and people are bound to look.'

Great-Aunt Elizabeth placed a large hand gently on top of Kate's head. 'Ah, my dear, you see I am *eccentric* – that's what people are looking at and it is my best disguise. People enjoy eccentricity in harmless old ladies; it is what they like to see. But I cannot afford to have people's curiosity aroused.' She patted Kate's cheek. 'Fortunately, most people aren't in the slightest bit curious about anything at all.'

After emerging via another tunnel on to a quiet Brooklyn pier, they began to make their way through New York to Great-Aunt Elizabeth's house overlooking Central Park. Kate and Phil pressed their faces against the glass and stared out of the sidecar at the streets of New York. Kate exclaimed aloud when she saw her first yellow taxi, and both children crouched down low in their seats in order to peer up at the buildings: gigantic towers that soared up into a clear blue sky. Things that they had seen only in films – such as fire hydrants and steaming manhole covers – had a welcoming familiarity about them.

While they were idling at some traffic lights, Phil's attention was caught by the strange sight of a man walking backwards out of a bank. Phil was about to lose interest when the man raised his arm and Phil saw that he was holding a gun.

'It's a hold-up!' Phil shouted. 'That man's robbing the bank!'

Great-Aunt Elizabeth had seen it too and had briskly dismounted, leaving the Harley at the head of a queue of traffic. She strode across the street towards the bank, each of her steps covering two metres of tarmac. As she reached the robber, he glanced around in alarm. From the sidecar they saw the fear leave his face and a smirk appear. It was just an old lady, he was thinking, tall – sure – strangely dressed – maybe – but an old lady neverthe- less. He turned away from her. No one quite saw what happened next but, quick as a green mamba's strike, Great-Aunt Elizabeth had one hand round his throat and was holding him off the ground. Her other hand held his wrist, which she was banging against the wall so that his Colt 45 clattered to the sidewalk. Still holding him aloft and at arm's length, she kicked the gun clear.

In his other hand the bank robber carried a holdall, which he dropped to the ground. His red face had now developed a tinge of purple and he was making little bicycling movements with his drooping feet. A security guard rushed out of the bank and retrieved the holdall. With his free hand he aimed his gun at the struggling robber. Now that the situation was under control, Great-Aunt Elizabeth loosened her grip and the man fell to the ground like a rag.

Great-Aunt Elizabeth nodded graciously to the security guard and strode back to the motorbike. Inside the side-car Fearless let out a joyous woof while Barking sprang about on the upholstery like a kitten,

'Did you see that?' Phil whispered to Kate, and she nodded, her eyes wide with amazement.

'Way to go, Aunt E.!' cried Fearless, throwing back his head and howling with triumph. Great-Aunt Elizabeth merely smiled and gave them all a small salute as she climbed back on the bike and roared away down the street.

The animals' spirits remained high throughout the remainder of the journey; when they finished discussing Great-Aunt Elizabeth's strength and had fallen quiet with their own thoughts, Fearless suddenly exclaimed, 'Did you see the look on his face?' and they started all over again. It was a noisy, lively group that arrived at last at Great-Aunt Elizabeth's house.

6

Some Baker Inventions

It was a large, detached house, ordinary enough from the outside in a grand but neglected kind of way. It was what lay beyond the front door and behind the windows that was completely extraordinary. Great-Aunt Elizabeth turned a key in the lock and they stepped into a large vestibule with a set of glazed swing doors leading from it. Once inside the door, Phil dropped his rucksack on the floor, just as he used to at home. However, instead of lying there at his feet, the bag slowly rose into the air and hovered gently in front of him.

'The Invisible Butler,' Fearless explained to the startled boy.

'Not a real *invisible person*, of course!' said Barking. 'It's based on a principle of harnessing static electricity and modifying it to behave in a certain way. It's quite limited – but useful for predictable situations.'

'One of Harold's inventions?' Kate queried.

'Who else?' Fearless grinned. 'He has programmed the static in the vestibule to respond to a whole range of possible events. It is likely that things will get dropped from time to time, carrying in shopping and such like, so retrieval is automatic.'

Barking joined in the description enthusiastically. 'If you come home soaking wet from a walk in the rain, you will be automatically helped off with your coat,' he said.

'That's if you come in on two feet,' said Fearless. 'Barking and I automatically get our muddy paws washed and blow-dried.'

'And if you ever forget your key, don't attempt to break in,' warned Barking. 'In the event of the front door being forced, you will be flipped into the air and slammed down on to the floor!'

Kate pushed the hovering bag into Phil's hands. 'It didn't know it would be getting an untidy boy though, did it?' she said gleefully. Since witnessing her Great-Aunt's triumph over the bank robber, she had felt increasingly carefree and optimistic.

'That's true,' Great-Aunt Elizabeth agreed, looking satisfied and smiling at Phil, 'but I do so love it when things turn out to be even more useful than first imagined. Come on, it's time you met the wonderful Harold Baker.'

Great-Aunt Elizabeth led them through the swing doors into a splendid, high dome-ceilinged room. Directly ahead of them they could see through an open door into a large room, lined with books from floor to ceiling, and which was home to an impressive oak desk and several elegant sofas and chairs. To their left were further doors, though these were closed and offered no clue as to what lay behind them. To the right, a broad staircase swept up and around to a balconied landing. As they followed Great-Aunt Elizabeth into the library, they passed a long corridor which disappeared beneath the curling staircase.

At the far end of the library, double doors stood open into what would once have been a conservatory or orangerie, but was now a gleaming office. Sitting at one of the computers and typing at great speed, they saw the back of a dishevelled head.

'Harold, dear,' called Great-Aunt Elizabeth, 'come and meet the children, Charlotte's children. Here they are, come to visit us at last.'

The dishevelled man spun round on his chair, leapt up and rushed towards them, holding out an arm in front of him. He grabbed Kate's hand first and then Phil's, and shook them vigorously, as if attempting to draw water from an old-fashioned pump.

'Kate, hello, hello. What do you like, Kate? Music? DVDs? And Philbert! Hello, hello! Got a catapult? How far can it fling a conker?'

'Philip!' Phil corrected him, but he smiled happily at this enthusiastic welcome.

Harold Baker looked every bit the inventor. He was tall and gangly, and his black hair, part twisted locks, part afro, stood up on end and out in every direction. His face was open and lit by a wide smile; his skin was remarkably smooth and flawless, apart from a ragged birthmark along his jawline that resembled a map of pale pink islands in a sea of coffee. After shaking hands with the children, he rubbed his palms up and down on his thighs as if trying to dry them.

'Stand back a moment!' he announced and, stretching out a long arm, he pointed towards the door. Suddenly an arc of lightning zapped from the tip of his finger to the door handle. 'Phew, I needed that!' he cried. Then, seeing Kate and Phil's open mouths and wide eyes, he added,

'Don't worry – just a bit of discharge! I've been getting your rooms ready, do you want to see them?'

With Barking and Fearless sprinting ahead and Harold leading the way, talking quickly and breathlessly about the unrealized potential of electricity as he went, the children followed him back through the library and up the grand staircase.

'I like the sidecar, Harold,' said Phil.

'Jolly good, Philbert – I hope you like your bedroom too. I've incorporated the Interior Expansion Device in there as well, much nicer room than it was – used to be a linen cupboard.' He reached out and opened the first door on their left at the top of the stairs then stood back to give Phil a full view of the room. 'I've been having a bit of a play around with virtual reality too,' he said modestly.

'Wow!' said Phil and Kate together.

In slightly less than a week, and despite the remarkable and extraordinary discoveries made each day, Kate and Phil settled surprisingly well into their new way of life.

The envy Kate had felt after seeing Phil's bedroom vanished the moment Harold stepped aside and showed her into her own room. She now settled down each night in a luxurious bed beneath a blossoming apple tree, and she was lulled to sleep by the sound of a gentle waterfall cascading into her very own pool.

In both their bedrooms Harold had installed his new invention, which he called a 'Dried-and-dressed'. While staying with Great-Aunt Elizabeth neither Kate nor Phil needed to think about washing, brushing their teeth or even what to wear. Each morning they chose how to dress by making a selection on a touch-screen keypad set into a revolving door that stood discreetly in the corner of each room. They would then disappear inside, only to reappear, a few moments later, comfortably dressed and sparkling clean. Kate spent an entire morning going through the Dried-and-dressed, trying to see herself in every garment, but she was happily defeated by the discovery of a collection of eighteenth-century silk gowns.

For Phil, his Dried-and-dressed was a convenience he soon took for granted, to be passed through while still half asleep, after waking up and swinging himself out of his hammock. This was slung between two prairie trees beside a corral where his palomino pony softly whinnied a morning greeting. Phil spent many a happy hour riding his horse; but the real source of endless fascination and pleasure for him lay downstairs in the kitchen.

This room was an extraordinary mixture of high-tech

ingenuity and old-fashioned durability. Across the ceiling, shiny steel pans hung from what looked like tiny metal tracks that disappeared through holes in the walls. Yet meals were eaten at an ancient and enormous table. Capable of seating at least twelve people, the circular table was made from dark hardwood and was fifteen centimetres thick. In the centre of the table was a stainless-steel cylindrical dome which had small doors like miniature cat flaps set into it. Across the surface of the table, an arrangement of tiny silver train tracks emerged from the central dome and criss-crossed their way to and from every place setting. A small panel beside each seat housed a touch screen just like the one on a Dried-and-dressed, except this screen displayed items from a delicious and seemingly endless menu. At every meal, Phil experienced the same thrill of anticipation he had felt the very first day when the touch screen had displayed the following message:

> May I recommend freshly baked chocolate brownies and a glass of cold milk?
>
> YES ⬤
>
> NO, PLEASE SHOW MENU ⬤
>
> • • •

The moment his finger had touched 'YES', the kitchen had whirred into life. Overhead, the gleaming pans had jerked into motion, gently swinging while gliding along the ceiling tracks. Then suddenly, through a flap door in the table's centrepiece, a chocolate brownie on a small china plate appeared. Phil had whooped with delight and watched in amazement as the cake hurtled towards him on its track, to be joined by his glass of milk arriving from another direction.

While the technology in the house was beyond their experience, it was not beyond Kate and Phil's imaginations – though this is not to say that things did not puzzle them.

One evening, after swimming in her pool, Kate stepped from her Dried-and-dressed wearing jeans and a blue T-shirt, and tucked her heartstone carefully out of sight. The exact nature of the heartstone's power was the one thing Kate found most bewildering. After their arrival Great-Aunt Elizabeth had sealed the stone by carefully touching it with a white-hot steel rod. Kate could not see how this would prevent her from removing or losing the stone, but she had tried to unclasp the chain afterwards and had to concede that it was impossible. At times the heartstone was cold, but it frequently surged with a buzzing energy and flared a glowing red at her throat. It was not entirely clear why this happened and she was eager to understand. Leaving her bedroom, Kate decided to seek out Great-Aunt Elizabeth and ask her a few direct questions.

As Kate passed Phil's bedroom she put her ear to the door and heard the sound of galloping hoofs and Phil's excited voice crying, 'Yeeha!' She decided to leave him be and went to find Great-Aunt Elizabeth alone.

Just as Kate reached the bottom of the stairs, Great-Aunt Elizabeth's strong voice rang out, making her jump. 'Kate, I'm in here!'

She followed her voice to the library, where she found her great-aunt sitting at a large desk.

'Hello, my dear. I'm busy catching up on my correspondence – I'll be with you in a gnat's wink.'

Kate peeped over her shoulder back towards the doorway. There was no way that someone sitting at the desk would have a view of the hall and staircase, yet Great-Aunt Elizabeth had known Kate was there. Accepting the chocolate she was offered, Kate wondered about this and idly picked up a brown and ageing postcard of Switzerland, showing the Alps in summer. Perhaps, she thought, this was somewhere her mother had visited. Without thinking, she turned the card over and read, with difficulty, the scrawling handwriting. Kate knew it was wrong to read another person's post, but she simply could not help herself. It began:

> *Dearest Lizzie,*
> *Thanks for the tip.*
> *I've tried it and you're*
> *absolutely right!*
> *It is $e = mc^2$.*
> *Much love,*
> *as always, yours,*
> *Albert x*
>
> © Schweiz postkarte

Suddenly, Great-Aunt Elizabeth was staring at her. Kate felt the heat in her face as she flushed pink. She let her hands drop to the desk but continued to hold the postcard loosely in her fingers. The intensity of Great-Aunt Elizabeth's gaze made her feel dizzy.

At last she spoke – but not to give Kate the reprimand she expected. 'I have noticed you constantly trying to make sense of things, my dear, and I am very impressed, very impressed indeed.'

Kate felt another surge of warmth rush to her face, but her fear subsided instantly.

'I'm so sorry, I didn't mean to read it,' she murmured.

Great-Aunt Elizabeth reached a large hand across the desk and took the postcard from Kate. 'Ah, dear sweet Albert!' she sighed, 'I have been lucky to have many remarkable friends over the years, Kate. Unfortunately, they all die and leave me behind.' Great-Aunt Elizabeth looked sorrowful for a moment, then she shot Kate another intense look. 'I think you would like to understand a bit more, wouldn't you? About me and about the heartstones?'

Kate nodded and smiled a little with relief, although she still felt hot and uncomfortable.

Great-Aunt Elizabeth stood and paced around the room. 'The heartstones are the key to it all.' She glanced back at Kate. 'But then I expect you've already guessed as much – a clever girl like you.'

Kate flushed again and looked down and away from Great-Aunt Elizabeth's intimidating gaze.

'It isn't magic – I don't want you filling your head with all that hocus-pocus nonsense. The heartstones are unique and have special properties. So, as they belong to us, our family is unique – we keep the legacy of the heartstones, and consequently we have some responsibilities.'

Great-Aunt Elizabeth paused as if trying to make up her mind about something. In the silence, it occurred to Kate that she should say something encouraging, something to show that she would understand anything that Great-Aunt Elizabeth might tell her. 'I don't think it's magic,' she heard herself saying. 'I think that you've developed technology further than I thought possible. I think the heartstones help you to do that.'

Great-Aunt Elizabeth leant her huge face towards Kate's small one and gently patted her cheek with her large, warm hand. 'Excellent!' she said kindly, and then to herself she murmured, 'Charlotte's child.'

Just then Barking trotted briskly into the room and leapt on to the desk. 'Harold asked me to tell you that he thinks he is on to something. His scanner has made a positive identification. He says it will take a while to download, then you should come and have a look.'

Barking stared for a moment or two at the bowl of chocolates wrapped in blue foil on Great-Aunt Elizabeth's desk, then he jumped silently to the floor and padded swiftly from the room.

Great-Aunt Elizabeth called after him: 'Tell Harold, very well done indeed!' She turned to Kate. 'We will talk again about the heartstones, my dear,' and for a moment she looked pensive, 'but there are a few things I must consider first.'

Great-Aunt Elizabeth's gaze seemed to settle far away and she nodded her head softly, as if making her mind up about something. Then, suddenly, her attention was back on Kate.

'I expect you've always known you were different from other people, haven't you, despite your parents' attempts to bring you up *normally*?' She spoke this last word as if she were unsure what it meant.

Kate thought for a moment before replying.

'I've always thought there was something not quite right,' she said slowly, then added quickly, 'I thought I was adopted.' She found herself blushing once again.

Great-Aunt Elizabeth smiled at her. 'Beans and bus tickets!' she exclaimed, 'You're certainly not that! Just look how well you wear the heartstone – there is an affinity between you and that stone, Kate.' Great-Aunt Elizabeth considered her for a moment. 'Come along, let's give the folks back home a call, shall we?'

'Oh, yes please,' Kate replied, suddenly recognizing with a pang that she missed home and her parents very badly. 'I'll call Phil.'

Up in his bedroom, Phil had tethered his pony to the corral and was lying in his hammock. Suddenly he found himself thinking about home, and it seemed a long way away. He thought about his mother, and immediately he could see her, in the kitchen, making him cheese on toast. He saw Charlotte push a curl of dark hair behind her ear as she bent down to peer under the grill. Two huge slices of toast, dripping with melting cheese, glowed beneath the flames. She turned and smiled at Phil. 'Blistering up nicely, just how you like it,' she said.

Phil was startled and looked around in surprise. The smell of toasted cheese, the sound of his mother's voice and the tick of the kitchen clock at home had been so vivid and convincing, he stared across the vast prairie of his new bedroom with a momentary confusion. Just then he heard Kate calling for him.

He clambered from his hammock and shot from his room, clattering down the stairs in time to see Great-Aunt Elizabeth settle with the phone on her lap and Kate beside her. He went and sat on Great-Aunt Elizabeth's other side.

'Hello, Michael, it's Elizabeth!' she boomed. After a

pause, in which Kate and Phil could hear a muffled, far-away voice, she continued, 'Absolutely fine, no problems. How's the roof? Good ... Well, here they are!' She passed the phone to Kate.

The first few words her father spoke made Kate feel sad, he sounded so far away, and a small hard lump settled in her throat, making it difficult to answer him. But as she began to tell him about the house and her bedroom, she spoke more and more enthusiastically.

While Phil took his turn at the phone, Kate reported back Michael's news to Great-Aunt Elizabeth. 'Dad says he is planning to go hang-gliding.'

'How interesting,' said Great-Aunt Elizabeth slowly. 'I wonder what made him think of that?'

'Oh, he's always wanted to do it,' Kate replied. 'He says he likes the idea of soaring through the sky,' and she shuddered involuntarily.

Great-Aunt Elizabeth stood up and returned to her desk. She seemed distracted, and Kate watched with interest as she flicked through a file. After several moments, she turned to Kate. 'Come and look at this,' she commanded.

Kate took the photograph that was being held out to her and studied it carefully. One edge was torn and the colour had faded. A very glamorous woman, who looked a little old-fashioned, like a beautiful movie star from olden days, seemed to be staring out at her. She had large, deep-set eyes beneath finely arched and slender eyebrows. Kate took a closer look at her great-aunt, comparing her to the photo. It occurred to her that this might be a photograph of Great-Aunt Elizabeth herself when she was younger.

'She's lovely,' said Kate simply.

To her horror, Great-Aunt Elizabeth, who had just unwrapped and popped a chocolate into her mouth, exploded. 'Crab's claws, Kate! This is the most evil woman in the world!'

Kate, her senses buzzing from shock, recoiled away from the desk. Great-Aunt Elizabeth struggled not to choke on the chocolate and, seeing Kate's alarmed expression, spoke more gently.

'I am sorry to make you jump, my dear. But you mustn't let yourself be fooled by appearances. This woman is my arch-enemy and I have reason to believe that she is at present up to no good. The problem is,' she said, taking back the photograph and peering at it with distaste, 'this photograph is nearly thirty years old. We have no way of knowing how she looks now ... or what she is up to.'

'Except for the eyes,' drawled Fearless, entering the room, his voice still soft after a recent nap. He paused just inside the doorway to lower his head on to his outstretched paws and stretch his back. 'She won't be able to disguise her eyes,' he added, leaning forwards and allowing his back legs to trail behind him as he lengthened his spine still further.

'Who's going to disguise her eyes?' asked Phil, holding out the phone 'Kate, Mum wants to speak to you.'

Kate withdrew to a corner of the sofa, and Great-Aunt Elizabeth passed Phil the photograph.

'This is Margot Jordan, also known as Crystal Farnsworth, Mariah Cruikshank and Penelope Parton. What she's calling herself now is anybody's guess, but she'll be up to no good – that's for certain.'

Phil studied the picture as Kate had done. 'She looks bossy,' he said.

'That,' Great-Aunt Elizabeth retorted, 'isn't the half of it!'

Kate, now fully composed, joined them once more at the desk and looked again at the photograph in Phil's hands. There was, Kate could now see, a coldness; a streak of cruelty in the gaze of those beautifully clear eyes.

Suddenly the door swung open and Barking raced in and sprang up on to a chair beside the desk. 'Harold says to come right away!' he announced breathlessly.

Just then Harold himself appeared in the doorway, looking agitated and even more dishevelled than ever. 'Aunt E., come and see. I think I've found her!' he said, stepping from foot to foot as if the floor were hot, then suddenly dashing back the way he had come. Great-Aunt Elizabeth strode after him, and Kate and Phil hurried along behind her. Moments later, they came to a halt in the threshold of Harold's lab and were astounded by what they saw.

'Woh!' breathed Phil.

There were computers and monitors everywhere, and large machines and generators, some sparking, some

71

passing violet-coloured liquids through tubes of glass piping. There was a telescope that stretched up to a glass dome in the ceiling, so big you had to lie beneath it in a big chair to use it. Kate and Phil entered the lab slowly, their necks craning left and right to take in all the equipment. Phil stopped completely for a moment or two in front of a robotic leg which was hanging in space and swinging back and forth from the knee as if kicking an invisible ball.

At last Phil joined Kate and the others at the computer where Harold had been working. On the screen was the home page of a website advertising a cosmetics company.

'Now this,' said Harold, holding up a computer print-out of an enlarged eye, 'is a high-definition facsimile of our target eye.' He passed the page to Kate and Phil. 'Every fleck and mark on the iris is in a unique position – no two people have the same eye. In fact, no one person has two eyes exactly the same as each other.'

'Just like fingerprints?' Phil asked.

'Exactly so, young Philibuster!' said Harold, rubbing his hands together. 'After scanning the target iris into the computer, I wrote a program to compare eyes on the Internet with our target. For the past few months this computer has been sorting, comparing and discarding images – until just now, when I got a positive match!'

He beamed happily round at them and Great-Aunt Elizabeth slapped him on the back and said, 'Yes, well done, Harold! Now, do please let us have a look!'

They stared as Harold streamed a video on to the screen.

They watched a strikingly beautiful woman glide gracefully down the steps of a private jet and shake hands with a smiling businessman. As the elegantly dressed woman walked confidently towards the camera, a syrupy male voice introduced her, accompanied by the muted strains from the Andante movement of Mozart's 'Symphony No. 40' in G minor.

'This is Lorabeth Lampton,' drooled the voice, 'the brains and the beauty behind the Lampton Cosmetics empire. In a little over a year, Lorabeth Lampton has taken the beauty and glamour world by storm. To mark the opening of eight new Lampton Laboratories around the world, Lorabeth Lampton has pledged her support to the environment. After a meeting with environmentalists, Lorabeth Lampton has been enrolled as a Global Guardian – protector of the Earth's endangered resources!'

At this point the voice broke off and Lorabeth Lampton, who had now crossed the tarmac and stood, smiling, before the camera, spoke.

'Join me, Lorabeth Lampton, and look lovely in a healthy world!'

'That's her! No doubt about it,' Great-Aunt Elizabeth growled, slamming her fist on the desk. 'So, Lorabeth Lampton is it?' she said in a mocking tone, 'Global Guardian my right foot! Skunk and hogshair! Find out what you can, Harold. I want to know her every move – she is up to something, I can feel it.' Great-Aunt Elizabeth usually wore her own heartstone tucked out of sight inside her clothes, but now it signalled its presence by radiating a soft red glow across her neck and throat.

Kate had looked hard at the video, trying to see the resemblance between this woman and the one in the photograph. There was *something*, she decided, but she couldn't quite place it. It puzzled her that the woman looked no older in the video than she had in the thirty-year-old photograph on Great-Aunt Elizabeth's desk.

Great-Aunt Elizabeth jabbed an angry finger at the monitor. 'Evil schemer! Vile betrayer!' she spat furiously, while Harold squirmed uncomfortably in his seat.

Kate noticed that Phil was subdued and she moved closer to him. It was a small gesture, but Great-Aunt Elizabeth, who had been pacing the floor and muttering angrily under her breath, watched by a nervous Fearless and Barking, suddenly became aware of the children.

She stopped and considered them. She stared from brother to sister, and Kate felt that she was about to tell them something important. But the moment passed, her expression changed and she clapped her hands decisively. She turned to Harold and muttered some instructions in his ear, then, facing the children, Great-Aunt Elizabeth's face lightened. She smiled and her shoulders visibly relaxed.

'Now then, Kate and Phil!' She looked them up and down appreciatively. 'You two will need to start a training programme . . .' She turned aside to Fearless and Barking and said quietly, 'Get on with planning that, will you? Stealth and Fitness Level One to start with.'

She drew a deep breath and turned her attention once more to her great-niece and -nephew. Just then Phil's stomach rumbled loudly and for a full three seconds.

'Right now, come along,' Great-Aunt Elizabeth said, rubbing her hands together briskly. 'I'm taking you out to dinner. That's what you two need. And we'll do some sightseeing to cheer ourselves up. I'll show you New York at night. How does that sound?' Kate and Phil looked up at her doubtfully. 'We'll visit my friend Jean-Paul,' she continued, undaunted. 'Lovely chap owns a hotel, marvellous food – fabulous panoramic view from the top.'

So saying, she strode from the lab and began to climb the stairs, three steps at a time. Kate and Phil, assuming their great-aunt was off to fetch a coat, followed her to the foot of the stairs and waited.

She had nearly reached the first landing when she

noticed that the children were not right behind her. 'Hurry up, you two!' she bellowed. 'The helicopter awaits us on the roof!'

Kate and Phil glanced momentarily at each other, grinned broadly, then sprinted up the stairs.

Fearless tilted his head enquiringly at Harold. 'You don't need me, do you?' he asked, repeatedly walking in a tight circle, briefly sitting, then circling again.

'I'll help Harold,' said Barking, his voice resigned. Fearless sprang up the stairs after the others while Barking jumped on to Harold's lap, his tail flicking around spasmodically.

'Remember to take care of Phil!' he called after Fearless.

Night Flight Over New York

Three thousand kilometres to the south-west of New York, in the chill of a desert night, Emily Carter fought the fatigue that invaded her body. Her limbs and fingers were numb with tiredness but her mind was fired with the thrill of the puzzle. In the few hours that she had held the heart-shaped stone in her possession, she had run every test she could think of. So far the stone had defied every attempt at classification. It was not, as she had first thought, a mineral at all; under the microscope Carter could see specks moving. So a life form, then? But there were none of the normal characteristics essential to life: it did not require food, light, air or water. It did not grow. Yet it did respond to being handled and, most remarkable of all, it appeared to respond to thought and human emotion. She had discovered this characteristic quite by chance. She had been re-examining the stone under the highest magnification microscope and was about to X-ray it when, suddenly, the telephone rang. Since giving Carter this task, Mrs Lampton had telephoned her several times, demanding to know what progress she had made. Carter had removed the stone from the microscope and was holding it in her hand when she answered the phone. She listened for a moment without speaking to Lorabeth Lampton's increasingly demanding and belligerent voice.

Carter held the stone tightly as she summoned the willpower and self-control to answer politely. 'I am doing everything I can, but scientific investigation must be rigorous and thorough. I need to repeat tests to minimize the possibility of error.'

As she spoke, Carter's mind was only vaguely on what she was saying. She felt her throat and chest tighten as anger welled up in her. When at last she replaced the phone on its cradle, she suddenly noticed the increasing heat radiating from the stone in her hand. It had turned from black to brilliant red and, as she looked and wondered, it began to cloud up and then darkened once more. It occurred to her that perhaps the stone was somehow responding to her: to her mood, her thoughts, her emotion. Incredulously, Emily Carter set about devising tests for this theory. She placed the stone on the lab bench and, putting her elbows on either side of it and resting her chin in her hands, she gazed at the stone for some time before at last picking it up once more.

For the first time, Emily Carter allowed herself to think about all that had happened since her arrival in Nevada. She flushed as she remembered the impertinent young driver laughing at her. She flushed more deeply at the disappointment of her first meeting with Lorabeth Lampton.

The discovery that her secret benefactor wanted at long last to meet her had aroused feelings in Emily Carter that she had long denied. She had hoped for more than a job, she had hoped for a family. The icy coldness of that first meeting had cruelly destroyed all such hope. She winced as she remembered how she had rushed towards Lorabeth Lampton, her arms ready to embrace her. But her benefactor had stood as still and as hard as a statue and had not returned her smile.

With tears in her eyes, Emily Carter opened her hand to examine the stone. It felt cool and had remained dusky black. She straightened her back, sniffed, and removed her glasses in order to wipe her eyes on her sleeve. That was enough, she decided; wallowing in self-pity would get her nowhere and could cloud her judgement.

'OK,' she said, looking at the stone in her palm. 'I am going to find out what makes you tick.'

Immediately the stone radiated heat and glowed a dark ruby red. Carter jumped a little, then quickly revised her theory. The stone did not respond to all emotion and thought – it was unresponsive to self-pity, fear, doubt and sadness. But more positive emotions – assertiveness, determination and controlled, justifiable anger – all these seemed to activate the stone's energy.

An hour later, Carter phoned Mrs Lampton to tell her of her discovery. She was unprepared for the response. For thirty-six hours without rest Carter had examined the stone, believing that Lorabeth Lampton was as ignorant of its nature as Carter herself.

'So,' her employer had told her calmly, 'the heartstone responds to you – I had hoped that it would.'

Carter spluttered. 'You knew all the time?'

'Of course. Now I want you to find a way of stopping it. I don't want it destroyed, mind you – I just want you to find a way to . . . switch it off. Let me know how you get on.' And with that she had hung up on her.

So, while Kate and Phil experienced their first night flight across Manhattan, Carter struggled through her second night without sleep in pursuit of scientific discovery.

Looking down from the rising helicopter, Phil had felt that he understood maps for the first time. It was clear where the land ended and the sea began and the roads criss-crossed beneath him. He could imagine himself down there, walking about. He loved the yellow-lit stream of traffic from the cars heading downtown next to the flow of red tail lights of the traffic heading uptown on a parallel street. And the glorious towering buildings reflecting shimmering light in glass and shiny metal. He imagined himself scaling those sheer walls like Spider-Man, swinging from roof to roof, crouching in the shadows and leaping up to grab hold of the underside of the helicopter.

Kate, meanwhile, sat stiffly and gripped her knees tightly with her hands. Her knuckles were white and her front teeth were firmly embedded in her top lip, although she was oblivious to any discomfort.

Her initial enthusiasm for the ride had left her as soon as they had stepped through the door at the top of the steep attic stairs and found themselves out on the roof. Looking down after the helicopter first took off, she tried to tell herself that Great-Aunt Elizabeth's diminishing house was a model in a model village and she was not, in fact, a hundred metres up in the sky. But as the machine banked and swerved, tipping her to a forty-five-degree angle, she was unable to fool herself any longer and she suffered a sudden dizzying sickness. And after they had landed on the pad on top of the hotel owned by Great-Aunt Elizabeth's friend, she soon discovered that even having her feet on firm ground – or firm roof – did nothing to quell her spinning head.

Phil had leapt from the helicopter and dashed across the roof to lie flat on his stomach at the very edge and peer over. His shouts of joy, and his exclamations at the things he saw, were snatched away by the wind and made unintelligible. Poor Kate couldn't even look at him without experiencing shooting pains down her arms and legs; the exact same sensations she was convinced she would feel if she really were to fall.

Fearless nudged her hand with his nose. 'What's up? Worried about Phil? I'll take care of him.'

He bounded away from her towards Phil and the sheer drop beyond. Kate's heart jumped and she closed her eyes. When she opened them again, Fearless was sitting on Phil's legs, holding the back of Phil's sweatshirt in his teeth. Phil was squealing with laughter.

Great-Aunt Elizabeth came and put a reassuring arm round Kate's shoulders.

'Is it the height that bothers you?' she asked.

Kate nodded and smiled weakly. Great-Aunt Elizabeth bent down so that she could speak quietly, her mouth close to Kate's ear. 'You must will yourself not to be afraid. Your heartstone will help you. Trust it. Don't give in to your fear; fight back.'

Kate shivered as her hand went to her neck and touched the heartstone. She looked at Great-Aunt Elizabeth, who smiled and nodded encouragingly before turning away to join Phil and Fearless. Kate held the heartstone in her hand and closed her eyes, tightly this time, as if making a wish. It had rained earlier and the ground was wet and the air felt damp. Kate noticed that, even with her eyes closed, her senses told her that she was high up. Perhaps, she thought, the air was perceptibly thinner up here. She imagined her toes on the edge and nothing in front of her but empty space and the fifty-seven storeys to the sidewalk. She swayed slightly and her legs gave a little; she managed to stay upright, but her knees were unsafe hinges. Opening her eyes, Kate saw the night sky and the adjacent towers swim before her. She had let the heartstone fall back against her throat and she held her hands in tightly closed fists by her sides. She could not feel her nails digging into her palms or her teeth sunk into her lip. She was transfixed by the image of a rapidly expanding ground hurtling towards her. Her stomach slipped away from her like silk sliding over satin.

Kate jumped as Great-Aunt Elizabeth's low whisper buzzed in her ear and her large hands rested heavily on Kate's shoulders. 'The heartstone can help you only if you are positive. You are not going to fall.'

Kate took a deep breath and stepped away from Great-Aunt Elizabeth and towards the edge of the building. She took hold of her heartstone tightly in her left hand and held her right hand out in front of her as if feeling her way in the dark.

'I am going to look down from this building,' she thought, 'and I won't be afraid.' As Kate moved her feet cautiously to the edge of the roof, she felt the heartstone warming her fingers. She took a deep breath and looked over. Peering down, through the cool night air on to the tiny, crawling vehicles, Kate began to laugh out loud. It was beautiful and she felt wonderful. She saw the space beneath her not as a void about to snatch her to her death, but as fresh, scented air gently transporting the sights and sounds of the streets to her senses. She looked back over her shoulder and grinned at Great-Aunt Elizabeth. Phil smiled and waved at her, while beside him Fearless wagged his tail.

It was just as well that Michael had not been there to witness his children teeter on the edge of the roof of the Meridian Hotel. He had been reassured by their phone calls and was no longer as distracted with worry as he had been after they first left. He had filled those first few days with self-reproach. Why had he allowed the children to go, against his better judgement? How had he let himself be bamboozled by his wife's crazy old aunt? For once he could not focus on his work: the complex mathematical formulae with which he endeavoured to prove theories of space and the universe. But hearing their happy voices on the phone had lifted his spirits, and the arrival of the builders proved a useful distraction. Soon he was able to get back to his desk, and he felt that at last he was making progress with his black-hole theory. But the absence of the children left Michael with time on his hands and an unsettling nostalgia for his own childhood, those few teenage years that he could remember.

One Saturday morning Michael decided to clear the attic and look for the remote-controlled plane he had built when he was fifteen. The attic was large and the stored boxes sloped in from the roof walls towards the hatch beside which Michael stooped, gazing around him and waiting for inspiration as to where to start. Close to him were the things they used infrequently but regularly, such as Christmas decorations, but he knew that his plane would be in the dark, long-unexplored territory of the eaves. There were masses of stuff that they would never need again, and with a sense of determination Michael began pulling out the things from the children's baby-hoods: the old cot, the wooden high chair, a large bag of baby clothes and blankets.

An hour later, Michael had passed a huge collection of items through the hatch to the landing below and had cleared a largish space around his feet. He was pleased with the progress he had made, but there was still no sign of his plane. He sat down for a rest, realizing with a sigh that he had a far bigger job on his hands than he had first thought. It was as he sat, catching his breath and wondering whether he could finish the job before Charlotte got back from town, that he noticed the corner of a shallow, lidded box tucked behind an old fireguard. Michael reached over and pulled it out.

As he shook the lid free of the box the strangest feeling came over him, as it did whenever he was confronted with his past. On top of the pile of papers in the box was a photograph of himself, aged about fourteen, standing in the grounds of Heathcote School, dressed in football kit. The photograph took Michael by surprise; he had never seen it before and did not remember it being taken. This lack of memory was a source of great sadness to Michael. Any reminder of the terrible accident that had stolen away all his childhood experiences, the joys and the sorrows, tended to be. And yet this photograph was taken after the accident, after the long months of being unconscious and the slow, painful recovery. The reason he did not remember this particular photograph being taken was because he could have had no idea at the time that he was being photographed. It had been taken from a distance with a telephoto lens. It surprised him that Charlotte should have a photograph of him that had been taken many years before they had met. Curious, he thought, that she should keep it hidden away and not show it to him. But the most surprising thing of all was that, in the foreground, partly obscured by a tree, Michael could just make out the back wheels of a motor-bike and the rear end of a large golden retriever.

Michael slumped backwards, his mind reeling. And then he saw the next photograph in the box. It was a faded portrait of three boys, standing side by side, smiling into the camera. The two younger boys Michael was sure he had never seen before in his life, yet they seemed somehow familiar.

The third and eldest boy, however, Michael knew well. He was looking at himself aged about twelve, long before the accident. Slowly turning over the photograph, he read: *Frank, Billy and Michael, 1984.*

8

Stealth and Fitness

Kate sat on a bench in Central Park with Fearless lying in the long grass at her feet. 'I can see you!' she called without lifting her eyes from the book she was reading.

Phil stepped out from behind a nearby tree and stamped crossly up the field where Barking was waiting for him. The stealth and fitness programme had improved their strength and agility equally, but so far only Kate had made any progress with the technique Barking called 'virtual invisibility'. The trick of keeping perfectly still and thinking about nothing at all proved an impossible combination for Phil.

Afternoons were spent sightseeing, and in this respect Kate and Phil shared similar feelings of joy and wonder. There were thousands of tourists in New York but only Kate and Phil had their trips organized by Great-Aunt Elizabeth. As well as numerous helicopter flights, they had enjoyed a speedboat trip along the East River beneath Brooklyn Bridge, and had taken a private launch out to Ellis Island to see the Statue of Liberty.

Harold remained busy in his lab and they saw little of him except at mealtimes. He usually arrived late, and as soon as he sat down Great-Aunt Elizabeth would fix him with a keen eye and demand any news of Lorabeth Lampton. While listening avidly to Harold's report, Kate felt more than a little sorry for him. Great-Aunt Elizabeth was a stern interrogator and an impatient listener. She would glare at Harold as if Lorabeth Lampton's very existence was somehow his fault. Harold gave his updates quietly and picked at his food while Great-Aunt Elizabeth banged her cutlery about and shook copious amounts of salt and pepper on to her plate. It was no wonder, Kate thought, that Harold was thin, and rather surprising that Great-Aunt Elizabeth remained healthy, since mealtimes were so stressful for them both.

Phil, meanwhile, so enjoyed mealtimes that he was oblivious to any tension between the adults. He was enthralled with the ancient oak table and its criss-crossing circuits of gleaming track. The fact that the purpose of this track was to deliver the food of his choice, from the central dome directly to his plate, delighted him. As to the choice of food, it appeared to be limitless; he merely had to make his selection on the touch screen and, all at once, there it was, swishing along on a stainless-steel dish via the track. If everyone ordered at once, the table looked like city rush hour, and although dishes sometimes careered towards the same junction they always just avoided a collision. Phil could have spent hours over every meal, but Kate found the speed and bustle disconcerting and kept a watchful eye on Great-Aunt Elizabeth as she digested Harold's latest news.

Back home in England, Charlotte had returned from town to find Michael sitting quietly at the kitchen table with the photos in front of him. She had entered the house noisily, dropping a couple of parcels in the hall and calling out that she had just been asked by their neighbour where Barking was.

'I hadn't thought about that,' she said, walking into the kitchen and putting a supermarket carrier bag on the worktop. 'I found myself saying that he'd gone missing, so Mrs Parker said he must be pining for the children and she'd help me put notices on –'

At last, Charlotte noticed that there was something odd about Michael's stillness and she stopped abruptly to look at him properly. He sat, motionless, at the table and did not lift his face to look at her. Charlotte's stomach tightened in anticipation of bad news.

And then she saw the photographs.

She lowered herself quietly into the chair opposite Michael and watched his face carefully.

Slowly, Michael raised his eyes to meet hers. 'Who are those boys, Charlotte?'

Charlotte bit her lower lip hesitantly. When at last she answered, her voice was a barely audible whisper. 'They're your brothers.'

Michael exhaled loudly and lowered his face into his hands. He rubbed his palms up and down, then lifted his head to look at Charlotte. He kept his hands in front of his face, his fingertips pressed together and his index fingers against his lips as if he were praying.

'Are they dead?' he asked quietly.

Charlotte stared steadily back at him. 'No, Michael, they're alive.'

Michael grinned widely and then began to laugh.

'Then I must meet them . . . Where are they? Why didn't you tell me?'

Charlotte smiled too, but when she saw his questioning expectant face her smile left her. 'They've changed, Michael . . . things are not the way they were, back then.'

Michael held out the other photograph to Charlotte. 'What's this?' he asked. He was not smiling this time.

'Let's have a cup of tea,' said Charlotte, rising from the table and turning to the kettle. Before she reached the sink, Michael was there, barring her way.

'I don't want tea, Charlotte. I just want to know where you got this photo from and how come your crazy old Aunt Elizabeth is in it?'

'Is she?' said Charlotte unconvincingly.

Michael jabbed at the motorbike with his finger.

'Come on, Charlotte,' he said, 'tell me what's going on.'

Charlotte put the kettle down and slid into her chair.

She sat still and studied Michael's face for a moment or two. Her eyes filled with tears but they did not spill over on to her cheeks.

'When I was kidnapped . . . you and your brothers

had been abducted too. You risked your life to save us, Michael. It nearly killed you. That's how you lost your memory. It wasn't an accident.'

Michael walked slowly round the table and sat down opposite Charlotte before speaking.

'And my brothers? I saved them?'

Charlotte sighed heavily. 'Yes, you saved their lives, but they had been through so much, they were never the same again. Great-Aunt Elizabeth brought you to England to keep you safe. She arranged for you to board at Heathcote; the headmaster was a friend of hers and he agreed to your staying on in the holidays.'

Charlotte reached for the photograph of Michael at Heathcote and turned it towards her.

'Sometimes Great-Aunt Elizabeth would pick me up and drive me out to your school to see you. But we kept out of sight – we were worried that if you remembered, it would make you ill again.'

Michael sat still, his eyes roaming the wall opposite while he thought things through. At last his gaze fell upon Charlotte's face.

'And my parents? What of them?'

'I don't know . . . We tried to find out. I think the three of you were taken from an orphanage.'

Michael nodded sadly. 'So, when I met you at the college dance?'

Charlotte blushed and smiled weakly. 'I sort of planned that,' she said quietly.

Michael's eyes suddenly widened with alarm.

'And this kidnapper? What happened to him?'

'Her . . . She went to prison. For life . . . only . . .'

'What?'

'She recently became eligible for parole . . . for good behaviour.'

Michael stood up violently, sending his chair crashing to the floor.

'And you choose this moment to send our children off with your batty old aunt when she has an enemy capable of kidnapping them and putting them into comas or worse?'

Charlotte, too, was on her feet and she came round the table to take hold of Michael's arms. Her face now wet with tears.

'Yes, Michael. She's out there and she's dangerous . . . evil. And if she has another evil plan, her only hope of success would be to get the children on her side. She would be after the children, wherever they were. The only safe place for them is with Aunt Elizabeth.'

Charlotte stared into Michael's eyes and held his gaze.

'I know what this woman is capable of: she nearly killed you. She has to be stopped, Mike, and I know you think my aunt is a dotty old eccentric but she is powerful and she is our only hope against this vile woman. Aunt Elizabeth can protect the children better than we can. I'm sorry to have kept this from you. It has been so hard. But you've got to understand. You were in a coma for six months. Billy and Frank were all but lost to you, you felt like you had failed them, and when you came round from the coma you didn't remember. It was kinder, safer not to tell you.'

Michael shook his head 'All these years . . .' he mumbled then cleared his throat. 'Right, well, I've been kept in the dark long enough. If our children are in danger, Charlotte, then we should be with them.' He hugged her briefly then turned quickly and left the room.

'Where are you going?' Charlotte called after him.

'I'm going to pack,' he shouted from halfway up the stairs, 'and I suggest you do the same.'

The Historograph

A strong wind ripped round the corner of the house and rattled the windows. In the privacy of her bedroom Great-Aunt Elizabeth paced the floor and growled with exasperation. From the bed, where he sat tall, his tail covering his small feet, Barking watched her, his head tracking left and right and back again as if he were watching a tennis match. At last she sank into the oak-and-leather swivel armchair at her dressing table and sighed.

'The children are very bright. And they're brave,' said Barking, continuing their discussion as he arrived at the dressing table in two graceful leaps. He picked his way among the antique French perfume bottles and ornately framed photographs, and sat down.

'Yes, they seem to be coping very well indeed,' Great-Aunt Elizabeth agreed, 'but are they ready to be shown the Historograph? That's what I must decide tonight. Just when I think I should show them everything, a picture of Michael lying lifeless in the hospital comes to mind and I feel less sure. Then there's Harold to consider – the children are so fond of him.'

'But Michael and Harold are both fine now. I think the children will be OK.'

'I have to get it right, Barking. I want knowledge to give them power, not cripple them with fear.'

'Well then, don't show them what happened last time, just show them how it all began,' said Barking.

Great-Aunt Elizabeth pulled a leather bag out of a drawer and carefully removed a large metal plate. It was made from a silvery metal and its surface was dimpled as if it had been beaten with meticulous care by a small blunt object. Across its broad flat base and the shallow outer rim, seventeen heartstones of varying size and shape were randomly set into the metal. Infinite distorted images of Great-Aunt Elizabeth were reflected across its silvery surface.

Barking moved closer to it and curled his tail round it protectively.

'There are other risks to consider,' Great-Aunt Elizabeth said. 'I shall have to remove my heartstone, and that is not something I do lightly.' She rose and instinctively went to the door, opening it to let Fearless in. He strolled over to the dressing table, where he nodded at Barking before sitting beside the swivel chair.

'I've checked on Kate and Phil – they're both fast asleep – and Harold reckons he'll be working in the lab all night,' said Fearless.

A particularly strong gust of wind shook the window violently and the lamp flickered. Fearless lifted his head and peered down his long nose as he took several deep sniffs at the plate.

'Are you going to use the Historograph?' he asked Great-Aunt Elizabeth, who had moved to the fireplace.

She took a poker from the hearth and placed it in the fire. 'I've decided I will,' she replied and, despite the heat from the fire, she shuddered to think how vulnerable she would be without her heartstone. 'They should know how it all began – it is their legacy.'

'You'll not tell them about the last time?' Fearless asked.

'No,' said Great-Aunt Elizabeth decisively. 'No, I shall spare them the sordid details of the Penelope Parton Pet Emporium.'

Great-Aunt Elizabeth had returned to sit at the dressing table, where she reached out her hand to touch Barking's face while her left hand found Fearless's head beside her knee.

'And you, my dears, I shall spare you that awful memory too.'

After several minutes of silence Great-Aunt Elizabeth stood and took the white-hot poker from the fire. She raised her arm to her neck and touched the ashen tip of the poker to her heartstone. A high-pitched note rose to a crescendo and became inaudible as the heartstone fell from her necklace into her hand. She dropped the poker back into the hearth and held the glowing heartstone cupped in her hands for a second, where it glowed with an intensity far beyond the rays that had ever shone from

Kate's. The energy emanating from it was audible and resembled the hum of a distant swarm of bees. The heartstones on Barking's and Fearless's collars glowed in sympathy, and all three faces, and the room itself, were lit with a red hue.

Great-Aunt Elizabeth brought the heartstone over to the Historograph and placed it against an embedded stone near the centre of the plate, turning it slowly until it locked into place. There was a sudden and momentary blaze that filled the room, reflected in myriad directions at once. Light danced between the heartstones as each of them in turn pulsed with energy.

Great-Aunt Elizabeth stood once more and returned to the door, opening it just wide enough for the animals to pass through. Fearless padded towards the door, but Barking hesitated, poised to jump from the dressing table.

'Shouldn't one of us stay with you?' he asked.

'No, no,' Great-Aunt Elizabeth replied, 'I'll not sleep tonight. I shall watch over the Historograph until events from the past have been absorbed from my heartstone.'

Barking joined Fearless at the door and they filed past her, Barking first, murmuring a low 'Goodnight', followed by Fearless, who padded soundlessly behind, his head and tail hanging down dejectedly.

'Goodnight, my dears,' said Great-Aunt Elizabeth, and she closed the door softly behind them.

The storm that racked New York that night was the worst since weather had first been recorded. Although the heat had been stifling that day, the temperature dropped drastically during the evening, and the rain that fell in torrents was icy cold. It stripped the leaves from the trees and stung the skin of anyone unlucky enough to be caught out in it. The highways were soon empty as cars and trucks that had begun to aquaplane across the tarmac, careering dangerously into oncoming traffic, were abandoned by their drivers. The swollen numbers of pedestrians who began to flow into the subways resembled the swirls of rainwater that poured down the storm drains.

By the time Lorabeth Lampton's limousine entered New York, shortly before 3.30 a.m., the storm had calmed and the streets were deserted. Litter and dustbin lids, billboards ripped from their hoardings and branches torn from trees were strewn across the roads and side-walks. The chaos, and the absence of any sign of life, was welcomed by Lorabeth Lampton, who was able to make quick progress towards Central Park.

In the driver's seat, Bardolph, one of her minders, exclaimed gruffly at the signs of devastation caused by the storm while beside him his brother, Frimley, grunted inarticulately. Bardolph's hairy knuckles slackened then regripped the wheel continually. He was excited. It had been a long time since their employer had required them for this kind of work. A bit of breaking and entering, a bit of demanding with menace, a bit of teaching some loser a lesson in a darkened alley: this was the spice of life for Bardolph and Frimley. For too long she had had them chauffeuring her about, opening doors, nipping into town on shopping errands. This, Bardolph thought with satisfaction, was more like it. Beside him, Frimley cracked his knuckles noisily.

Bardolph parked the limousine in the shadows of an unlit street. 'Looks like there's bin a power cut, heh, heh,' he chuckled as he switched off the engine.

From the blackness of the rear of the car, Lorabeth Lampton's clipped voice cut him dead. 'Be quiet, Bardolph,' she said coldly, 'and get on with it.'

Bardolph and Frimley exchanged glances, before stepping out of the car.

'And don't forget I want the phone lines intercepted *before* you get inside the house,' she hissed after them.

Both men were tall and squarely built and walked with the far apart, slightly waddling gait of bodybuilders. Slowly they crunched their way across the leaf- and branch-strewn street towards an impressive house, which stood behind wrought-iron gates. Parked in the drive was a beautiful black-and-silver Harley-Davidson with a state-of-the-art sidecar. What a shame, Bardolph thought. If he didn't have the limo with that stuck-up broad in it, he would have had that bike.

In the back of the car Lorabeth Lampton watched them approach the house with her lip curled in disgust. What idiots they were, she thought. She slipped her hand into the deep pocket of her fur coat and pulled out what looked like a small torch. She smiled faintly. Thank goodness not all her employees were mindless fools. Carter had excelled herself. With remarkable competence she had invented the Inhibitor which Lorabeth held in her hand. It disrupted the flow of energy through a heart-stone, changing positive energy to negative, and vice versa. The effect would be to weaken and confuse the heartstone's owner. The altered, negative energy would fuel insecurity and doubt. The old, positive energy which had heightened awareness and understanding would be weakened.

'Well done, Carter,' she whispered into the darkness as she squeezed the device in her thin hand. 'Now, if I can place a direct hit with the beam on the old fool's heartstone, she will be off my back forever.'

She watched through the car window as Bardolph and Frimley struggled with the front gate, then disappeared inside. She had little confidence in their ability to succeed, but they would serve the purpose of a decoy. Slipping silently from her fur coat and stepping out from the back of the limousine, Lorabeth Lampton, dressed in a black leather catsuit, made her way to the rear of the house. A few moments of agile climbing gave her access to the bedroom windows.

Lorabeth Lampton could not believe her luck when she saw the soft red glow radiating from one of the highest windows. She held Carter's Energy Inhibitor in her teeth and flattened her sinewy body against the wall, where she clung, out of sight, ten metres from the ground. Slowly inching her way across to the window, Lorabeth Lampton peered inside and saw the back of Great-Aunt

Elizabeth's head slumped forwards on to her chin. She could also see the large heartstone resting in the Historograph. With one claw-like hand clinging to the ornate security bars at the window, Lorabeth Lampton aimed the Inhibitor at the heartstone and fired a thin ray directly at it. Great-Aunt Elizabeth's slumped shoulders gently rose and fell and she snored softly.

In her bedroom, along the hall, Kate was asleep and at the mercy of a dream that ran, pleasant one moment, then terrifying the next. She dreamt that she was standing on a rock on the shore of a blue and gentle sea. A fragment of high cloud slowly passed overhead as the sun sparkled on the water. A gentle wind lifted her hair, and she raised her face skyward to feel the warmth of the sun on her skin. Suddenly the rock beneath her bare feet squirmed and shifted slightly as if it were alive, the sea rolled an oily black and the sky darkened and dropped oppressively close until it was hanging above her head like a dungeon ceiling. Screwing her eyes tight shut, Kate fell to her knees and placed her hands flat on the rock. Instantly, she felt the warm sun on her back, and the rock felt reassuringly hard and stable beneath her grasp. Kate opened her eyes and found the sea blue and inviting. She slipped into the water and began to swim. She marvelled at how the droplets of water, shot through with sunlight, dripped from her fingers like jewels. Then her foot touched something thin and slimy, a length of weed which, even as she kicked it free, began to curl and tighten round her ankle. All at once the water seemed to thicken and clutch at her skin. She struggled to pull her arms and legs through the water until she could not make another stroke. Frantic with fear, she found herself being sucked under by the glutinous water, and this last sensation woke her. Kate lurched upright, noisily filling her lungs with air. She kicked her legs free of her duvet and glanced uneasily round her room. Above her head was a skylight in a ceiling where she had been used to stars and moonlight. In the dim half-light she could just make out a series of strange shapes where her pool should have been. As her eyes adjusted to the gloom she was able to identify a large, kidney-shaped bath, propped up on several breeze blocks. Jutting through the cracked plasterwork of the adjacent wall, an overflow pipe trickled water into the bath.

Kate opened the door of her room and found the house in darkness. She trailed her hand along the wall and found the light switch. She flicked it on and off a few times, but it remained dark. Stepping out on to the landing with the intention of going to Phil's room, she noticed a curious red light shining under Great-Aunt Elizabeth's door. She turned and walked along the hall, then paused outside the door to listen. Her fist hovered, a fraction away from the door, and it wavered there as she hesitated to knock. She held her breath and leant her ear towards the door; she could hear a strange humming sound accompanied by a sporadic and rhythmic rumble. Deciding not to knock, she lowered her trembling hand to the doorknob and held it there for a moment as she took two or three deep breaths. She gripped the doorknob in her hand and slowly began to turn it clockwise until she felt the lock click free.

Outside the window, Lorabeth Lampton had clung, motionless, for five minutes. Her aim was true; a thin ray of light bisected the room, passed over Great-Aunt Elizabeth's shoulder and focused on the tip of the large heartstone resting in front of her. Lorabeth Lampton's narrowed eyes considered the Historograph and the advantage she would have if she were to possess it. Suddenly, a small movement beyond the dressing table caught her attention. The door handle was slowly turning. Swearing under her breath, Lorabeth Lampton snapped off the Inhibitor and ducked back, away from the window into the shadows. She clenched the Inhibitor in her fist. Had she had long enough to destroy the heartstone? Perhaps not. But hopefully, surely, she had weakened and damaged it. Her face twisted into an angry frown, Lorabeth Lampton began a swift and silent descent.

Kate had stood so long outside Great-Aunt Elizabeth's door, poised to enter, that the handle felt warm and her palm had begun to sweat. She chewed on her bottom lip as she deliberated about whether to lean against the door and enter the room. She could feel her heart thumping in her chest and the sound of her pulse roaring in her ears. Kate placed her face against the wooden door and willed herself to listen hard. She suddenly recognized the strange intermittent rumbling which at first had confused her: it was the sound of Great-Aunt Elizabeth snoring. Kate slowly released her grip on the doorknob and allowed the lock to click back into place.

Shivering, she scuttled away from the door and hurried along in the dark, back to her own room: stark and comfortless now without the enchanting effects of virtual reality. Yet her bed still held the warmth from her body and Kate pulled her duvet tight around her and curled up small. It was some time before sleep came and released her from a confused stream of thoughts. Perplexing questions formed in her mind and Kate decided that, first thing in the morning, she would go to Great-Aunt Elizabeth for some answers.

Michael replaced the phone after another unsuccessful attempt to call the Central Park house.

'I can't understand it,' he said, coming into the sitting room where Charlotte had just switched on the television, 'the line must be out of order.'

'This might explain it,' Charlotte said, turning up the volume. The programme was interrupted by a news flash.

'Extraordinary climatic conditions have devastated New York and the Eastern Seaboard tonight. High winds gusting up to ninety miles an hour and a freak ice storm have brought down power lines, and the city of New York is without electricity.'

'I hope they're all right,' said Michael, his voice tense.

'They'll be fine,' said Charlotte. 'Let's send an e-mail, and phone when we get there.'

'I just hope our flight isn't delayed too much,' Michael replied wearily. 'There will be a backlog of planes trying to land in New York.'

'Come on,' said Charlotte, switching off the television and getting up to leave the room. 'We had better get some sleep, we've got a big journey ahead of us tomorrow.'

'Yes,' said Michael, 'or a big wait.' And he switched off the light.

10

Intruders in the Night

Harold, haggard and numb from lack of sleep, stepped from his laboratory at six a.m. and saw the splintered doors to the vestibule and the light flashing on his intruder alarm in the hall. His brow furrowed with disbelief as he reached out a long, thin arm and took hold of the nearer of the swing doors. He pulled on the handle and the door swung off its hinges.

Clawing his slender fingers through his bedraggled locks, Harold stepped timidly into the chaos of the lobby. Broken glass and some drops of blood proved disconcerting evidence of a struggle. His hands flew to his face as he realized, with a stabbing pang of guilt, that he had made a terrible mistake. Accustomed now to working all night, developing various espionage gadgets and tracking Lorabeth Lampton's business developments on the Internet, he had allowed his security arrangements to lapse. When the power had failed, he had been excitedly preoccupied with his 'Insult Fermenter' and had switched to his basement generator. It had not occurred to him to connect to the back-up security system. He had previously sealed the lab with soundproof doors and was wearing earplugs to protect himself from the impact of a fermented insult during the trials. He had heard nothing. An overwhelming sense of guilt and failure swept over him and he groaned out loud.

Just then, Barking and Fearless, looking wet and bedraggled, appeared at the front door. The locks had been smashed, and here, too, the wood was split and damaged and the antique glass panel had a large fist-sized hole in it.

'What on earth ...?' Fearless began, frowning at Harold, then looking around at the mess.

Barking picked his way across the broken glass and sped up the stairs to alert Great-Aunt Elizabeth.

Feeling morose after being reminded about the Pet Emporium, Fearless and Barking had taken a long walk through town, ending up at dawn beside Grand Central Terminal where they had managed, all those years ago, to escape from Penelope Parton. They were too far away, in their minds as well as in distance, to have been alerted to any danger.

As Barking ran past her bedroom, Kate appeared at her door. She had woken, minutes before, with a pounding headache and a hollow, sick feeling in her stomach. Her face was pale and dark shadows circled her eyes. She hugged her arms round herself and called after Barking as he bounded up to Great-Aunt Elizabeth's door.

'What's the matter? What's happened?'

She hurried along the hallway to where Barking was

scratching and calling out to Great-Aunt Elizabeth. Kate joined him and began banging on the door with her fist. She remembered how she had been reluctant to knock a few hours earlier, and now regretted it deeply.

'If she's not OK, I'll never forgive myself,' Kate thought.

Just then Great-Aunt Elizabeth flung her door open. In one hand she held a poker, and she immediately turned and took it to the fireplace. Her dark grey hair tumbled in chaotic curls about her head and shoulders. Her skin was sallow and waxy – she was an alarming sight.

She stooped and lifted Barking into her arms. 'What is it?' she asked. 'Tell me.'

'It would seem,' said Barking, 'that there has been a burglary of some kind.'

As Great-Aunt Elizabeth dropped Barking to the floor and strode off along the hallway, her hand flew to her heartstone and pushed it out of sight inside her dressing gown. Kate got only a quick glimpse of it, but there was something about it that troubled her; her own heartstone was glowing intensely whereas Great-Aunt Elizabeth's was dark and foggy.

Kate was about to say something when Phil flung open his bedroom door. 'Look at this!' he cried, waving his arm in a broad sweep, inviting Kate to look at his bedroom. The expanse of prairie, the corral and his palomino had all gone. There was still a hammock, slung between two scaffolding poles, and, behind a length of two-by-four, a saddle on a wooden frame.

'There's been a power cut,' said Kate, 'and the virtual reality is off. Come on, something's happened.'

Kate and Phil rushed downstairs and arrived at the lobby to find Harold standing on the top of a small stepladder.

'Who did this, Harold?' Great-Aunt Elizabeth demanded.

'We shall soon see,' said Harold as he reached up to the intruder alarm monitor and removed the memory card.

'I don't think they got further than the vestibule,' Fearless said, appearing from down the hall.

They all followed Harold through Great-Aunt Elizabeth's library and gathered round a computer monitor in the office. Harold pushed the memory card into the drive.

On the screen, a flickering image of the darkened vestibule appeared. In the bottom right-hand corner of the screen the time was recorded: 02:58. Everything looked normal.

Harold forwarded through the film until 03:36, when suddenly a large, gloved fist appeared through the glass in the front door. The gathered group exclaimed and jumped back a little. Kate watched, horrified, as the gloved hand withdrew for a moment, then reappeared with a steel wrench and swung viciously at the lock. The hand disappeared a second time, and after a moment's pause the door began to shake intermittently as if being rammed from the outside. Suddenly the wood gave way in the frame and the door swung inwards. Two large, dark figures hurtled into the lobby. They seemed to steady themselves for a moment and, just as they drew themselves up to their full height, ready to proceed through the next door, the Invisible Butler went to work.

It was too dark to see their faces, but suddenly both men flew two metres into the air and then slammed to the ground as if dropped. One of them, apparently life-less, stayed down; but the other scrabbled to his feet, only to be thrown again. This time he was flipped forwards and his head smashed against the swing doors into the house; they splintered from top to bottom from the impact. Both figures slowly scrambled up and, looking flustered, they bumped into each other in their haste to retreat back through the front door. Seconds later, they were both yanked into mid-air, where they dangled as if impaled by their bottoms on invisible butcher's hooks. The shocked little group of watchers winced as the men's heads swung violently together then bounced apart. There was another momentary pause, then both figures were propelled through the front door, head first. The timer registered 03:39.

Phil cheered, while Kate, whose own head was thumping, grimaced.

Great-Aunt Elizabeth was the first to speak. 'Lorabeth Lampton will be behind this – of that I am certain.' Her hand moved fleetingly over her heartstone.

'At least they didn't get in,' said Harold. 'We were rather caught with our guard down.' He lowered his head and shuffled his feet nervously before mumbling, 'Sorry.'

Fearless and Barking looked at each other guiltily.

'Well, it can't be helped now,' said Great-Aunt Elizabeth, 'and, by the looks of things, no real harm's been done. I'll phone for a carpenter to come and see to these doors.' She turned and strode to her library.

Her head still pounding, Kate went back to the vestibule and stood, surveying the mess for a moment or two. She frowned at the debris of glass and wood and felt that something was more wrong than a smashed-up lobby. Deep in thought, she slowly fingered her heartstone as it glowed warmly against her neck. At last she turned and quietly followed her great-aunt into the library. Great-Aunt Elizabeth, discovering the telephone line to be dead, reached for a mobile phone and was towering over her desk as Kate came up behind her.

'Great-Aunt Elizabeth,' Kate began, but she got no further. Her great-aunt jumped and the mobile slipped through her fingers on to the desk.

'Rats' ears, Kate! Whatever are you creeping up on me for?' she asked crossly.

Startled, Kate stepped back.

'Well? What is it?'

'I don't feel well,' Kate murmured, for want of a way to express her sense of foreboding.

Great-Aunt Elizabeth smiled sympathetically as she placed the phone to her ear. 'Run along and ask Harold to give you a pill or something,' she said. 'I'll be there directly.'

*

Everyone was subdued over breakfast until Great-Aunt Elizabeth cleared her throat and frowned questioningly at Harold. 'Well, Harold, apart from a thwarted attempt at house-breaking, did you glean any more news of what that woman is up to?'

Harold lowered the thinly buttered toast and Marmite from his lips and put it back on his plate. 'Apparently, yesterday Lampton Cosmetics officially opened the eight new laboratories,' he replied and lifted his toast to his mouth.

'Where are they? Do we know?'

Harold looked at his piece of toast before putting it down again. 'They're in Washington, Paris, Milan, Tokyo, Madrid, Moscow, Canberra and . . .' he paused and swallowed before finishing, 'and Stuttgart.'

This last name caused one of Great-Aunt Elizabeth's more violent reactions. 'Germany?' she exploded, getting up from the table. 'I can't believe she'd dare go to Germany, not after the way she encouraged that vile little man, back in the nineteen-thirties.' Great-Aunt Elizabeth, spluttering with agitation, began striding round the table and was followed, with matching speed, by her scrambled egg.

Kate, who had been quietly sipping water and holding her temple to ease the throbbing, thought she would vomit as the plate of quivering egg, dashing along on its little track, hurtled past beneath her nose.

'What are these laboratories for, Harold?' Great-Aunt Elizabeth demanded.

Harold looked wretched and stared miserably down at his plate. He was wearing a shirt and jacket above pyjama bottoms: a style of dress caused by absent-mindedly pushing his way back out through his Dried-and-dressed the way he had gone in. He clasped and unclasped his long fingers as he told them what he had been able to discover.

'I'm still gathering information, but I know that some of the laboratories are producing a much-prized anti-ageing cream which makes the skin look drastically younger.'

Harold reached for his glass and took a sip of water before continuing.

'She is hosting a conference on "Environmental Protection" at the new Washington laboratory, where she is launching a new perfume ...' Harold paused, then added quietly, 'It's called "Legacy".' Great-Aunt Elizabeth strode past him menacingly and he grimaced. 'Aunt E., please do slow down. I'm afraid your egg will suffer wind damage.'

Great-Aunt Elizabeth stopped dead, causing the plate to halt abruptly and the egg to splatter against a jar of tawny marmalade.

'I want to hear what she has to say at this conference,' she announced, 'and I would like to take a closer look at one of these laboratories of hers. Can we do that, Harold?'

Harold scratched his head. 'Well, yes, I thought you would want to do that. Invitations have already gone out to the press, and there are organized tours of the laboratory. If we can get inside, we should be able to navigate around the ventilation system. I have hacked into the database of the Washington architects who designed the building.'

'Excellent, Harold!' Great-Aunt Elizabeth bellowed, sitting down at last. A forlorn-looking piece of toast, soggy and without its topping of scrambled egg, slowly arrived in front of her.

Phil was staring at Great-Aunt Elizabeth, his mouth full of pancake and maple syrup. 'Wajzsh uhrbarht ujzsh?' he asked, then, reaching for his water, took a slurp and repeated, 'What about us, Great-Aunt Elizabeth?'

'Oh, we're all going. Don't worry, my dear, I need you with me,' she replied.

Kate felt her stomach lurch. Something was terribly wrong, but what? She frowned hard, trying to fathom out the cause of her anxiety. She looked at Great-Aunt Elizabeth, who was staring quizzically at her plate of bare, wet toast. 'I have no choice,' thought Kate, 'but to trust her.' The thought did not comfort her.

'So, when is this conference?' Great-Aunt Elizabeth asked.

Harold coughed and mumbled, 'Ah, well, there's a thing, you see – meant to tell you first thing, only, what with all the upset – it's all a bit of a rush – it's ... tomorrow.'

Great-Aunt Elizabeth leapt to her feet once more.

114

'Then we have no time to lose! We must prepare to go at once!'

She marched towards the door, then spun round to face the table again.

'I will need you to be able to work when we get there, Harold. How much time do you need to get ready?'

Harold jumped jerkily to his feet. 'I can probably do it by this afternoon – perhaps Kately and Philling can help me,' he suggested.

With breakfast abandoned, Phil went happily to assist Harold in the lab while Kate, in a more sombre mood, followed behind, struggling to keep in check a small trickle of anxiety that persisted in creeping around her stomach.

11

An Encounter with the Enemy

Even with both animals and Harold, plus all the luggage and extra equipment, the sidecar was spacious. They were heading across town towards the interstate freeway through block after block of untidy streets – all casualties of the previous night's storm. They saw a car that had smashed through a shop front and a child's bike dangling from the top of a tree. It was late afternoon and the city-wide power cut continued. The absence of neon shop signs made the streets look dreary. The gloom matched Kate's mood perfectly, while Phil, excited by the prospect of adventure, chattered happily to whoever would listen.

Once they were speeding along the highway, Kate peered up at a dark, thunderous sky and soon it was pouring with rain. Great-Aunt Elizabeth lowered her goggles to her eyes and gritted her teeth as the Harley and sidecar sped south towards Washington. As the journey progressed, Kate's unease grew. It was a horrible feeling: the pit of her stomach felt chilled and unstable. Her instinct was telling her that they should not have left New York, and the long drive on the freeways beneath menacing, dark skies and rain was compounding her feeling of dread. This time, as she had glanced through the sidecar's dome at Great-Aunt Elizabeth, Kate had been dismayed to see her looking vulnerable and strained as she grimaced against the driving rain.

Inside the sidecar, Harold, who had been tapping away at the computer, suddenly gave a low whistle. 'Unbelievable weather at the moment – and not just here in the States either,' he added as a gust of wind and rain buffeted the sidecar. Harold accessed a digital radio station in London and they listened to reports of torrential rain causing problems of flooding in Milan, and a *tsunami* that had devastated the coast of Japan. Barking explained that this was a huge wall of water which could destroy coastal towns. While he was talking, their attention was suddenly drawn back to the radio, which told of another strange and unconfirmed report about molten lava running down the gutters in Paris.

'As soon as we get back to New York,' Harold mused, 'I'd like to get hold of some seismology equipment and set up a weather station. There's some weird stuff going on at the moment.'

'What's seismology?' Phil asked.

'Seismology,' replied Harold, 'is the study of geological movement – earthquakes and so on.' He sighed ruefully. 'However, I am preoccupied with the study of Mrs Lorabully Lampton at the moment, so excuse me while I get on.'

While Phil chattered away to Fearless, Kate stared out

at the rain in silence. Barking had curled himself up on her lap and she stroked him absently.

Harold continued to tap away at his computer and at last he clapped his hands together. 'Eureka!' he cried and told them that he had found the perfect accommodation. 'It's not far from the centre of Washington and will make a discreet operations headquarters. I've entered it in the Harley's navigation system.' He paused and glanced at his watch. 'We should arrive about 8 p.m. . . . which just gives me time for a doze.'

So saying, Harold reclined his seat, closed his eyes and snuggled down. To Kate's surprise, within a couple of seconds he began snoring softly.

After four hundred kilometres in the driving rain, the Harley finally left the freeway by a slip road just as a patch of faint light broke through the relentless sheet of rain clouds overhead. As they proceeded into the city the weather changed completely and a weak evening sun began to shine. At last the Harley turned a corner and slowed down beside the barren forecourt of a second-hand car showroom which had fallen into disuse.

The building was of two storeys, with a workshop and showroom downstairs. The glass doors of the showroom, behind which the most prestigious cars had once been displayed, were smashed and the garage had long since seen the last of its tools and equipment. It now contained nothing but grease, a few old rags and a couple of flat tyres that had been thrown into the inspection pit. The forecourt had once provided parking for thirty cars. In the past, rows of valeted and gleaming cars had displayed their prices across stark white banners on their windscreens. Brightly coloured bunting had stretched overhead, fluttering noisily like a flock of exotic birds. Now the little plastic flags lay, shabby and torn, in a pool of motor oil and the one remaining car, an old green sedan, sat on its flat tyres, its driver's door and various lights missing. Two large wheelie-bins had long ago been hauled out from their recessed accommodation beside the garage workshop and were not only full to overflowing, but were surrounded by more dumped household items. A wooden-framed armchair, the sort that is used to furnish staffrooms and institutions, stood between a bin and the abandoned car, its tweedy fabric ripped away to reveal the crumbling yellow foam underneath.

Great-Aunt Elizabeth drove the Harley past the chair and parked out of sight of the road behind the bins. She dismounted briskly and stood tall with her arms akimbo as she surveyed the scene. 'Perfect!' she announced crisply, 'Well done, Harold, a superb hideout. No one will come bothering us here.'

Kate stepped out of the sidecar, and broken glass crunched beneath her feet. There was a terrible smell, thick and fusty-sweet, and a viscous liquid oozed in the shadow of the bin. Fearless began to charge round the lot, nose down and tail wagging as he investigated every nook and cranny. After stretching his lanky limbs and yawning loudly, Harold wandered off round the side of the building. He reappeared a moment later and beckoned them to follow him.

Beneath a sign that said 'Reception upstairs' a door opened easily and they were assailed by a smell of damp.

'Good work, Harold!' Great-Aunt Elizabeth snapped as she brushed past him and followed Barking up the stairs. Kate and Phil covered their noses and mouths with their hands and followed cautiously behind Harold, stepping over a large pile of unopened mail.

There was a small landing, and a door led to a bathroom at the top of the first flight of stairs. The next flight ascended at a right angle to the first, and Barking hesitated at the foot of these steps, his nose and whiskers twitching as he took in the heady cocktail of smells wafting from the floor above. 'Wait here while I check it's not already occupied,' he whispered.

Great-Aunt Elizabeth followed Barking up the stairs while Kate and Phil loitered nervously beside Harold on the half-landing. They heard a sudden clattering disturbance overhead, followed by Great-Aunt Elizabeth's huge voice bellowing, 'Rats!'

Immediately, thirty or so rats came hurtling towards them down the stairs, a flowing, turbulent mass of squealing, leaping brown fur. Phil cried out and leapt into the air. His arms and body flailing, he managed to throw himself off the landing and into the bathroom as the rats descended. Kate, however, was horrified to discover that she was rooted to the spot. As rats passed on either side of her feet, Kate felt one of them run up her leg before launching itself down the next flight of stairs from her shoulder. For a fragment of a second, its little claws were entangled in her hair and Kate felt a tiny, shocking tug at her roots. She began to scream and fell against Harold, whom she then attempted to climb as if he were a ladder. The rats were followed by Barking, who bounded down the stairs in pursuit and managed to mutter, 'Sorry about that!' as he shot past. Kate shuddered and the hairs on her arms and legs rose and her skin and scalp crawled. Her face was as white as an empty page.

Phil was laughing hysterically in the doorway to the bathroom, where he had watched, fascinated, and felt a small thrill of disgust as the sea of rats washed over his sister.

'Come along, up you come!' boomed Great-Aunt Elizabeth's voice from above their heads.

Harold placed his hands on Kate's shoulders and began guiding her forwards. She shuddered again; first her fingers, then her arms and back and finally her legs tingled, as she dragged herself up the stairs.

The reception area was large and covered the entire top floor of the building. A window ran the length of the room and overlooked the forecourt. Beneath the window a deep sill served as table and desk, and was cluttered with empty takeaway boxes, ashtrays, old newspapers and rats' droppings. The walls and ceiling had once been white but were now stained a sticky yellow-brown from the thousands of cigarettes that had been smoked in the room. The floor was covered in a brown-and-green dog-tooth-checked carpet that was stained by numerous grey, shiny patches. In the middle of the carpet, three vinyl sofas were arranged around a glass coffee table. The centrepiece was an enormous ashtray containing several dozen wrinkled cigarette stubs.

At the far end, a small glass office jutted into the room. It had broken venetian blinds at the windows and a sticker saying MANAGER on the door. In the little galley beside the office and opposite the window, a sink, a kettle, a two-ring electric hob and a microwave served as a kitchen.

'This will do nicely!' Great-Aunt Elizabeth announced, marching towards the office and pulling open the flimsy door. The entire structure wobbled. 'You can get yourself set up in here, Harold!'

Kate went over to the window and looked down through the grimy glass to where Barking and Fearless were still dashing about in the forecourt. Phil came over and stood beside her.

'Come along, you two, no shilly-shallying. Go help Harold get his stuff in!' Great-Aunt Elizabeth commanded, fixing Kate and Phil with a glare and nodding her head towards the stairs. 'I'll make a start with clearing up this awful scragpit of a mess.'

As they cautiously retraced their steps, Kate asked her brother what he thought of Great-Aunt Elizabeth. 'Do you think she seems different? I mean, I know she's odd, but does she seem even stranger to you?'

Phil shrugged. 'I guess she's got a lot on her mind, worrying about Lorabeth Lampton.'

As they reached the sidecar, a passing bus caught their attention. 'Speak of the devil,' Kate whispered. The now familiar face of Lorabeth Lampton was emblazoned on the entire length of one side of the bus, along with the time and date of the conference and a slogan.

'That'll make Aunt E. mad,' Fearless mumbled, passing by with a roll of cable in his mouth.

'Maybe she won't see it,' Phil said hopefully.

Harold, covered in cobwebs and carrying wire cutters, emerged from a cupboard under the stairs as they staggered back with as much equipment as they could carry.

'Thanks guys,' he beamed. 'Just got the power back on. If you don't mind bringing the rest up, I'll start wiring in the hardware.'

'"Looking Lovely in a Healthy World!"' Great-Aunt Elizabeth roared in disgusted tones as they entered the room. 'Can you believe it?' She was busy stuffing magazines and takeaway cartons into a rubbish sack.

Kate, Phil and the animals continued back and forth, bringing things up from the sidecar. On their last trip up, Phil collapsed into one of the plastic sofas while Kate stood in the doorway and watched Great-Aunt Elizabeth's grey and haggard face. After a moment, Kate wandered into Harold's office, where he was setting up his temporary lab.

'Hi there, Kate-kadoodle,' he said, glancing up from a

minute circuit board, a soldering iron in his hand. He was wearing magnifying safety goggles which made his eyes appear enormous. 'Thanks for helping with my stuff.'

Kate looked around for somewhere to sit and, finding nothing apart from a paper shredder and an empty water cooler in the corner, leant against the table where Harold was working.

'Harold, do you think it was good idea to come to Washington?' she asked.

Harold turned his gigantic eyes to the ceiling while he frowned in thought.

'Well, we shall find out more about what she's up to – I think we will be able to get inside the lab. But if you're asking me, do I think we will get to the bottom of it all here, then I doubt it.'

'Why?'

Harold sighed, set down the soldering iron on its stand and pushed the goggles up over his forehead, where they disappeared into the wiry spirals of his hair.

'It's all too public: the cosmetics, this Global Guardian bit. There will be a side to the Lampton enterprise that she has to hide away, and that's where we'll need to have a look-see. I expect that the headquarters of her operation will be in a secret location.'

'How can you be so sure?' Kate wondered.

Harold tapped the side of his nose. 'Well, you can put me to one side and label me out-of-service if I'm wrong,' he said and, winking at Kate, he put the goggles back over his eyes and picked up the soldering iron.

Kate watched him for a moment, then went out of the office and slumped on to the sofa beside Phil and Barking, and surveyed the room. Great-Aunt Elizabeth had removed the rubbish and wiped down the surfaces, but it was still bleak and horrible and smelled musty.

Barking leant close to Kate's ear and she felt a whisker tickle her cheek.

'What do you think of the place?' he whispered.

'It's hideous,' Kate replied.

Just then, Great-Aunt Elizabeth appeared at the top of the stairs carrying armfuls of camping equipment. She beamed at them, her silver-streaked black hair wild about her face and shoulders.

'I knew these would come in handy one day!' she cried, dropping the bundles on the floor. 'It's a marvellous all-in-one tent and sleeping bag.' She began to undo one and roll it out on the carpet. 'We can put them up in different corners of the room – that way we'll get some privacy.'

It unrolled just like a sleeping bag until, two-thirds of the way along, the top end popped up to make a small tent.

'Now isn't that clever?' she said, smiling round at them.

'Personally, I don't think it's very suitable for the children to be sleeping on the floor,' said Barking, staring down his nose at the carpet. 'It's filthy.'

Great-Aunt Elizabeth drew herself up to her full height and glared at him.

She reached into her pocket for a chocolate and stuffed it into her mouth.

'Perhaps,' said Barking, 'the children would be better off in a hotel.'

'Oh, yes please!' cried Phil, while Great-Aunt Elizabeth narrowed her eyes and seemed to be considering Barking's suggestion.

After a moment she gave a small smile. 'I would prefer it if we all stayed together, but if you could come too, Barking?' she suggested, casually scooping her hair up into a bun.

'Yes,' he said. 'Of course I'll come.'

'Good, that's settled then,' she announced, heading for the door once more. 'I'll just go and get you a cat basket.'

'Now hang on a minute,' Barking called as he leapt from the sofa and dashed after her.

After a few minutes, Great-Aunt Elizabeth and Barking returned, she carrying a large wicker cat basket with a metal mesh grid for a door, and he striding at her side, his hackles raised. Barking went straight to the window, where he sat with his bristled back turned against them, and he would acknowledge no one, not even Phil or Kate. His tail trailed out stiffly behind him. It was thick and bushy, and every so often it whipped about jerkily like a black viper.

Great-Aunt Elizabeth stood and watched him for a while, popping one chocolate after another into her mouth. At last she said, 'You only need get in it in public places.'

At this concession Barking calmed down; his tail became slimmer and gave only an occasional flick.

Harold emerged from his office and said he would be glad to have Fearless help him test the surveillance hardware.

'We shall be back first thing tomorrow,' Great-Aunt Elizabeth told Harold. 'You will be ready, won't you, Harold? Will that give you enough time to brief the children?'

Harold nodded and smiled at Kate, who was gazing at him. His long, lean face looked tired, and shadows the colour of ripe aubergines lurked below his eyes. 'He looks as though he could do with a long hot bath and a good night's sleep in a comfortable bed,' Kate thought, and she felt sorry for him.

As they traipsed back down to the sidecar, Great-Aunt Elizabeth murmured, 'Let's ride by this laboratory of hers. I wouldn't mind a closer look at it before tomorrow.'

The Harley pulled away from the forecourt and hurtled towards the intersection. Pulling out into the flow of traffic, they saw another advertisement on a gigantic hoarding on the opposite side of the street. Across the ten-metre-high billboard, a stunningly beautiful woman stood, one hand resting on the delicate shoulder of a startlingly beautiful child. The woman held her other hand stretched out in front of her, and nestled on her palm was an elegant bottle of perfume. In cupped hands, the little girl cradled a vibrant and healthy-looking planet Earth. The slogan read:

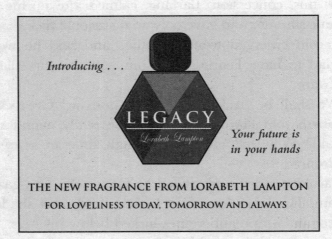

Introducing . . .

LEGACY

Lorabeth Lampton

Your future is in your hands

THE NEW FRAGRANCE FROM LORABETH LAMPTON

FOR LOVELINESS TODAY, TOMORROW AND ALWAYS

Kate glanced out at Great-Aunt Elizabeth and saw her face flicker and twitch. They took a right turn at the next junction and followed the temporary signs for the conference that had been attached to traffic lights and signposts. At last they turned the corner – and there it was.

Great-Aunt Elizabeth stood astride the Harley and gazed up at the building while Kate, Phil and Barking peered out through the sidecar's glass dome.

Vast concrete, windowless walls stretched as far as they could see. On top of the building, up at the skyline, metal tunnels twisted and turned across the roof like some giant robot's misplaced intestines. They stared in silence. Clearly, Kate thought, it had nothing to do with 'looking lovely' or a 'healthy world'.

Slowly Great-Aunt Elizabeth revved the idling bike and put it into gear, then she turned the Harley in a broad sweep and drove them back the way they had come. Kate put her hand to where the strange feeling in her stomach loitered. Quite suddenly she knew that she must be prepared to face danger; that her instinctive unease was a signal to be wary and on her guard. As they drove away from Lampton Laboratories, Kate imagined the building looming menacingly behind her and she shuddered, but as she glanced back they turned the corner and it disappeared from view.

They drove for a few minutes until Great-Aunt Elizabeth waved her arm aloft and pointed. Kate and Phil saw a grand hotel coming up on the left.

'Basket time for me, I suppose,' Barking remarked grimly.

As they pulled up, a hotel porter in a red uniform approached and did a poor job of hiding his curiosity and amusement as he took the Harley's keys from Great-Aunt Elizabeth and oversaw the unpacking of their luggage on to a trolley.

Passing through the revolving door into the hotel's lobby, Kate felt a sudden shocking surge of warmth from her heartstone. Perhaps, she thought, it was because she was reminded of her Dried-and-dressed, and she glanced down to confirm that she was in fact still dressed the same.

The hotel was grand, and neither Kate nor Phil had ever seen anything like it, except in the movies. They followed Great-Aunt Elizabeth to the beautifully carved mahogany reception desk, where a perfectly composed man greeted them respectfully as if he were accustomed to welcoming gigantic elderly women dressed in motorcycle leathers. Light from an enormous glass chandelier danced about the brass buttons of his uniform and the gold rims of his spectacles. Phil noticed one of his bushy black eyebrows twitch slightly as Great-Aunt Elizabeth placed Barking's basket on the desk while she signed the hotel's register.

Suddenly Great-Aunt Elizabeth started and jabbed an agitated finger at the top of the page.

'Lorabeth Lampton is a guest here?' she inquired of the concierge.

'I believe so, madam,' he replied.

'In that case I'm afraid we shall not be staying after all,' said Great-Aunt Elizabeth firmly, pushing the register back towards him. 'Kindly have our luggage brought back down.'

Great-Aunt Elizabeth took Kate and Phil by the hand and began to pull them away.

Just then, Barking, who had been suffering the humiliation of a cat basket with some dignity, hissed loudly from the reception desk. Great-Aunt Elizabeth lifted the basket up to her face and, for the benefit of the concierge, made kissy noises at the wire-grid door.

'What is it, pussums?' she asked, moving discreetly away.

'Enemy at twelve o'clock,' Barking whispered, 'and don't call me "pussums"!'

Spontaneous applause broke out in the lobby, and they turned to see a glamorous woman descend the stairs. Great-Aunt Elizabeth jostled the children out of view behind an enormous potted palm and placed Barking at their feet.

She put her finger to her lips. 'Not a sound,' she warned and, turning away, she stepped purposefully into the lobby.

Peeping through the foliage, Kate and Phil saw an imposing figure standing at the bottom of the marble staircase. She was a fantastically tall woman, perhaps one metre eighty in her bare feet, though now she wore a pair of emerald-green shoes that added a further fifteen centimetres to her height. She was as lean and bony as Great-Aunt Elizabeth was broad and muscular. Her dress was made from a curious metallic fabric and was deep midnight-purple in colour. It was shorter at the front than at the back, and this gave her a languid appearance. Her eyes were deep-set and her gaze piercing beneath high, arched eyebrows. She stood straight and held her head high as if she were peering over the top of some invisible person. Her platinum-blonde hair was combed close to her head and held at the nape of her neck by a diamond-studded clasp. She blinked slowly then, equally slowly, smiled slightly as she stepped forwards.

'Elizabeth . . . what a surprise.' Her voice was cold and the words were pronounced perfectly and drawn out to give each syllable equal weight. She said 'surprise' as if she were saying something faintly disgusting.

Kate took hold of Phil's hand and he did not pull away.

Great-Aunt Elizabeth moved closer. 'Margot,' she said. 'It's been a long time.'

The woman frowned. 'Actually, my name is Lorabeth Lampton, and you must excuse me, I am very busy.'

Great-Aunt Elizabeth took another step forwards. 'I didn't expect to see you here,' she persisted.

Lorabeth lifted one perfect eyebrow. 'Really?' she said inquiringly. 'It seems to me, Elizabeth, that you pop up every time I turn round.'

'How strange,' countered Great-Aunt Elizabeth. 'It is twenty years since we last met . . . you were in rather a hurry then, as I remember.'

'I think you must be mistaken, Elizabeth; twenty years ago I was a mere girl. You are getting confused in your old age.'

Lorabeth Lampton raised a lean arm and clicked her fingers. In an instant, two men in identical brown suits and electric-blue ties appeared at her side. They trailed between them a silk-lined fur coat which they draped across her shoulders. The men were very similar in appearance and could have been brothers. They shared square, bullish heads with bald pates, wide shoulders and, both children noticed as they dangled at their eye-level, large, hairy hands. Both men had angry-looking bruises on the opposite side of their foreheads.

Kate was horrified by the fur coat; it was luxuriously

soft and the palest of golds – so like Fearless that it made her skin prickle with outrage.

As the coat dropped on to her shoulders, Lorabeth Lampton made to leave. For a terrifying moment she seemed to stare directly at the potted palm, and Kate held her breath.

'Well, Elizabeth,' Mrs Lampton said, turning towards Great-Aunt Elizabeth once more, 'I'm afraid I can do nothing for your mind, but you will find several Lampton products which will prevent further decay of your face and body. Goodbye.'

'She's gone too far this time,' Barking hissed from the cat basket at Kate and Phil's feet.

Flanked by the two men, Lorabeth Lampton swept past the children and out of the hotel. Kate came out from behind the palm and stared after her.

Great-Aunt Elizabeth, her lips pressed tightly together, stormed past. 'Blasted bumbling bogweed!' she spat under her breath.

'She's the one who kidnapped Mum, isn't she?' Kate asked suddenly, turning to where Great-Aunt Elizabeth was gathering up the cat basket. Great-Aunt Elizabeth stopped in her tracks, absent-mindedly holding the basket at a forty-five-degree angle so that Barking struggled to stop himself sliding into the mesh door. She stared at Kate as a porter emerged from one of the lifts with their luggage.

'Shall I take this to your car, madam?' he asked.

'To my motorbike, yes,' said Great-Aunt Elizabeth,

while to Kate and Phil she said, 'Let's get back to Harold and Fearless. We can't talk here.'

Kate was quiet in the sidecar, while Phil chattered excitedly to Barking. 'She wasn't that scary, I'm sure we could duff her up!'

'We need to find out first what she's up to. Believe me, if there's any duffing up to do, I'll be in there with a left-paw swipe – claws fully extended, don't you worry. I hate that woman,' said Barking forcefully.

This revelation interrupted Kate's train of thought. 'Barking,' she asked, 'have you met that woman before?'

For once Barking did not answer immediately and instead began coughing.

'What is it?' asked Kate.

'Furball,' Barking replied and continued to cough.

'Barking,' Kate pleaded, 'please tell me what's going on.'

Barking glanced at Phil, who sat staring and smiling, lost to the world. In his imagination he was karate-chopping Lorabeth Lampton on the side of her long, sinewy neck.

'Be patient, Kate,' Barking said at last. 'Aunt E. is going to tell you all about her when we get back.'

The Origin of the Heartstones

The Harley wove its way through Washington's traffic, and in ten minutes they were pulling up in the forecourt of the second-hand car dealer. Having heard their approach, Harold and Fearless appeared at the dingy upstairs windows.

'What brings you back so soon?' Fearless asked as they climbed the stairs and arrived in the office.

'We've seen her! Vile, hideous woman!' Great-Aunt Elizabeth cried, crossing the room and turning to face them so that her back was to the window.

While Kate and Phil sat down on the sofa and watched with some trepidation, she went on to tell Harold and Fearless that Lorabeth Lampton had been at the hotel.

'It was a stroke of luck, seeing her name on the register,' said Great-Aunt Elizabeth, 'but unfortunately she came down into the lobby before we had time to leave.'

'Why didn't you hide with us?' Kate asked.

'Oh, she would have sensed my presence,' replied Great-Aunt Elizabeth. 'The energy from my heartstone is especially strong because I have you with me. You will have noticed, Kate, how your heartstone glows strongest when we're all together.' Kate nodded uncertainly, her hand automatically reaching to her throat where she felt the reassuring warmth of her heartstone with her fingertips. It was true: her own heartstone was positively humming with energy.

'Does she have a heartstone, then? How did she get it? Did she steal it from you?' Phil asked, and Kate, too, was anxious to hear the answers to her brother's relentless questioning.

Great-Aunt Elizabeth looked carefully from Kate to Phil, and Kate sensed a reluctance, a holding back, and it made her even more determined to get some answers.

She got to her feet and, looking directly into her great-aunt's dark eyes, took a deep breath. 'Didn't *you* sense that she was there?' Kate asked. 'It seems so odd – you used to know who was in the next room. I felt it as soon as we went into the hotel, but I didn't know what it meant.'

Great-Aunt Elizabeth had been leaning against the window sill; she suddenly stood alert and stared at Kate, her forehead lined in a deep frown. 'No, no, I didn't expect her to be there – that is very odd.' She turned to where Harold hovered in the doorway of his makeshift office, 'What do you think of that, Harold?'

Harold shrugged and shook his head.

'I haven't been feeling too good recently,' Great-Aunt Elizabeth murmured, shaking her head slowly.

Fearing that she was about to be side-tracked yet again, Kate pressed on, determined now to get some answers.

'Tell me about Lorabeth Lampton ... I'm right, aren't I? She did kidnap Mum, didn't she? I heard you say that you hadn't seen her for twenty years and I remember Dad saying that was the time of Mum's last trip with you. Is that when it happened?'

The look of confusion left Great-Aunt Elizabeth's brow and she studied Kate's face as if impressed by her cleverness. Phil, too, was looking at his sister with a face that suggested a mixture of admiration and bafflement.

Encouraged, Kate said, 'And there's something familiar about her, and it's not just the photograph. When I watched her in the lobby ... there was something ...' Kate's voice trailed away and she shrugged. She couldn't quite put it into words, but she stared hard into Great-Aunt Elizabeth's shining, dark eyes.

'Oh, Kate, my dear,' her great-aunt sighed.

Fearless padded quietly over to Kate's side and put his nose against her hand. On her other side, Barking reached out a paw and touched Kate's leg tentatively.

'What is it?' Kate demanded, glancing down at them, then in a quieter voice she added, 'Please tell me.'

Phil looked at his great-aunt anxiously and for once his imagination failed him.

At last Great-Aunt Elizabeth spoke. 'Yes, she is the kidnapper, but I'm afraid it's worse than that, children. Lorabeth Lampton, as she now calls herself ... is Charlotte's mother.'

There was a stunned silence for a moment, then Kate collapsed on to the sofa behind her. Phil said slowly,

'If she's Mum's mother and you're Mum's aunt ...' He hesitated.

'Yes, Philip,' said Great-Aunt Elizabeth grimly, 'that woman is my sister – as misfortune would have it.'

'Then she's our ... grandmother!' Phil added quietly, making the connection he had been looking for.

''Fraid so,' said Barking, nudging Phil's shin with the top of his head.

'No, she's not!' cried Kate, jumping to her feet once more. 'Our gran is in England – she knits us sweaters and makes marmalade and rock cakes, and she loves us. That woman is a monster! Did you see her disgusting coat? Animals were killed to make that coat.'

Fearless groaned in sympathy, sounding more like a dog whining than his usual self. Phil looked thoughtful and gazed calmly at everyone in turn.

'What I don't understand,' he said after a moment's silence, 'is how you can kidnap your own daughter.'

Phil's eyes narrowed as he imagined himself stepping out of Mackenzie's corner shop back home and his mother running at him, throwing a sack over his head and bundling him into the back of a van. It made no sense at all.

Great-Aunt Elizabeth took a deep breath and exhaled a long sigh. 'Yes, it is all terribly confusing – that is why it has been so hard, knowing how to tell you. Your mother came to live with me when she was a little girl ... she ran away from her mother, and of course I took her in. My sister was furious and vowed to get your mother back –'

Great-Aunt Elizabeth waved her arms and ushered them to settle on the sofas.

'Sit down, Kate. Sit down, both of you. I will tell you everything, but it's a long story and you might as well make yourselves comfortable.'

She turned to where Harold stood, fidgeting from foot to foot.

'Harold dear,' she said kindly, 'you needn't stay. Perhaps you could pop out and get us some pizzas?'

Harold smiled and nodded and then he bumped into the door as he left the room and went clattering down the stairs.

Phil had settled himself on to one of the sofas and Fearless clambered up beside him. Opposite him, Kate curled her feet up under her legs and Barking, his eyes half closed, nestled against her. They waited quietly, expectantly looking at Great-Aunt Elizabeth as she stood gazing ahead, wrapped in thought. Slowly she took a chocolate from her pocket, carefully unwrapped it, and put it with luxurious care into her mouth. She breathed deeply a couple of times then began to speak.

'Many, many years ago . . .' She paused to stare at the children in turn, who gazed steadily back at her, 'according to the story passed down to me by my mother, my great-grandmother accidentally fell into the concealed entrance to the sub-Atlantic tunnel and she found, clutched to the chest of a brittle skeleton, a large leather bag. At first she thought she had discovered treasure – the bag contained a large silvery plate, fashioned from an extraordinary metal, and what she at first believed to be gemstones. But as soon as she held each of the stones, she experienced their power and energy. She understood how special they were and how dangerous it would be if they fell into the wrong hands. She believed that she had been chosen to protect the stones and to make sure they were used for good and not evil.'

Kate had been expecting a proper explanation, not some fairy story, and she felt a twinge of irritated disappointment as Great-Aunt Elizabeth continued.

'You have already learnt a lot, you are observant and can see for yourselves that I am different. I think you both understand that my heartstone makes me what I am.' She paused. 'But a heartstone will not respond to just anyone. It is clear as soon as a person touches a heartstone whether there is a bond. The heartstone must then be worn next to the skin, and there it develops, sharing the experience of the person who is wearing it. Just as children learn and understand more about themselves and the world, the heartstone also adapts from experience and in turn enhances and accelerates the development of the wearer. The heartstone will increase a person's potential in every respect: they will become many times stronger and far cleverer than an ordinary person.'

Two chocolates were swiftly unwrapped and popped, one after another, into her mouth.

'Did you know that even the most intelligent person uses less than ten per cent of the brain's cognitive capacity?' Great-Aunt Elizabeth smiled at them, her eyebrows raised in respect to this little-known fact. 'Wearing a heartstone enables a person to access the rest. And, of course, when you inherit a heartstone, you reap the benefit of the experience of the person who wore it before you.'

Kate put her hand to her throat and experienced a sudden and almost overwhelming surge of love and gratitude for her mother. When she looked up, Great-Aunt Elizabeth was smiling at her and tapping her own heartstone.

Watching from the sofa, Phil felt small and left out until, suddenly, Great-Aunt Elizabeth told them something so utterly unbelievable and amazing that his self-pity vanished. 'I shall be eternally grateful to my grandmother, for it was she who discovered how to use the heartstones for time travel.'

Kate felt her muscles tense, while Phil let out a loud gasp. Great-Aunt Elizabeth dug deep into her pocket and took out another chocolate. The room was silent, apart from the rustling of cellophane.

'Time travel!' said Phil at last in an awed whisper.

Great-Aunt Elizabeth absent-mindedly followed the chocolate with yet another and shook her head sadly. 'Not any longer, I'm afraid, Phil. Those days are gone.'

She sighed and pulled several chocolates out of her pocket and began unwrapping them and pushing them into her mouth. She began to pace the room slowly as she resumed her story, noisily sucking up the chocolate drool that had begun to escape from her lips.

'Time travel is only safe if the travellers are united in purpose, and one heartstone in particular is essential: the keystone.'

Great-Aunt Elizabeth paused beside Phil, unwrapped a chocolate and tipped it out of its shiny paper into his mouth.

Barking wriggled slightly beside Kate, shifting his weight from paw to paw as he watched the delivery of the chocolate through half-closed eyes.

Great-Aunt Elizabeth continued to pace the room, her heavy leather boots making a soft ticking sound as she lifted them from the sticky carpet.

'We always had to be discreet, wherever and whenever we lived; as I have told you, it doesn't do to attract attention. We had the technology to live in great comfort, of course, but mostly we lived simply and kept our talents to ourselves.' Great-Aunt Elizabeth stared sadly into space for a moment or two before continuing. 'Then, one day when I was about twelve years old and my sister Margot was ten, my mother discovered that someone was using the power of the heartstones in a selfish and evil way.' Great-Aunt Elizabeth closed her eyes and kept them shut as she continued. 'I do understand the awful shock you have had, my dears. You see, that traitor, that vile perfidious betrayer,' and her voice dropped to a whisper, 'was my own father.'

Fearless whimpered sympathetically. Great-Aunt Elizabeth stood still for a moment. Her hair, a mass of grey-streaked black curls, was pinned precariously on top of her head. She shook her head slowly from side to side and a heavy curl worked loose and fell across her face. Great-Aunt Elizabeth removed a pin, opened it with her teeth and, pushing her hair up roughly, replaced the pin with a sharp jab as if fixing the wayward curl permanently to her skull.

At last, Great-Aunt Elizabeth smiled, first at Kate and then at Phil. She unwrapped two chocolates, one after the other, and gave them one each. Barking's head followed Kate's chocolate as it passed by in her hand, his nose and keen eyes tracking its path exactly. As Great-Aunt Elizabeth turned and resumed her story, Barking hopped on to the arm of the sofa and watched her intently as she slowly paced the room.

'My mother was able to trick my father out of the heartstone she had given him when they married, and then she took my sister Margot and me and we travelled around for a few years before settling down in sixteenth-century Suffolk.'

'The sixteenth century?' Phil exclaimed. 'Where were you before?'

'France, eighth century,' Great-Aunt Elizabeth replied matter-of-factly.

At this point Harold returned and placed three boxes of pizzas and a two-litre carton of orange juice on the table, before slipping away to his glass office, mumbling that he still had much to do. Great-Aunt Elizabeth came to the table and poured herself a large mug of orange juice.

Despite his excitement, Phil was hungry. He lifted the steamy lid of the nearest box and tore off a slice of pizza, which drooped beneath the weight of its toppings.

'What happened to your father?' Kate urged, retrieving a string of mozzarella that dangled from her slice.

'Left him to explain his sudden lack of influence to Charlemagne,' Great-Aunt Elizabeth replied matter-of-factly as she downed her juice in four steady gulps and slammed the mug down on the table, 'so he never became the big shot he hoped to be – he'll be nothing but a heap of dust by now.'

She folded her arms and leant against the window sill as she studied both children's faces in turn while they hungrily ate their pizzas.

Kate glanced over to where Phil was squirming in his seat, his eyes shining with excitement. His life of day-dreaming fantasies had prepared him to accept all this easily, but a mere few weeks ago, Kate knew she would have dismissed this story as ridiculous. Great-Aunt Elizabeth remained silent and Kate allowed her thoughts to wander, conjuring up memories of her old life. She saw herself filling her days, as she used to, with friends, school, TV, computer games and rollerblading. Having fun had meant sleepovers and midnight feasts, catching the bus into town or just sitting on the swings in the park and chatting with her friends. Yet, Kate recalled, even then she had felt different; she'd had a sense that something was missing from her life. She knew that she would not be able to tell anyone about Great-Aunt Elizabeth, and now she completely understood why her mother had kept her secret. You need evidence to back up stories of time travel. Without seeing Great-Aunt Elizabeth, or meeting Harold, or having Barking and Fearless speak to you, it would sound like childish nonsense. Kate looked over once more at her brother. He had just helped himself to a third slice of pizza, and she realized that he too was different; for one thing, he had just spent half an hour sitting still. Kate wondered if people would notice a change in her. Would she be able to go back to school in the autumn and live her old, ordinary life?

'Might it be possible to travel through time again one day?' Phil asked, taking a huge bite of his pizza.

'In theory, yes. But sadly, the keystone is missing. In any case, my sister and I would have to co-operate – which, my dears, is not very likely.' Great-Aunt Elizabeth fell silent and had a faraway look in her eye.

She was interrupted in her reverie by Phil. 'What I don't understand is, how . . .' He stopped in order to chew vigorously and swallow his mouthful. 'I mean, what happens to all your things when you time travel?'

Great-Aunt Elizabeth ruffled his hair, 'Excellent question. Good, logical thinking. Well, anything in close proximity can be taken too. Otherwise we would hide things in the tunnel. If there was time, of course; we lost some very precious things over the years. Mother, Margot and I moved about a lot – from place to place and from time to time. It was a wonderful life in many ways.' Great-Aunt Elizabeth beamed with pleasure. 'Our mother was a marvellous woman, very striking and terribly influential. No matter where we pitched up – Babylon, Constantinople, Tudor England, the Roman Empire, seventh-century Cornwall – we always dined in the best houses. I was particularly fond of Mother's friend Arthur, he was such a lovely man – now, I do still have the parting gift he gave my mother. My beautiful kitchen table.'

At this piece of information Phil jerked up straight in his seat. 'Holy shamoley!' he cried, echoing one of Harold's sayings. He loved that table but had been so taken with the mechanics and the slick silver tracks that covered it, he had barely noticed the hefty oak beneath. Yet, for all those meals he had been sitting at *the* Round Table.

'King Arthur's table?! I've eaten my dinner at King Arthur's Round Table? I can't wait to get back to New York and have a closer look!'

Great-Aunt Elizabeth appeared to be enjoying Phil's enthusiasm until a new weariness crept into her expression and she sighed deeply. 'Yes,' she said sadly, 'for some years we were very happy, and then something unspeakably terrible happened.'

Great-Aunt Elizabeth stood still and gazed steadily ahead of her as if she were standing in respect beside someone's grave. Slowly, she turned her gaze to the children. Eventually she nodded her head as if she had come at last to a decision.

'There are certain things I cannot bring myself to speak about, nor could merely being told them let you appreciate the full horror of what came to pass. You must see for yourselves.' Great-Aunt Elizabeth reached forwards and placed her large hand under Barking's chin. 'Go in and ask Harold to bring out the Historograph, will you?'

Barking nodded and padded silently across the carpet.

13

A Vision of the Past

'Come near, my dears,' said Great-Aunt Elizabeth and she put her arms round Kate and Phil's shoulders and pulled them closer to the large metallic plate that Harold had produced from a battered leather bag and placed on the window sill. The plate, which looked as if it might have been a gift from an ancient king, was half a metre in diameter and made from a curious shiny metal which seemed as though it were only just opaque and only just solid.

'Look out across the surface of the heartstones,' said Great-Aunt Elizabeth, her voice hushed and intense. 'Ignore your reflections; look into the space just above the plate and try to focus.'

What came next happened so quickly that neither Kate nor Phil could describe it. They were both aware of some kind of shock, but whether it was a flash of light, a sudden shrill scream or a fleeting but intense odour neither could say. But they both felt the disturbance of it tingling their spines and, had it not been for Great-Aunt Elizabeth's strong arms holding them close, both would have jumped away.

'Look carefully,' said Great-Aunt Elizabeth, 'and tell me what you see.'

Phil saw a thousand upside-down versions of himself reflected in the shiny metal dimples. The embedded heartstones began to glow in random sequence; as one dimmed, so another flared.

'I can see the heartstones,' said Kate, 'but what is it?'

'It's called a Historograph,' said Great-Aunt Elizabeth softly. 'Now, you must take your eyes away from the surface; ignore the reflectors and look *above* the heartstones, not at them — focus your attention in mid-space. What do you see now?'

Phil and Kate gasped. Suddenly, where there had been nothing, they were looking through wisps of cloud and then down on treetops and rolling countryside. An image, like a moving hologram, but clearer and more lifelike, had appeared in front of them. As they watched, the scene grew and seemed to completely surround them.

'Yes, dears,' Great-Aunt Elizabeth said in her slow voice, 'keep watching carefully. What you see is the English countryside of the sixteenth century — the last time my mother, sister and I lived together as a family.'

As they continued to watch, they became less and less aware of the room around them; it was as if they were now invisibly placed inside the scene they viewed.

A few straight roads had been left by the Romans but most were unmade and wound their way from village to village. From each village you could see the church spire of the next in the distance. In the woodlands between the villages lived wolves, along with wild pigs and deer, the fox and the badger. In one of these villages two girls lived with their mother. No one remembered when or how they had arrived and, as well as being strangers, there was something strange about them. The people of the village grew suspicious of this family of women who appeared to live in some comfort despite having no man to provide for them. The mother and elder daughter particularly aroused suspicion; they often walked and talked together and appeared to be plotting something. The younger daughter fought in the dirt with the local children and usually won, and when the miller's son had come home with a black eye and bloodied nose, the miller had grabbed hold of the girl in order to give her a good hiding. He soon let go of her and told afterwards how his hands had become hot and had tingled painfully when he touched the child. One day (and this is the day Kate and Phil witnessed with the clarity and immediacy of having actually been there) the villagers had had enough.

It was a beautiful summer morning and Elizabeth stood watching from the doorway as her younger sister ran off to play. She turned to where her mother sat at the table and quietly closed the door behind her.

'As the eldest you will inherit responsibility and must learn how to manage, should anything happen to me,' the mother said, beckoning her daughter to sit beside her. She was a striking woman, tall and dark haired and with a strong, proud face. Despite the warmth of the day she had lit a fire in the hearth. Now she took a hot poker from the flames and carefully touched it against the stone she wore round her neck. She removed Elizabeth's in the same way and the girl held them while her mother lifted a familiar leather bag out of a chest beneath the shuttered window. From it she removed the Historograph and placed it on a small table by the fire. Elizabeth watched her mother position the heartstones on the base of the plate and lock each into a unique position on top of a matching stone. From a smaller bag containing several heartstones, she removed the largest one and held it over the Historograph. This, she said, was the keystone, and its power would enable time–place travel. The young Elizabeth watched and listened carefully as she bent over the Historograph.

Suddenly, there was a hammering on the door and a great clamour of shouting and cursing outside. The door burst open and several men charged into the room and immediately seized the mother, handling her roughly.

'Protect the Historograph and the stones!' she hissed at Elizabeth as she was dragged from the house, upsetting the table and chairs.

One man grabbed hold of Elizabeth's shoulder, but he quickly snatched his hand away and stared at his palm in alarm. In her own hands, hidden behind her back, Elizabeth could feel the warmth and energy of the stones. The man hesitated before turning and following the rest of the villagers out of the house.

As fast as she could, Elizabeth held each heartstone

against the chain round her neck and touched it with the poker. Turning, she snatched up the Historograph and the small pouch, thrust them into the leather bag and slung it over her shoulder.

By the time she ran out of the house there was no sight of the crowd, but she turned in the direction of the village green, following the sound of distant shouts and curses.

At the green a large crowd had gathered, jostling one another and shouting, 'She's a witch! Kill the witch! Kill the dark one!'

Elizabeth ran forwards and screamed at the men, who had lashed their mother to a ducking stool, while Margot dodged the spit and stones aimed at her by the local children. The ducking stool was roughly fashioned from wood and hastily forged iron hinges. Leather straps with large buckles were fixed to a crude seat, and these were pulled cruelly tight round the accused's legs and chest.

Three men hauled on a length of plaited ship's rope, and the chair was dragged on to its side before it rose jerkily into the air and was swung out over the water.

Elizabeth screamed again and began to force her way forwards through the crowd, but her mother's penetrating glare stopped her in her tracks. Elizabeth stared back at her mother and reluctantly began to nod through her tears. Just then the men released the rope and, accompanied by gasps and cheers from the crowd, the chair plunged into the water.

Elizabeth stepped back into the crowd and shouldered

her way through the jeering mob until she stood beside Margot. Moving as if to walk past her, she leant close to her sister's head and whispered, 'Follow me – we have to get away from here.'

Elizabeth walked on until she was behind the first house, and then she began to run. More cheering reached her ears and she realized that her mother must have survived the first ducking and was being doused a second time. Her survival would confirm to the villagers that she was indeed a witch. The punishment would continue until she was dead, and then they would come looking for the daughters. Glancing back, Elizabeth saw Margot tearing through the trees behind her, followed by the miller's son. Elizabeth flung herself through the door of the house and snatched the poker from the fire; she removed the two heartstones from her neck just as Margot tumbled into the room. Elizabeth pulled her close and touched the glowing poker to Margot's heart-stone. The younger girl gasped as it fell from her neck into Elizabeth's hands. Wrestling the Historograph from its bag, she took both their heartstones and the keystone, and hurriedly turned them over and round until each was in the correct position to click into place on top of its partner.

As the miller's son arrived in the doorway, he saw the sisters bent double over a low table. A strange high-pitched sound pulsed through the air and he shielded his eyes with his arm as a bright flash of red light rose up in front of the girls and filled the room. A moment later, it was silent and the miller's son lowered his arm and squinted into the gloom.

The room was empty.

Kate and Phil became aware of Great-Aunt Elizabeth's hands slipping from their shoulders; suddenly the sights, sounds and smells conjured by the Historograph were lost to them. Kate felt the tears, previously unnoticed, damp and cold on her cheeks.

'Fate can be cruel,' said Great-Aunt Elizabeth. 'Or perhaps the time and place were ill chosen. My super-human mother, confidante of kings and presidents, architect of pyramids, adviser to Leonardo da Vinci, was cruelly, needlessly drowned in a Suffolk duck pond in 1568.'

She shook her head dolefully and, taking a large handkerchief from her pocket, blew her nose loudly. Her face was grey and had collapsed into an expression of grief and fatigue.

'I could never live in England after that,' she said nasally. 'Margot and I reacted very differently to our mother's death. For me, it strengthened my resolve to fight ignorance and evil; whereas Margot became increasingly greedy and cruel – she is our father's child, I'm afraid.'

As she spoke, Great-Aunt Elizabeth slipped the Historograph into its leather bag and gently nudged Kate and Phil towards the sofas.

'Where did you go, when you disappeared?' Kate asked, sinking into her seat.

'Mother had taught me well, but as you saw there was little time to think. I headed for the future – my plan was to get us as far away from such barbaric practices as I could. By chance, not design, I transported us to the twentieth century, and we arrived in Chicago in 1924.' Great-Aunt Elizabeth took a deep breath and exhaled loudly. 'And what a challenge that was! At first I was far too wrapped up in myself to notice that Margot was hanging out with some unsavoury characters. I was aware that her friends had rather odd names: Bugsy, Mickey the Hat, Dave the Dog – that sort of thing. Within five years, Margot was calling herself Crystal Farnsworth and was single-handedly running the mob.' Great-Aunt Elizabeth snorted. 'I had the devil of a job crushing that one!'

From the sofa where he had wriggled his way back in beside Fearless, Phil sat up eagerly, his eyes shining, as shoot-out scenes from gangster movies flashed through his mind.

'Some years later, she ran off to Europe,' Great-Aunt Elizabeth continued. 'The next thing I knew, she was consorting with a lunatic called Adolf and had changed her name to Mariah Cruikshank.' Great-Aunt Elizabeth shuddered. 'But that is another nasty story.'

'But,' Kate persisted, fearing that Great-Aunt Elizabeth was about to change the subject, 'how did she come to be our . . . mum's mother?' She could not bring herself to say the word 'grandmother'.

'We had a brief reconciliation in 1945 – at least Margot

needed to get away and she needed my help to time travel. We didn't go far in time or distance – just to California in 1962 – but what a difference! At last we could relax and be ourselves,' and Great-Aunt Elizabeth began to smile at the memory. 'I bought my Harley and dyed my hair fuchsia pink and no one batted an eyelid. But it wasn't long before Margot went her own way. I can't say I tried to stop her, and I didn't see her again for several years. Then, quite suddenly, she just turned up at the New York house one day carrying a tiny baby – your mother. Her husband, she told me, was a zoologist and they had settled in Africa. She seemed changed: much calmer, happy even. She wanted some of our mother's heartstones for her new family.' Great-Aunt Elizabeth sighed and shook her head sadly. 'To my eternal regret I gave her the heartstones she wanted. It wasn't until your mother ran away and came to me, some nine years later, that I realized what a terrible error of judgement I had made.'

'How many heartstones does she have?'

Great-Aunt Elizabeth tilted her head as she considered Kate's question.

'She has six now, but only her own is of any significance. The others have their uses but are not as powerful. That's why it was such a blow to her to lose your mother – she lost the power of Charlotte's heartstone as well.'

Kate glanced over at Phil, who was slumped into the sofa, staring quietly into his lap.

'What about Phil?' she asked. 'Is there a heartstone for him?'

Phil looked up quickly, but the expression on Great-Aunt Elizabeth's face warned him to expect a disappointing response.

'The heartstone that should be Phil's has been missing for many years.'

Fearless raised his enormous head and put it down on Phil's lap while Barking jumped up and lay on the back of the sofa behind Phil's head.

Great-Aunt Elizabeth gazed at him for a moment or two.

'Make no mistake though, Phil, you are no ordinary nine-year-old boy.' She smiled at him. 'The legacy of the heartstones is as much yours as your sister's. The heartstone that is rightfully yours is special, and so are you.'

Phil felt his body tingle with a thrilling mixture of hope and pride.

'Meanwhile,' Barking said softly in Phil's ear, 'Fearless and I are here to look after you.'

'What happened next?' Kate asked. 'You said you regretted giving her the heartstones. What did she do with them?'

Hearing a creak, they turned their heads and saw Harold standing in the doorway of his glass office.

'I thought perhaps we could discuss plans for tomorrow now, since you're all here – you know, get the children all kitted out.'

Kate and Phil looked quizzically at Great-Aunt Elizabeth.

'Sorry, my dears, the rest of my story will have to wait. I need you two to do a little spying for me.'

Arrivals and Departures

Their flight had been delayed for sixteen hours and, as time slowly crawled by, Michael became increasingly restless and agitated. Charlotte had every faith in her aunt and she knew the children would be fine, so she attempted to reassure Michael as best she could. Yet she, too, found the waiting hard. It was as if, somehow, a whole age had compressed itself into that wait. Every second was a fraud and felt as though it were of a minute's duration. Ten minutes had somehow cunningly concealed an hour inside itself. Each half-hour was illegally smuggling three hours into a future that felt as if it might never arrive.

In comparison, the flight itself felt short and was a relief. At least now they were getting somewhere. Michael was calm and patient now, but he was quiet and seemed troubled by private thoughts. Charlotte tried to cheer him, but he would neither be coaxed into conversation, nor read his book, nor watch the in-flight movie. He ate his meal in silence.

Charlotte refused to let Michael's anxiety unnerve her. She knew better than anyone the threat that Lorabeth

Lampton posed, but she had invested a lifetime of trust in her aunt, and she was determined and confident that it would be no different this time. Great-Aunt Elizabeth would take care of everything. Yet, as they stepped into the arrivals lounge at John F. Kennedy Airport, Charlotte was more than a little relieved when Great-Aunt Elizabeth justified the faith she had in her so soon.

A smiling young man approached them. 'Excuse me,' he asked them politely, 'am I right in thinking you're here to visit your aunt? Only, she asked me to come and get you.'

'Aunt Elizabeth did? She will have got our e-mail then,' Charlotte said, glancing at Michael, her eyebrows raised as if to say, 'You see? I told you everything would be OK.'

'How are the children?' Michael asked, putting down his case and flexing his fingers.

The young man made a grab for the luggage while flashing a broad grin at Michael and Charlotte. 'Well, they're out of town for a couple of days. All I know is, your aunt said to come and fetch you.' He turned and strode away, and Charlotte and Michael hurried after him.

'Where have they gone to?' Michael asked the young man's back as he put the case in the boot of a waiting car and slammed it shut.

He moved swiftly from the back of the car to the passenger door and opened it wide for Charlotte and Michael to climb in. 'Well, you see, it's not me that works for your aunt. I'm just holding the fort – strictly speaking, it's my dad and uncle, only they're away too . . . so I don't exactly know where they've gone . . . only that they'll be back soon.' He fixed them with his widest smile, and first Charlotte, then Michael slid into the back of the car. With the sound of the door slamming shut still ringing in their ears, they watched the young man leap into the driver's seat.

He turned briefly to face them before starting the engine. 'The name's Eddie, by the way, Eddie Bardolph – pleased to meet you.'

Striding through the long white corridors of Lampton Laboratories in Washington, Lorabeth Lampton spoke crisply into a mobile phone the size of a credit card. 'Good, well done.'

Trailing at her side, Bardolph and Frimley struggled to keep up and sweated in their crumpled suits. Their day had begun badly, with Lorabeth Lampton berating them for bungling the break-in in New York.

Now she snapped the phone closed and passed it, without looking, in Bardolph's direction. 'Well, Bardolph, at least your son, thank goodness, knows how to do a job properly; apparently my guests have arrived and are on their way to Nevada.'

The mobile slipped through Bardolph's thick fingers and clattered to the floor. He and Frimley both stooped to retrieve it.

'Oh yes, ma'am,' Bardolph said breathlessly. 'He's a good boy, my Eddie.'

Forced to stop while the two men scrabbled at her feet, Lorabeth Lampton growled, 'And you two are useless. Now stand up and listen carefully. I am inviting the press into the lab and I want you to be alert in case anyone is foolish enough to snoop around. You clearly aren't capable of more . . .' she paused, 'demanding work. But even you should be able to manage this.'

Bardolph and Frimley nodded. Lorabeth Lampton, with an exasperated sigh, strode away, forcing them into a trot to keep up.

'The snooper I am expecting is an old woman – you saw her at the hotel, so keep your eyes peeled. She used to be a tough old bird, but she's past it now.'

They reached the door to Lorabeth Lampton's office and she stopped abruptly as she reached for the handle.

'Now get out of my sight and make sure you check the security systems.'

The Insult Fermenter

Outside the car showroom a full moon hung between an office block and a neon sign; both were reflected in the pools of motor oil on the forecourt. At the long table inside, Kate and Phil stood with Harold as he traced his lean finger through the corridors and in and out of the rooms in the architects' drawings of Lampton Laboratories.

At last he tapped his finger on one room in the centre of the building. 'This is where you should head for. There is a computer in this room that is not networked to the system. From its central location I imagine this is Lorabeth Lampton's private office and that computer will have vital secret information on it.'

'We can't just stroll into her office though, can we?' asked Kate.

Harold lifted several pages and frowned. 'I must have left the service blueprints in the other room,' he said. 'I need them to show you how to get inside the ventilation system.'

'I'll get 'em,' said Barking, leaping down from the table.

He soon returned and dropped the plans at Harold's feet. As Harold stooped to pick them up, Barking smelt the sweet aroma of chocolate on Harold's breath. He glanced at everyone in turn and found them either licking their lips or chewing, and Great-Aunt Elizabeth stuffing her bulging pockets with empty cellophane wrappers. Barking strode purposefully across the room and sat, a little removed from everyone else, his jet tail swishing thickly behind him.

'Oh, do stop being a grouch,' Great-Aunt Elizabeth warned him affectionately. 'You know full well that your stomach plays up if you eat chocolate.'

After entrusting the map to Phil, Harold showed them the surveillance system and his latest invention. Fearless and Barking were to wear tiny cameras and micro-transmitters fitted to their collars, and Harold had adapted wristwatches for Phil and Kate which would enable them to make audio contact with Harold and Great-Aunt Elizabeth, who in turn would be able to track their progress.

'We will be stationed outside the building in the sidecar,' said Harold.

'I saw the perfect spot earlier,' Great-Aunt Elizabeth added.

Phil held his watch up close to his face and grinned. 'This is so cool!' he breathed.

Kate was more fascinated by the new invention which Harold proudly placed in her hands. She turned it over, appreciating its sleek design. She was holding a steel canister with a screw lid; it resembled a miniature drinks flask.

'I'm calling it an "Insult Fermenter",' said Harold.

'How does it work?' Kate asked, slowly unscrewing the lid.

'That's it,' said Harold. 'You take the lid off, then place the container to your lips and whisper your insult into it.'

Kate peered thoughtfully into the canister.

'Here, let me,' said Barking, jumping on to the table beside Kate where he daintily leant his face towards the flask and mewed softly into it.

'OK,' said Harold. 'Now, Kate, screw the lid back on tightly and turn the small dial on the bottom to set the timer. Four seconds should be enough for a pretty dramatic effect. As the insult ferments, it will become more powerful and capable of inflicting deeper wounds, the longer you leave it. Insults left brewing for more than twenty-four hours could prove fatal, so be careful you don't forget to switch it off.'

'What effect will a four-second insult have, Harold?' Great-Aunt Elizabeth asked.

'Well, let's see, shall we? You all know the shock you get if someone offends you – it is a physical reaction, right? You feel it in your stomach and you tense up: it's like time stops for a moment. Well, the fermented insult is a much more exaggerated version of this.' Harold smiled proudly. 'It is completely debilitating!' Harold called across to Barking. 'You weren't directing your insult at anyone in particular, were you, Barking?' he queried.

Barking flicked his tail. 'I was merely expressing a general peevishness, that's all.'

'OK,' said Harold. 'Open it up, Kate. Careful now, brace yourselves, everyone.'

As Kate turned the last screw on the lid of the Insult Fermenter, a small wisp of vapour curled up from it. The gathered group watched with interest until suddenly the open canister emitted a deep and terrifying curse that blew the door of Harold's office off its hinges and caused the venetian blinds to drop noisily to the floor.

Everyone in the room gazed around in shock, until the sight of one another with their hair standing completely on end and Kate's loud, uncontrollable hiccups made them burst out laughing. All, that is, except Barking, who sat on the table, sleek and tall, fur unruffled. He looked thoroughly smug, as proud and composed as an Egyptian temple cat.

'A well-aimed insult to a deserving human, fermented for ten seconds, will leave the recipient shocked rigid and immobile for up to three minutes,' said Harold, once they had all gathered their wits and Kate had suppressed her hic-cough to a rib-racking silence.

'Excellent, Harold, excellent!,' Great-Aunt Elizabeth beamed, smoothing down the frizzed hair that had escaped from her bun. Then, to the children she said, 'Use it wisely, my dears, use it wisely.'

*

The day dawned chilly and damp, and they began their drive into Washington's centre before the sun had mustered enough strength to disperse the fog that had settled on the forecourt and drifted along the local streets. In the sidecar, Harold had installed the operation's nerve centre. A small suite of computers, a video monitor and digital listening equipment occupied one side. Opposite these, the children and animals sat, quietly gazing through the window at the traffic and listening to a news bulletin that Harold had just tuned in to. As the Harley purred through the grey streets, they heard how high winds had ripped roofs off in Milan and how fire-fighters were tackling the flow of molten lava that had begun to bubble up from the drains and run down the gutters in Paris.

'It's hard to believe it's summer,' Fearless remarked casually.

'It feels like the whole world is falling apart,' said Kate.

Great-Aunt Elizabeth avoided driving past the laboratory, and she parked in a side street round the corner. Joining them in the sidecar, she fixed Kate and Phil with a serious look and spoke in a sombre voice, reminiscent of her lectures to them at the beginning of their stay with her. 'Remember, my dears, I am here and will come straight away if there is any trouble.'

Both children nodded, and they followed Great-Aunt Elizabeth's gaze through the window, where a light rain was beginning to further obscure their view.

'And be discreet. Remember what we've taught you,' Great-Aunt Elizabeth continued. 'Trust your instincts, Kate, you must let your heartstone guide you.'

To Phil she said, 'Make sure you stay with Fearless or Barking.'

Phil nodded. He would, he promised, he definitely would.

Kate and Phil stood on the sidewalk opposite the car park of Lampton Laboratories and surveyed the building. Several vehicles were queuing to get in, presenting their invitations to the car-park attendant in his booth and a moment later receiving a permit and proceeding under the raised barrier. They could see the main entrance and reception area clearly. A broad flight of shallow steps edged by a low brick wall led to double glass doors that opened automatically whenever someone approached. Kate looked down at her watch and timed how long the doors remained open before closing again. If they waited behind the wall, she reasoned, they might have time to jump over it and slip in behind someone. Before she could confirm the accuracy of her calculations, a coach passed through the barrier and parked, blocking her view of the building.

'Come on,' she said and started to move across the road.

'Wait a minute, look!' Phil said, pointing towards the coach, where a group of children were clambering out on to the tarmac. 'Maybe we can slip inside with them.'

'Brother, you are a genius,' Kate grinned. 'I'll tell Harold and Aunt E.,' and she raised her watch to her lips.

'Oh, let me!' Phil cried, grabbing at her arm. 'Please!' He lowered his mouth to his sleeve and whispered, 'We're going in. Over.'

Kate shook her head in mock despair. She could see the excitement shining out from Phil's eyes like beams of light from a torch. 'Be careful,' she warned. 'This is for real, you know, it's not a game.'

Phil glowered at his sister. He'd had years of experience, daydreaming about similar situations to this, and each and every one of them had felt real to him; he never considered himself to be playing games.

It began to rain heavily and they hurried across the road just as the noisy party of schoolchildren set off in a haphazard, tangled group towards the main reception area of Lampton Laboratory. Fearless peeped out from behind a bush and Phil winked at him and jerked his head towards the group of children. Fearless understood and bounded off to find his own way into the building while Kate and Phil tagged on to the end of the school party. The teacher stopped in front of the automatic doors and turned to quieten and count her charges while the glass doors slid open behind her. Kate and Phil ducked down and pretended to fasten their shoelaces while sidling forwards to be near the front of the group.

'Now, children,' the teacher said brightly, 'I imagine many of you will have mothers who were rather excited this morning? Perhaps they asked you to be on the lookout for any free samples? We are so lucky to have a Lampton Laboratory in our city – and you, children, you are lucky because with Mrs Lampton's amazing advancements in the cosmetic industry, you need never suffer the pain of seeing your faces wrinkle with old age.'

Out of the corner of her eye Kate saw a drenched Barking run along the wall in a sleek, straight-legged fashion. Like a slick black liquid flowing uphill, he slipped inside the building.

All at once the schoolchildren began to move forwards, and Phil and Kate dodged their way into the middle of the group, keeping their heads down so as not to catch anyone's eye. Once inside the doors, they sidled towards the toilets in the reception area. Barking was sitting serenely beside the entrance to the women's toilet and he nipped neatly inside as Kate pushed open the door. As Phil opened the door to the gents', Fearless bounded out from behind a large stainless-steel rubbish bin and was inside first.

The plans Harold had shown them were perfectly accurate: they had merely to stand on a toilet seat in order to push the grating off a ventilation duct and climb inside. Barking and Fearless stood guard at the doors while the children hauled themselves into the dark space above their heads. Once inside, Kate and Phil could see each other quite well in the dim light; just a few metres of smooth steel tunnel separated them. Phil grinned and waved at his sister.

Suddenly Barking sprang into the tunnel beside Kate and hissed, 'Close the grate and tell Fearless to get a move on.'

At that moment Fearless's massive head, shoulders and two huge, scrabbling paws appeared in front of Phil. 'It's no good,' he grunted. 'I'm too big.'

'You'd better get down before someone comes in and sees your great blond backside dangling from the ceiling,' Barking hissed, at which point Fearless, his paws scratching vainly at the polished metal, suddenly disappeared. They heard a loud splash.

'Oh, for heaven's sake!' Barking spat. 'Didn't you put the seat down?'

To his credit, Phil kept perfectly quiet, but Kate could see his shoulders shaking with silent laughter.

Phil nodded to Fearless and closed the grating. He crawled carefully over to Kate and Barking. 'Fearless says he'll keep track of us from below and make his way to the central office.'

'OK,' said Barking. 'There's not much else we can do. Let's go.'

They began to crawl through the ventilation duct, Barking leading the way, closely followed by Kate, then Phil. Ahead of them they could see the light shining up from another grating. As they passed over it, Phil lowered his face to the mesh and peered down into the corridor below. There was no sign of Fearless except for two pairs of wet pawprints, close to the wall. Phil crawled on; ahead of him he saw the sole of Kate's trainers as she turned a corner. He crawled faster, shifting the weight of his rucksack from shoulder to shoulder. When he caught up with Kate, she was glaring back at him with a finger to her lips. Phil raised his eyebrows questioningly and Kate pointed straight down. In front of her was a grating and, leaning in towards it with his face close to Kate's, he could hear a pair of gruff voices floating up from the corridor below. Barking sat on the far side of the grating, frowning. Leaning forwards, Phil could see the tops of the heads of two men wearing identical brown suits. Although he could not see their faces, he recognized the two large pairs of hairy hands from the hotel the day before.

'The counter shows that forty-five people passed through the door into reception.'

'How many in the school party?'

'Forty-three. Some of the kids say they saw a cat and a dog.'

'Huh, kids! You don't want to talk to kids! Kids know nothin'.'

'What do we do, Bardolph?'

'What d'ya mean, what do we do? You heard what she said. We look out for anyone snooping around, that's what we do.'

The two men moved out of earshot, but up in the ventilation duct they had heard enough to put them on their guard.

Kate took the Insult Fermenter from her belt. 'Kids know nothin',' she murmured, imitating the man's thick monotone. 'Well, Mr Hairy Hands, we'll show you.' And she unscrewed the lid and whispered inside.

'What did you say?' Phil asked.

'Wait until you hear the fermented version,' Kate said, screwing down the lid and setting the timer for ten seconds. She tucked the Fermenter back into her belt. Changing her mind, she retrieved it and altered the timer to twelve seconds.

Up ahead, Barking was waiting at a crossroads where the tunnel branched to the left and right. 'Hurry up, you two!' he hissed softly. 'We have to decide which way to go.'

Phil pulled his rucksack round in front of him and took out Harold's map. 'Both these ducts meet up at the circular room where Harold says we'll find the computer that is not networked to the system.'

Barking considered the map for a moment. 'I'll go left, as that way will take me over the canteen, and I have a hunch I'll find Fearless,' said Barking. To Phil he added, 'Just keep close to Kate and we'll meet up on the other side, OK?'

Kate and Phil nodded, and Barking darted off up the left-hand tunnel.

Phil placed his watch to his lips and reported back to the sidecar.

Great-Aunt Elizabeth repeated Barking's caution. 'OK, but make sure you two children stay together,' she warned.

*

In the sidecar, Great-Aunt Elizabeth paced about and Harold either had to slide out of her way on his castored chair or tuck his legs in, to prevent a collision.

'I don't like them being separated,' said Great-Aunt Elizabeth. 'Barking should have stayed with them.'

Harold glanced up from the computer screen at Great-Aunt Elizabeth. 'Aunt E., there's an e-mail here you should see. It's from Charlotte and Michael.'

Great-Aunt Elizabeth hurried to the computer and read over Harold's shoulder.

```
Couldn't reach you by phone — must have been some
storm — we saw it on the news last night. Anyhow,
we've decided to come to NY — flying tomorrow. Be
with you by supper time. Love, C and M.
```

'There must have been a problem with the server, because it's dated three days ago,' Harold pointed out.

'Gnats and noodles,' Great-Aunt Elizabeth said. 'What on earth is Charlotte thinking of?'

'It can't be easy for her,' said Harold. 'Michael was always so determined. Lottie can't keep him in the dark forever, not now the children are involved. You must have thought of that, Auntie.'

'I would be happiest if Michael knew everything. I am just frightened what the shock may do to him.' Great-Aunt Elizabeth shook her head sadly.

They were interrupted once more by Barking. 'Fearless and I are together now – we're on a floor directly above the central control room. The children are still in the ducting. There is a grating that gives access to the ventilation system by a store cupboard. We're going to meet up with the children there.'

'I think we had better concentrate on the matter in hand and worry about Michael later,' Great-Aunt Elizabeth said, flicking the switch on the microphone so that she could relay Barking's message to Kate and Phil.

Inside their stainless-steel tunnel, Kate and Phil had been making slow progress. They were now above the control room, but the ceiling was much higher than in the corridors and they could not find a grating over a quiet, discreet place to jump down. The ducting was maze-like, spiralling round over the control room, and the children were beginning to feel tired and confused. Worse than that, Phil, who had been too excited to eat any breakfast, was now hungry, and the gnawing in his stomach made him feel sick.

At last they found a grating close to a desk and, as far as they could see, no one was in sight.

'Probably having lunch,' said Phil.

'Look,' said Kate, beckoning Phil down closer to the grating, where she could see the far side of the desk and beyond into an open cupboard. 'That'll be the storeroom where we're to meet them.'

Phil squinted through the mesh and saw what Kate could see, the unmistakable familiarity of soft, light-gold fur.

'It's Fearless!' Phil whispered, lifting his head.

'OK,' said Kate, 'I'll lift the grating and you go first, drop on to the desk and hide under it until you're sure it's safe, then join Fearless in the cupboard. I'll follow in a minute.'

As Phil moved forwards, eager to be off, Kate put her hand on his shoulder. 'Be careful,' she said, but then, embarrassed at how tender her voice sounded, she added, 'Don't mess up.'

Phil grinned happily. He had forgotten his hunger, his stiff back and aching knees, and was enjoying the tingle of anticipation.

Her fingers working nimbly, Kate unscrewed the four corners of the grating and carefully slid it to one side. She returned the screwdriver to her belt and held her breath while Phil dropped silently on to the desk below. She watched him slip to the floor and disappear beneath the desk. Kate leant slowly from side to side as far as the tunnel's width would allow.

She looked out into the ceiling space of the large open-plan room, then quickly looked back into the shaft. For a moment she had a flash remembrance of her fear of heights. She held her heartstone and concentrated on not being afraid. If she didn't think about the height or about how far she was going to fall before she alighted on the desk, but instead imagined her effortless, light-footed landing, she would, she was sure, be fine. Her heartstone encouraged her by glowing warmly. Another quick glance around told her that it was safe to follow Phil. As she prepared to jump down, she heard a small noise behind her. Squinting back into the dim light of the tunnel, Kate recognized, with alarm, the sight and sound of a large rat running fast towards her on tiny feet. Kate watched in horror as the rat veered from one side of the duct to the other, occasionally pausing to sniff the air with its pointed nose.

Kate stole a furtive glance down through the grating and considered jumping without waiting for Phil's signal. The distance to the desk she had judged to be about two metres, but she had been prepared to tackle it as if it were less than one. Now it suddenly plummeted to a greater depth as if the desk were an elevator that had been summoned to the basement. Sickened, she looked back along the tunnel to see that the rat was closer and had spotted her. He was staring directly at her, nose twitching, little pink hands reaching in front of him. Kate returned his gaze and didn't dare move a muscle.

Beneath the desk, Phil could see Fearless's back partially hidden inside the cupboard. He noticed how still Fearless was keeping and wondered if perhaps someone was round the corner that he couldn't see. Phil held his breath and listened hard, but all he could hear was the soft *throb-throb* of his own heartbeat. He wondered what was keeping Kate, and he decided that there was not room for both of them under the desk. He glanced around at as much of the room as he could see and decided to run for the cupboard. At least then he would be with Fearless as he had promised. Remembering everything he had been taught in stealth lessons, Phil crept forwards silently until he was close to the cupboard, then he darted inside.

He reached out to touch Fearless but, as his hand brushed against the soft golden fur, Phil felt a shock at its coldness. The shock swelled into horror as his hand continued to pass through the fur . . . and it fell over his arm. Phil gasped and jumped back as the voluminous folds of Lorabeth Lampton's fur coat slipped from its hanger in the cupboard and fell to his feet.

Kate heard Phil's cry and her stomach lurched in terror, but she could not take her eyes off the rat that was now approaching cautiously, one step at a time, its whiskers twitching, its sharp little nose jabbing at the air as it craned its neck forwards. Then, behind the rat, in the darkness, another movement caught Kate's attention. With relief she recognized Barking's sleek figure galloping through the tunnel.

Phil's heart banged against his ribs. He was alone and he realized he was in danger, but for several moments he stood transfixed with shock that the golden fur he had mistaken for Fearless was now lying sprawled on the floor. He had to get back to Kate. Starting into action, Phil turned quickly away from the horror of the cupboard, only to smash into the solid wall of a shiny brown suit. A large, hairy hand clasped his arm and pulled his entire body upwards so that his face was so close to a pair of saliva-spitting rubbery lips that Phil could feel the moist warmth of the man's garlic breath against his skin.

'Not so fast, yer little squirt.'

'Aah, help!' Phil cried as a salty hand slapped across his mouth, stifling his voice and making his stomach churn with its smell of tobacco.

Back in the tunnel, Barking swiftly closed the gap upon the unsuspecting rat. With one swift pounce the rat was pinned down, its chin crushed to the floor. Kate held her breath as, less than a metre away, Barking's jaw flexed and clamped shut on the rat's head. Barking's whole body whipped violently from side to side, flinging the rat over and back in an arc. Suddenly the struggling rat's little legs stopped thrashing and it fell dead from the cat's mouth. Barking picked his way over the corpse on delicate paws.

'That was disgusting!' he groaned, then noticed Kate's distress. 'Where's Phil?'

Kate lowered her whole head through the grating into the room below. When she came up, her look was desperate.

'Barking!' she cried, bursting into tears. 'Oh, Barking, I think Phil's been caught.'

Barking disappeared through the hole into the room below and almost instantly reappeared beside Kate.

'Follow me,' he hissed, 'and get the Fermenter ready. We may need it.'

He dropped silently on to the desk and Kate followed, slipping quickly out of sight beneath it. She grasped the

Insult Fermenter in both hands, one gripping it tight, the other poised, ready to unscrew it.

Barking appeared beside her and whispered in her ear, 'Be ready to jump out and aim that thing when I say the word. One of those thugs in the brown suits is holding Phil. They're waiting round the corner by a lift. I'm going to try and get him to follow me.'

Barking disappeared and Kate wiped her smarting eyes roughly with the back of her hand. If she was going to be of any use to anyone, she had better not have blurred vision. She forced herself to take a deep breath, wishing she were braver and, as she did so, she suddenly felt that she was. The heartstone began to warm her throat, and she put her hand to it. The moment she felt its warmth, she felt brave and powerful and ready to take on the world. How dare anyone hurt her brother.

Barking peered round the corner to where the brown-suited man stood by the lift holding Phil roughly by a shoulder. The man had his back to Barking but as Phil struggled in his grasp he faced the direction where the cat was crouched. Barking willed Phil to see him and inched closer while he planned what to do next.

Phil spotted Barking's nose twitching round the corner and hope leapt in his heart. He decided to try and distract his captor. Wriggling free of the sweaty palm that gagged him, he took a deep breath and yelled, 'I want my mum, you're hurting me!' He twisted and writhed in the vice-like grip.

'Shut it,' came the gruff reply. 'You were snoopin' about. That's wrong, that is!'

Out of the corner of his eye, Phil could see Barking in attack position, his face crouching over his front paws, his back end swaying from side to side. As Barking pounced, Phil swung all his weight on to the man's arm, lifted his leg and placed a well-aimed kick on his left shin. With a flying leap, Barking sailed through the air and landed perfectly on the thug's bald head, into which he sank his extended claws and held fast. The man roared and Phil felt his grip loosen. Seizing the advantage, he struggled free and ran as fast as he could. Even so, Barking overtook him, shouting as he went, 'Now, Kate, now!'

As Barking and Phil hurled themselves round the corner with the man raging behind them, Kate jumped out from under the desk and pulled the lid off the canister. She thrust it in front of her at arm's length. Parting on either side of her, Phil and Barking skidded for cover.

For a second the man hesitated and there was a flicker of amusement in his eyes as he stared in disbelief at the small girl brandishing a – what was it? a coffee flask? – as if it were a sword. Then suddenly it happened. The canister smoked slightly and a barrage of vile contempt flew at the man, stopping him in his tracks and lifting him a full thirty centimetres off the floor.

To the others in the room the sound was unintelligible, but Frimley heard it clearly and he recognized a voice he had not heard for fifty years and had never expected to hear again. The angry, spiteful words were being spoken by his mother: a reprise of the humiliation he had received as a boy and which he had managed to eradicate from his memory.

A shrill voice entered his brain as if each word were a knife being thrown into a plank. '... Look at you, wet your trousers, well you can stay in them. Come and see the big baby who can't get to a toilet. I'm sick of you, sick of the sight of you. I don't love you: I've never loved you. The day you were born I wished you were dead. You're nothing but a piece of –'

Kate held out the canister with difficulty; it roared with some kind of internal power and almost wrenched itself from her grip. She fought to hold it steady and aim it at the man as a fierce vibration passed up her arm and down her body where it buzzed through the soles of her feet.

Kate watched as the puce colour drained from the man's complexion and his face went slack and his body limp. As the vicious scorn continued to stream from the Fermenter, the man slowly drifted to the floor, where he stood, slumped in his shiny suit. A pathetic expression of hurt and dismay filled his eyes and he began to cry silent tears. At last the tirade ended and the man stood, rooted to the spot, quite incapable of speech or movement, his soft mouth hanging open and a trail of saliva escaping on to his stubbled chin.

'Quickly,' said Barking. 'There's no time to lose.'

To Kate and Phil's astonishment, Barking leapt up to the computer, and his paws were soon flying over the keyboard. Kate dragged the camera Harold had given her from her rucksack. Phil pulled the filing cabinet open and yanked papers from the folders, laying them out for Kate to photograph.

Suddenly they heard a soft 'ding' from an arriving lift. Phil looked alarmed but Kate and Barking, their heartstones glowing intensely, spoke in unison.

'It's Fearless,' they said, and continued hurriedly rifling through the office's contents.

Sure enough, Fearless appeared round the corner and, after glancing momentarily at the drooping, frozen man, rushed over to help. Soon they had downloaded all personal files from the computer and photographed the contents of the filing cabinet.

'We'd better get out of here,' said Barking just as the remote radio on the thug's belt began to crackle and fizz.

'Frimley, you pea-brained idiot,' came a distorted gruff voice. 'Where are you?'

Frimley's face twitched and his hairy hands flexed slightly.

'Quick,' said Kate. 'He's coming round!'

'Get on to the desk and climb back through the grating,' Barking hissed.

Phil and Kate began scrambling up and Barking sprang up behind them. Kate's foot slid on a sheet of paper and she banged her shin painfully on the edge of the desk. Behind her, Frimley was beginning to moan softly.

'Just get yourselves up there,' said Fearless, 'I'll keep him at bay,' and he began to snarl menacingly and circle round the dazed man. First Kate, then Phil hauled themselves breathlessly into the ventilation duct. Kate sat, hunched over, holding her throbbing shin and rocking, tears stinging her eyes as she fought not to cry. Phil crawled a few paces away and sprawled flat on his back, panting. A streak of black fur sprang into the duct behind them, then turned to peer back down.

'Get going, Fearless,' Barking called. 'We're safe.'

But Fearless had stopped dead in his tracks. In circling Frimley, he had come to face the open cupboard . . . and there, in front of him, was Lorabeth's fur coat trailing across the tiled floor. Fearless walked slowly towards the coat, his head lowered and his tail tucked in beneath him. He reached the coat and pulled at it with a curled paw and pushed at it with his nose while whimpering softly.

'Come on, Fearless, get out of there!' Barking hissed.

But with a heart-rending howl, Fearless threw himself down on the coat and began sobbing loudly.

'Fearless, Fearless!' Barking called. 'There's nothing you can do, they're gone. You can't help them now. Come on, Fearless, move! Get out of there.'

Just then, Frimley groaned loudly and began to rub his eyes and scratch his head. Barking ducked back out of sight for fear of betraying the whereabouts of the children. With his teeth and claws he hurriedly slid the grating back in place.

Kate looked up. 'What are you doing? What about Fearless?'

'It's no good, Kate, we have to go. He can't get up here anyhow, there's nothing we can do.'

The urgent shuffling crawl back through the ventilation duct was unbearable for the children. Kate, who had managed to keep back the tears despite her painful shin, now wept copiously. She felt completely wretched about leaving Fearless behind. And that disgusting coat; Kate felt horror well up inside her as her mind rebelled against the thought that the cruel, vile Lorabeth Lampton could somehow be her grandmother.

Meanwhile, Phil was tormented by the enclosed space of the tunnel; he desperately wanted to jump up and stretch and run and run until he could no longer feel the man's fingers pressing into his skin. On first raising himself up into a crawling position, he had nearly put his hand on a dead rat, and the shock had made him feel sick. As he crawled on, he shuddered with disgust and felt his stomach begin to heave, although it was completely empty.

They proceeded as quickly as possible with Barking leading the way, Phil following closely and Kate, miserably, bringing up the rear. Beneath them they could hear a persistent alarm klaxon and a request over the tannoy for all visitors to return to the reception area.

Barking turned back to the children and whispered, 'We must hurry. Hopefully, you two can get out the same way you came in.'

*

Barking's hopes were realized as there was a great deal of confusion at the reception. Kate opened the door to the women's toilet cautiously and was reassured by the chaos. The alarm was deafening and visitors were converging on the area from all directions; most were demanding to know what was going on. The school party was adding to the pandemonium, shouting to one another in shrill, excited voices while their teacher attempted to count them. Phil cowered behind Kate, mortified at the thought of being seen in the women's toilet.

'Remember, think *invisible*,' said Barking. 'Once you're out through the door, don't look back. Get to the Harley as fast as you can.'

Following Barking, they dodged their way through the noisy crowd and out into the rain. Once off Lampton Laboratory premises, they hurried across the road and round the corner to the side street where Harold and Great-Aunt Elizabeth were waiting in the sidecar. At first Kate refused to get inside, and she stood on the tarmac, insisting that she was not going without Fearless, and that was that. Great-Aunt Elizabeth placed a large hand on her back and swept her inside. 'Fearless will be all right, believe me. Now sit down and tell me what happened.'

Kate stumbled into a seat, and once more the tears welled up. 'It was the fur coat, that hideous coat she was wearing when we saw her at the hotel.'

'And those men were there,' said Phil. 'One of them got me.' He lowered his head and looked down at his lap, feeling suddenly foolish at the way he had carelessly walked right into his captor.

Kate was experiencing a huge wave of anger rising inside her as she remembered Lorabeth Lampton sweeping through the lobby in her fur coat. Why hadn't she done something then, when she had had the chance?

'It should be against the law to wear a coat like that!' Kate sobbed. 'It's disgusting.'

'I thought it was Fearless in the cupboard,' said Phil dolefully. 'I touched it and it was cold and horrible.'

'When Fearless saw it, he started whimpering,' said Kate through her tears.

Great-Aunt Elizabeth shook her head and frowned. 'It is monstrous, monstrous!' she said. 'Poor Fearless. It might have been his family – perhaps his brothers and sisters lost their lives to make that coat! But you must rest assured, Fearless is brave and strong; he will not let that woman get the better of him.'

Kate was about to ask how Great-Aunt Elizabeth could be so sure when she was interrupted by Barking and Phil, who had been staring anxiously back towards Lampton Laboratory.

'Here he comes!' they cried suddenly.

Sure enough, bounding up the road towards them was Fearless, his golden ears flowing behind him. As he reached the sidecar, Harold operated the door so that the domed roof rolled back and Fearless leapt inside. Kate and Phil flung their arms round his huge, muscled neck, and Great-Aunt Elizabeth ruffled the broad flat top of his curly head as she stepped outside. 'Well done, Fearless. Now let's get away from here.'

As the dome rolled down over the sidecar, Great-Aunt Elizabeth stepped astride the Harley and pulled out into the traffic.

The rain continued stronger than ever as they approached the car showroom and, by the time Great-Aunt Elizabeth had parked the Harley and they had all clambered out, the downpour was forming a shallow lake and they had to run for the stairs.

Inside, it was gloomy and the rain hammered noisily on the metal roof. The weather suited everyone's mood. Once upon a time Kate and Phil would have grumbled about being bored and cooped up. But now they sat quietly side by side on one of the sofas, not caring how long they had to wait for whatever was coming next.

The news, when it came, was totally unexpected. 'Mum and Dad are in New York!' Kate cried, grinning widely. 'That's brilliant!'

Great-Aunt Elizabeth smiled and touched Kate's cheek. Her small face was flushed and puffy from crying, and her hair had begun to frizz from the rain.

'You two have done very well today. I'm proud of you, and I know Charlotte will be proud of you too.'

'But not Dad?' asked Kate.

Great-Aunt Elizabeth considered Kate carefully. 'No, no need to worry Michael with this little adventure.'

Phil was pleased at the prospect of seeing his parents

and smiled wearily; he was more tired than he had ever felt in his life before. With his head on the arm of the sofa he slowly drifted off to sleep and was soon deep in a dream with his mum and dad, back at Great-Aunt Elizabeth's New York house. While his dad rode the horse round Phil's prairie room, he and his mum sprawled in the hammock, eating cheese on toast. Even in his dream it tasted perfectly delicious.

Seeing her brother quietly sleeping, Kate began to yawn. She was longing to see her parents and was particularly looking forward to discussing things with her mother. However, being told, yet again, to keep secrets from her dad was deeply unsettling. She fretted about this for a while, until fatigue overwhelmed her. Silhouettes of Harold, Fearless and Barking moved round the office behind the venetian blinds, and as Kate watched them her eyes began to close. She too settled her head against the sofa and allowed herself to sleep.

Every so often, Fearless or Barking would shoot down the stairs to fetch another lead or some software from the sidecar; but neither this nor the frequent gusts of wind that sent squalls of rain hammering against the windows disturbed either of the children.

16

A Lost Watch

Inside the Washington laboratory, the doors were at last closed to the public and the security alarms had been reset. In the panelled control room, Lorabeth Lampton sat on a raised swivel chair. With her head inclined slightly to one side, she blinked slowly and purposefully. Carefully she reached out a long thin arm and pressed a button, triggering the tannoy. She paused momentarily before speaking. 'Bardolph, Frimley, come to the control room.' She lifted her finger for a second and then replaced it on the button. 'At once,' she added sharply.

In the corner of the room stood a thin young man wearing a Lampton Laboratory white coat. Lorabeth turned slowly towards him. As she stared at him, the man coloured and began to shuffle from foot to foot.

'You say my computer has been tampered with?' Lorabeth asked him at last.

'Ya, it ... it ... vould zeem zo.' The man used the forearm of his sleeve to wipe the sweat from his brow.

'Remind me, what is your name?'

'Bernhard Kleimer, Frau Lampton.'

'Ah yes, Bernhard,' she repeated coolly. 'Well, Bernhard, I am very pleased with the work you have done for me. Very pleased. Those e-mails you intercepted for me have been most useful. With your help I learnt that some very important visitors were due to arrive in New York. They might have turned up at the airport without anyone to meet them if it hadn't been for you. That would have been very bad for Lampton Cosmetics, Bernhard, very bad indeed.'

'Zank you, Frau Lampton. Shall I go now?'

'No. I have another job for you.'

Just then the lift door opened with a 'ding' and Bardolph and Frimley's voices could be heard mumbling crossly. They appeared round the corner and eyed Lorabeth Lampton uneasily.

'Blasted kids, Mrs Lampton! I don't know why you allowed them in in the first place. They've got no respect. If you ask me, one of them tripped the alarm by mistake, or mischief-makers, more likely – messing about. Little scumbags, I can't stand them,' Bardolph grumbled in his gravelly voice.

Lorabeth Lampton blinked at him a few times then turned her head to gaze directly at Frimley.

'A dog,' said Frimley in a croak, then cleared his throat, 'bit me on the ar– pardon me, no offence, bit me on a tender spot, he did. Tore my trousers, Mrs Lampton. Sunk his teeth right through them, he has. Like a wolf he was, ma'am.'

Lorabeth swivelled the chair and stared at Bernhard.

'Who do you think has tampered with my computer, Bernhard? A child or a dog?'

'I-I-I don't zink it iz very likely to be either,' said Bernhard in a small flat voice, nervously twisting his fingers together.

From the other side of the room Bardolph and Frimley glowered at him, and all the blood seemed to drain from his face into his lips, which turned purple.

Lorabeth Lampton opened a drawer, slowly put her hand inside and drew out a small silver gun.

'Now, please, Mrs Lampton,' Bardolph blurted, 'Frimley may have been sleeping on the job, imagined the dog maybe, but don't shoot him, Mrs Lampton, it won't happen again.'

Lorabeth raised an eyebrow and pointed the gun at Bardolph. Frimley squealed and stepped away from him.

'No, please, I'll be nicer to the children. I'll try, I really will,' Bardolph murmured.

From the corner of the room Bernhard allowed a small whimper to escape from his lips.

Continuing to gaze steadily at Bardolph, Lorabeth slowly raised the gun so that it was pointing up towards the ceiling. 'I hate children,' she said. 'Don't you know even that, you stupid man?'

She pressed the trigger and a soft jet of perfume sprayed up into the air and settled in a gentle mist on her hair. She replaced the little gun in the drawer and slid it shut. She reached lower, to the drawer below, and produced a small watch, which she held aloft on one finger.

'A child's watch, would you say, Bernhard?' she asked, holding it out to him.

'It zertainly looks like it, Mrs Lampton,' Bernhard said, stumbling forwards to take it from her, his voice now a rasping whisper.

Across the room, Bardolph and Frimley were exchanging dark looks. While Bardolph snarled, Frimley was mouthing, 'It's not my fault!' and shrugging irritably.

'So,' Lorabeth said, rising to her feet, 'we have a child's watch – which I found here under my desk, and my fur coat is wet and has been slobbered on by a dog.' She turned to stare accusingly at Bardolph and Frimley. 'What will you two do now?'

Bardolph and Frimley looked at each other and shrugged.

'You will go to the gymnasium and punch each other silly and if you don't both have black eyes next time I see you, I really shall shoot you. Understood?'

'Yes, ma'am,' Bardolph and Frimley replied and as they turned towards the lift they began punching each other's arms and slapping each other around the face, swearing furiously in strained, hushed voices.

Lorabeth Lampton closed her eyes slowly and then turned to Bernhard. 'I have a job for you which I suspect you may not like.' Lorabeth gazed fixedly at Bernhard's thin and rapidly reddening face.

'I have been very unlucky with my employees in the past. Too many of them have had – *accidents*. We don't want anything nasty happening to you, now do we?'

Bernhard mouthed the words, 'Nein, Frau Lampton,' but only an ear touching his lips would have heard him. He stared at her from frightened eyes that blinked rapidly beneath a deeply furrowed and sweating brow.

Mrs Lampton gazed steadily back at him for several moments.

'I suspect the watch will have a transmitter in it. Can you locate the receiver?'

Shocked and shaken, Bernhard looked down at the watch he had been turning over and over in his hands. 'Erm, it might be possible, if zere iz two-way transmission,' he mumbled. 'You zee I could –'

'Just do it, Bernhard. I am not interested in how.'

Lorabeth Lampton stood up from her desk and gestured towards the lift.

'Off you go, Bernhard.'

'Er no, Frau Lampton, I mean, yes,' Bernhard murmured at he retreated backwards from her towering form.

'Oh, and Bernhard,' she called after him, 'do it by midnight. If I must kidnap a child, I'd rather do it when it's dark.'

A soft 'ding' and the lift doors opened and Bernhard stumbled inside.

Leaving Harold to analyse the data they had stolen from Lorabeth Lampton's office, and Barking to a session of laborious washing, Fearless announced to Great-Aunt Elizabeth that he was going out for a run.

'The weather is atrocious,' she warned him.

'There'll be fewer people around,' Fearless replied. 'That's how I like it.'

As he passed the sofa, his tail brushed Kate's face and she came swimming back out of a deep sleep. Phil, too, began to stir and stretch. He raised his arm, noticing with a shock that he was no longer wearing his watch. Kate yawned and mumbled beside him as he began to look in the corner of his sofa and under the cushions next to him.

'What are you doing?' Kate asked, rising from the sofa and stretching her arms over her head.

Phil shrugged as he got up. 'Nothing,' he scowled at her.

'Ah, good! You're awake,' Great-Aunt Elizabeth interjected from across the room. 'Now, my dears, I haven't been able to contact your parents but I expect as we weren't at home they will have checked into Jean-Paul's hotel – your mother knows it well and is fond of Jean-Paul.' Great-Aunt Elizabeth turned her head sharply and sneezed violently over her shoulder. 'Ooh! Bless me!' she said, then, to herself, she murmured, 'This is most unusual, I am never ill.'

She returned her attention to Kate and Phil.

'Now, I've been thinking and, with your parents coming for a visit, I have decided that there is something more you should know about the family history.'

Kate was immediately alert, her eyes focused intently on her great-aunt's face, but Phil was distracted as he tried desperately to remember when he had last seen his watch.

'As you know, Kate, now that you have your mother's heartstone it is your destiny – as it was hers and is mine – to use your developing power and expertise to combat evil.'

Kate nodded and waited while Great-Aunt Elizabeth frowned and scratched the side of her head. She did not look well, Kate noted. She used to have an inner energy that lit her face and danced in her eyes. Right now her eyes appeared cloudy and dull, and her skin looked grey and clammy. Kate resolved to keep a close eye on her as Great-Aunt Elizabeth continued.

'Now, your father is not fully aware of things, as you know, and I can see that this *deception* is making you uncomfortable.'

Kate said, 'We know about Dad's accident and that he mustn't get shocks.'

Great-Aunt Elizabeth surveyed them gravely. 'I suspect your parents will not have told you very much about the so-called *accident*; your father because he cannot remember and your mother because she knows what is at stake.' She raised an eyebrow. 'Well, am I right? Do you know what happened to him?'

The subject caught Phil's attention at last. 'I thought he fell out of a tree,' he said, 'but I don't remember who told me.'

'You're in for another big surprise, my dears.' Great-Aunt Elizabeth dragged the back of her hand across her brow. 'You see, your father had an encounter with Lorabeth Lampton when he was a boy. When she was Penelope Parton, that is.'

'Dad did?' Kate blurted out. 'But I thought Mum –'

Great-Aunt Elizabeth held up her hand to silence Kate. 'Your dad was there, too. She kidnapped him and used him in the most appalling way. We did everything we could to reverse the damage, but he very nearly died. He was terribly ill for a long time – unconscious for months. When he came to, he had no memory of what had happened to him. Any small reminder sent him into a delirium. Which is why everything has been hushed up all these years.'

'So, the phone calls every summer?' Kate said, trying to understand.

'The story about my wanting to take you on holiday? That was for your father's benefit,' said Great-Aunt Elizabeth. 'Marg– *Penelope Parton* was given a life sentence, and with her safely behind bars your mother chose to remove her heartstone and live an ordinary life. Each year I phoned Charlotte to let her know that everything was all right.'

'And this year,' said Kate, 'everything wasn't all right.'

'No,' Great-Aunt Elizabeth said regretfully, 'everything was very wrong . . .' Her voice trailed away and Kate again had the feeling that the full story was being kept from her. What had been Penelope Parton's crime? What exactly had she done to their father?

Just as Kate took a breath to ask these questions, Harold called them. 'Hey! Come and look at this!'

As Kate followed Great-Aunt Elizabeth and Barking, she noticed that Phil had not moved but stood where he was, staring into space, a small frown furrowing his brow.

'Hey, dopey!' Kate called to him, and Phil slowly moved towards the office.

'You did an excellent job in Lampton Laboratory, kids – really first-class espionage!' Harold said as they gathered round the monitor in a huddled semicircle.

Phil smiled half-heartedly and squirmed uncomfortably.

'We couldn't have done it without Barking and Fearless,' said Kate, though pride flushed her cheeks.

'No, and they couldn't have done it without you,' said Great-Aunt Elizabeth, adding, 'Let's see what you've got, Harold.'

Harold's hands flew across the keyboard.

'Right,' he said. 'This should be it.'

They watched the screen as a fog cleared and an extraordinary landscape emerged.

'It's the moon!' said Phil wondrously, despite himself.

'No,' said Harold, 'it's a lava field in Iceland, near Reykjavik.'

The ground was broken and blistered in a curious way. There was no visible sign of vegetation, apart from a few slimy patches of green that must have been moss or lichen. As the camera rolled across the terrain, they saw more patches of fog in the distance. They closed in on the foggy area and could see, beneath it, a pool of bubbling milky-blue water.

'It's water vapour evaporating off the boiling water,' Harold explained.

Suddenly the water in the pool surged up into a huge aquamarine blister and exploded in a jet of spray that shot twenty metres into the air.

'Wow!' Phil and Kate gasped together.

'And that,' said Harold, 'is a geyser. Gases build up and every so often it blows like that.'

'What has all this got to do with Lampton Laboratories?' Great-Aunt Elizabeth asked irritably.

Harold typed at the keyboard again and they watched as a beautiful milky-blue lake appeared on the screen. You could see that the water was hot, gentle wafts of mist were rising from its surface. Here and there people floated or swam in the water, and around about were ragged slopes and small hills of the same bubbly-looking rock from the lava fields they had seen before.

'This is a health spa in Iceland. It is a natural phenomenon because the earth's crust in that place is thin and the heat and gases from inside leak out.'

'What? Does she own it?' Great-Aunt Elizabeth asked.

'She is about to open similar spas all over the world. The first one is in Milan, opening next week,' Harold replied.

'Can she do that?' Kate queried.

'Well, it seems she can, and she claims it's safe, but I don't see how it can be.'

'What do you mean, Harold?' Great-Aunt Elizabeth asked, sounding edgy.

'Well, I suspect she has found a way of sinking bore-holes deep down into the earth, penetrating the crust and releasing the geothermal energy she needs for the spas.'

'Won't that be dangerous?' Kate asked.

'Yes,' Harold said, scratching behind his ear, 'it will destabilize the earth. There have recently been rather a lot of earthquakes and volcanoes in new areas.'

'Remember the news this morning,' Kate cried, 'lava in the streets of Paris!'

'Oh my goodness!' Great-Aunt Elizabeth breathed. 'Surely not even she would risk wrecking the entire planet.'

'There's more,' Harold said, tapping at the computer keyboard. A world map appeared on the monitor. Heart-shaped icons embossed with the initials L. L. were placed at various locations. 'This map shows the sites of the new Lampton Laboratory developments. Notice anything?'

Kate's eyes trailed across the map. 'The laboratories are close to where the storms have been reported!'

'Exactly so,' said Harold. 'In fact, there is a laboratory smack bang in the eye of every storm.'

'Look, there's one in Tokyo,' Phil said, pointing to Japan on the map, 'near where the *tsunami* hit.'

'Each of these laboratories,' Harold continued, 'either produces the anti-ageing cream or is the site of a proposed spa. But there's one that is different from the others. And it doesn't appear on this map.'

He closed the window on the screen and opened the disk that Barking had downloaded from Lorabeth Lampton's computer.

A familiar building appeared on the monitor but, unlike the Washington laboratory, this one stood isolated in a desert, its metallic facade shimmering in the strong sunlight.

'This is what scares me most,' Harold said. 'This is where the prototypes for all her cosmetics have been developed and where her Legacy perfume is produced.' He rubbed his bony fingers into his scalp and his twisted locks bounced around his head. 'This laboratory is not listed on the Lampton company files, nor is there a record of it on the state land registry. As yet, there seem to be no unusual seismic or climatic disturbances in the vicinity. But I just don't like the look of it.'

'Where the devil is it?' Great-Aunt Elizabeth asked impatiently.

'Nevada,' Harold replied.

'What do you think she's up to, Harold?' Great-Aunt Elizabeth asked. There was something in her tone of voice, an insecurity that made Kate glance up at her. Great-Aunt Elizabeth's face was drawn and grey, and her lips were pressed together in a thin line.

'Er, well, I don't know,' Harold said, fidgeting in his seat, 'but it doesn't look good, Aunt E., it really doesn't. There's one file that is in code and as yet I haven't been able to crack it.'

'Well, keep trying,' Great-Aunt Elizabeth said. 'I have

some serious thinking to do – and we have Charlotte and Michael to think about – we don't want them worried unduly ... We should get back to New York ...' Her voice trailed away.

Kate looked at each of them in turn. At Harold, with his every-which-way hair and his stubble, his shirt untucked and misbuttoned so that one side hung down lower than the other. On top of this he wore his jumper inside out and back to front. Behind him stood Great-Aunt Elizabeth, as tall as ever but somehow less of herself. Her shoulders sagged and everything about her seemed slumped and depressed. Kate noticed how quiet and pale Phil was as he stood beside her, and she thought that the mere sight of them all would be enough to worry her parents.

That night, Kate lay awake in her sleeping-bag tent, pondering the questions she wanted Great-Aunt Elizabeth to answer. She was looking forward to seeing her mum and dad, but the anticipation was not pleasant enough to override her worries about Lorabeth Lampton. When sleep came at last, her anxieties surfaced in her dreams.

She dreamt she was in a vast, rocky wasteland, barely able to stand against a fierce wind. Her hair was being whipped across her face and she was frantically trying to see. She didn't know where Phil was and she was desperately shouting for him. Her voice was snatched from her mouth by the wind, and she knew that wherever

Phil was he wouldn't hear her. The ground beneath her feet began to shake, and she fell awkwardly on to barren earth, where she was jostled and tossed like a popping corn in a hot pan. Suddenly she heard a distant rumble that grew rapidly to a crescendo and she staggered to her feet, pressing her hands over her ears. On the horizon, trees seemed to be disappearing from view – and then the line of toppled and falling trees came rushing towards her. With a mind-splitting roar the ground beside her was ripped apart and a deep chasm appeared. Kate started screaming.

When Great-Aunt Elizabeth yanked the zip on her tent open, she found Kate struggling to free herself, tear-stained and drenched in sweat, her body shaking violently. Great-Aunt Elizabeth pulled her to her feet and held her close, hushing her, while Harold, Fearless and Barking stood blinking in the darkness.

'It was terrible,' Kate gasped at last. 'It was like the end of the world.'

'It is all right, Kate. You've had a nightmare after an upsetting day,' Great-Aunt Elizabeth said soothingly. 'Get some sleep. Fearless will sleep beside you and keep you company.'

Kate sniffed and nodded gratefully as she settled back down on the floor. Taking a last look round the room, Harold and Barking returned to the office; Great-Aunt Elizabeth, after glancing into the far corner where she could just see the tip of Phil's sleeping bag in the shadows, retreated to her own bed.

Fearless slumped to the floor, knocking the breath from his body with a loud sigh.

'Fearless,' Kate whispered in the dark.

'Uh-huh?'

'I'm so sorry you had to see that coat.'

Fearless sniffed and fidgeted a little.

Kate heard his heartstone chink softly as he scratched his neck. 'Fearless.'

'Hmmm?'

'I won't let anyone hurt you, I promise.'

'Thank you, Kate,' Fearless said softly. After a pause he added, 'You did a good job with that Fermenter thing. You stopped that Frimley guy in his tracks, didn't you?'

'What happened after we left, did he wake up properly?'

'Well, he certainly seemed to when I sank my teeth into his bottom.' Fearless replied dryly.

Kate giggled. 'Good. I wish I'd seen that. 'Night, Fearless.'

'Goodnight, Kate.'

Kate Takes Over

'It's not like Phil to be last for breakfast,' Fearless said next morning. They were seated round the low coffee table where Great-Aunt Elizabeth had placed a loaf, bagels and preserves after an early trip to the store.

'He was always last at home,' Kate said, peering into a jar of apricot jam before screwing the lid back on and replacing it on the table unused. 'He used to be terrible at getting up.' She pulled a small piece of bread from the slice in her hand and nibbled it.

Harold emerged from his office, stretching his arms above his head and yawning.

'Go and get that boy up will you, Harold dear?' Great-Aunt Elizabeth said, nodding her head towards the far corner of the room where Phil had made a little den for himself under the long window, the sill making a roof over his head.

Still yawning loudly, Harold crossed the room and crouched down beside Phil's sleeping bag. 'Come on, Philbert, you old slug-a-bed. Rise and shine!' he said, giving the sleeping bag a gentle shake. He leant forwards and unzipped the tent. Where Phil's head should have

205

been there was nothing. Harold yanked the sleeping bag open and saw that it was stuffed with Phil's clothes and his rucksack. 'Phil's gone!' he cried, jumping up and banging his shoulder on the sill.

Barking sprang across the room and stared at Phil's bed as if Harold might not have looked properly and he expected to find Phil curled up asleep after all.

'Maybe he's just gone for a walk. I'll look for him,' Fearless said and he ran down the stairs.

Great-Aunt Elizabeth stared in disbelief at Harold. She was sitting on the low sofa beside Kate and began struggling to get up.

Kate sprang to her feet, jogging the table so that her glass of milk slopped over. 'Phil wouldn't go off alone, I know he wouldn't,' she said, tears beginning to fill her eyes.

Fearless, yelping and growling, darted up the stairs. 'I don't understand, I was right here in the room. I was with Kate,' he said anxiously. 'He definitely went down to the forecourt, there's a fresh scent but –' He broke off and stared at Great-Aunt Elizabeth, who had got to her feet at last.

'What is it? Where's Phil? Where is he?' Kate demanded, glaring at everyone in the room in turn.

Great-Aunt Elizabeth composed herself and lifted her chin. 'Let's not despair,' she said in a bold voice. 'I shall go to Lampton Laboratories at once and demand him back.'

Kate looked into Great-Aunt Elizabeth's face and noticed a small tic flickering beneath her eye. Fearless and

Barking had gone back downstairs and she could hear them calling for Phil.

'I'm going to find him. We can't just stand here doing nothing.' Kate pushed past Harold and ran down the stairs and out on to the concrete.

She immediately noticed something strange about the Harley and she went directly towards it. As she approached it, she discovered a bright red message written across the glass dome of the sidecar. As she shouted to the others to come quickly, she saw something shiny lying among the litter and grease round the bins. She stooped to pick it up. It was a silver lipstick case with the initials L. L. embossed on the cap and 'Lorabeth Lampton's Luscious Lips' scrolled down the edge. Kate pulled off the lid and twisted up the base to reveal a completely blunt scarlet lipstick.

Just then, Great-Aunt Elizabeth came crashing down from the reception area and let out a roar of rage and frustration when she saw the message scrawled in lipstick on the glass dome of her sidecar:

I have the boy
Meet me at
The Modena
8 p.m. tonight

Fearless sniffed round the bins and the motorbike and retrieved Phil's watch. Harold, who had been hovering in the background, reached out and took it from him. 'I was hoping he might contact us with this,' he said sadly.

'What about Phil?!' Kate cried. 'What will she do to him?'

Great-Aunt Elizabeth turned to Kate and fixed her with her powerful gaze. 'She will take good care not to harm Phil, I can promise you that. She wouldn't dare hurt him.' Great-Aunt Elizabeth paused and her eye twitched again. 'I am certain of it,' she added emphatically. But Kate had seen that moment of uncertainty flash across her great-aunt's face, and her insides turned to ice. Yesterday she had been told that this evil woman had all but killed her father and now she was expected to believe that Lorabeth Lampton would not harm her brother.

She looked away and squinted up into the early morning sky, and the idea formed in her mind that Great-Aunt Elizabeth had let them down and was perhaps incapable of looking after them or of making the right decision. It was a terrifying thought, but Kate put her hand to her throat and felt the warmth of the heartstone, and she willed it to help her be strong. As she held the heartstone in her fingers, Kate thought about Phil and struggled to work out what to do next. She tried to imagine where he was, what he would be doing and thinking. Suddenly Kate felt the heartstone's energy surge through her. An image of startling clarity came to her and she felt, with total conviction, that she knew exactly what they should do. Phil needed her help and he needed it soon, not at eight o'clock that night.

'Nevada,' she whispered. 'Great-Aunt Elizabeth!' she exclaimed. 'I have to go to Phil *now* – he needs me.'

Great-Aunt Elizabeth straightened up sharply from where she had been inspecting Lorabeth's lipstick message. 'Now, my dear, I know you're upset, but we will get him back tonight.'

'No, no, you're wrong,' Kate interrupted her fiercely. 'Not tonight. Tonight will be too late. We must leave straight away.'

Kate looked at her great-aunt and again saw a flicker of confusion in her eyes. Had she had any doubt at all, then that was the sign Kate needed to make her trust her own instincts. Her Great-Aunt Elizabeth may have had all the answers once, but now Kate was sure it was she who was right. 'It's a trap; if we wait until tonight, they'll get away. Phil isn't even in Washington any more – she's taken him to Nevada.'

Great-Aunt Elizabeth began to move towards Kate, reaching out her arms as if to embrace her. 'Now, Kate, listen to me –'

'No! You listen to me this time.' Kate's eyes flashed wildly. 'You may be right most of the time, but you're not right now. My brother is in trouble and we have to help him.' Kate was breathing deeply and staring steadily at her great-aunt, her thick, unbrushed hair hanging untidily about her face.

Great-Aunt Elizabeth hesitated and Kate knew she was nearly persuaded.

'You're not well or something, Great-Aunt Elizabeth,' she said more gently. 'Something's wrong with you. Remember how you didn't know that Lorabeth Lampton was at the hotel? And that morning after the break-in, when I wanted to talk to you, you didn't know I was behind you. Do you remember how I made you jump?'

Having stood still, as if frozen, Great-Aunt Elizabeth nodded slowly.

'You've already been down here this morning when you went to the shop – didn't you see the message? Do you think Phil could vanish from under our noses if you were OK?'

For some time they stood on the forecourt in an awkward silence.

'That is what your nightmare was about, dear,' Great-Aunt Elizabeth said at last, meeting Kate's persistent stare. She began her characteristic pacing back and forth. 'You foresaw the danger Phil was in.'

'And I'm seeing something now – something important, Great-Aunt Elizabeth. Just now, when I thought of Phil, the Lampton laboratory in Nevada came into my mind. It was perfectly clear – I could see it: the desert, the orange sun flashing on the metallic walls. We must go to Nevada –' Kate glanced around at Barking, Fearless and Harold, who were all watching her intently, and she sensed that they believed in her. 'That's where Phil is,' she said confidently, 'I'm sure of it.'

It is always easy, looking back afterwards, to see what you should have done, Phil thought. Now he did not know why he had not told Harold or Great-Aunt Elizabeth that he had lost his watch. At the time, he had desperately wanted not to be the one who made a mess of things. He was the youngest, he was the one who needed extra stealth and fitness coaching, he was the one who had got caught inside the laboratory. He just could not bear to tell them that he was the one who could not be trusted to look after a watch. But that was not the worst of it; he knew now that the worst thing he had done was to go out alone.

After everyone was asleep, he had slipped from his sleeping bag and waited in the bathroom on the landing below until he was sure he hadn't disturbed anyone. He planned to search the forecourt of the showroom and look in the sidecar to see if he could find his watch. If he had it again by morning, then no one need ever know what a loser he was.

Dense black rain clouds drifted across the sky so that the moon seemed to be on a dimmer switch, swinging the forecourt haphazardly between brilliance and gloom. The neon sign opposite worked intermittently and, when it was off and the moon was hidden, it was alarmingly dark.

Phil had been crouched over, trailing his fingers below the Harley, when a cloud obscured the moon and darkness fell on him as if a blanket had been thrown over him. Phil held his breath, waiting for the neon's flash to illuminate the shadows beneath the bike when he sensed a presence behind him. He glanced up and found the tall, shadowy figure of Lorabeth Lampton towering over him.

'Looking for this?' her cruel voice hissed at him.

Phil jumped up and darted round the side of the Harley, only to stumble into a horribly familiar grasp and an overpowering stench of garlic and tobacco. His eyes staring wildly from over the top of the large hairy hand that was clasped painfully across his mouth, Phil saw Lorabeth Lampton toss his watch on to the ground. This time he was held too firmly and roughly to make it possible to struggle or resist. Gulping silently on sobs of fear, pain and frustration, he was lifted awkwardly and bundled across the forecourt to a waiting car.

At first, he thought with alarm that they were going to put him in the boot, but instead Phil was pushed roughly into the back seat, guided by a large hand pressing on his head. The owner of the hand clambered in beside him and placed a heavy arm across Phil's chest, pinning him back into his seat.

In front of him, in the driver's seat, sat the other man from the hotel and the laboratory and, Phil was now certain, from the wood-splintering, head-crashing battle with the Invisible Butler in the lobby of Great-Aunt Elizabeth's house.

The door next to him opened and Lorabeth Lampton

sat down beside him. 'Drive to the heliport, Bardolph,' she told the driver, staring straight ahead of her.

'We going to Nevada, Mrs Lampton?' he asked gruffly.

'The boy and I are going,' Mrs Lampton replied coolly. 'I want you and Frimley to return to the Hotel Modena. At eight o'clock tonight that decrepit old woman is coming to meet me there. Unfortunately, I shall not be able to keep our appointment. I'd like you ...' she hesitated, '... to *entertain* her for me. Do you understand?'

Bardolph and Frimley chuckled softly. 'Yes, Mrs Lampton, we understand.'

Prisoners

As Great-Aunt Elizabeth steered the Harley through the Washington suburbs to join the freeway, each of the sidecar's passengers silently suffered the pain of Phil's absence. Harold worked feverishly at his computer, trying to crack the coded information about the Nevada laboratory, while Fearless, Barking and Kate stared sadly through the windows.

The all-too-familiar rain lashed against the glass and blurred their view, but Kate did not notice. She was trying to focus her attention on Phil, concentrating all her mental energy on him. She held his rucksack on her lap. She felt as if she were able, by thought alone, to fill him with power so that he would guide them to him like a pulsing light on an electronic map. Kate did not allow herself to think about whether such a thing was possible or not; she could only trust her heartstone and be strong, it was all she had. She had fleeting spasms of concern for her parents which she struggled not to think about. In this instance, she would have to assume that Great-Aunt Elizabeth was correct and her mum and dad were biding their time, seeing the sights of New York while waiting for them to return.

They drove through the strangest weather conditions anyone could remember. Despite it being summer, the north-eastern states had already had the highest monthly rainfall since records began, and temperatures were uncharacteristically low. As the Harley sped south-west, traversing the broad plains of central North America, they saw little other traffic and few people out and about under the gloomy skies. The farm buildings had storm windows in place, and twice they saw tornadoes on the horizon: gigantic blue-black cones staggering precariously across a flat grey sky like towers of badly stacked plates.

They pressed on without stopping and had covered more than a thousand kilometres by evening when gale-force winds buffeted the Harley and the temperature fell to just two degrees above zero.

In the shadows beside two large wheelie-bins in the car park of the Modena Hotel, Bardolph and Frimley lurked. They shook from the cold until their teeth chattered as they waited in vain for their employer's elderly adversary.

Charlotte sat still and watched Michael pacing the narrow strip of carpet that surrounded the bed. Like all basic motel accommodation found across America, the room had twin beds, a wardrobe, chest of drawers, television, a kitchen and breakfast bar in one corner and a shower room and toilet in another. It was small and cramped but fine for an overnight stay ... except that Charlotte and Michael were now in their second day and motels do not usually lock their guests in.

Michael marched to the door and tried the handle for the hundredth time. He didn't bother to check the windows. He had been convinced that the security grid was locked and immovable when in a fit of rage and frustration he had gripped the bars in his fists and shaken them with all his strength. The phone beside the bed, he had quickly discovered, was dead. Shouting and hammering on the door brought no one running in response.

Neither he nor Charlotte had slept during the previous thirty-six hours, and both were now seriously worried. Eddie had told them, as they left New York and headed for the freeway, that Aunt Elizabeth would meet them in Nevada. They had driven continuously, making only brief stops at remote gas stations, with Eddie becoming increasingly surly and uncommunicative. He had finally delivered them to this roadside motel, in the middle of a barren and desolate nowhere, in pitch darkness. He loaded the small fridge with food, told them gruffly not to thank him, and left the room.

Since then, they had heard nothing and were becoming more and more anxious about the safety and whereabouts of the children. The television fuelled their distress. The continuous reports of earthquakes, volcanoes, storms and landslides made it hard to imagine that there was anywhere left that was safe. At first Charlotte had tried to reassure Michael, but in the last few hours her own fears were beginning to occupy her thoughts, so she kept quiet.

On the evening of Charlotte and Michael's second day of captivity, Phil stepped out of an air-conditioned limousine beside the entrance to Lampton Cosmetics Research Laboratory, Nevada. His legs buckled beneath him as he struggled to breathe in air so thick and hot it seemed to swirl about him like soup. He was pulled to his feet by Lorabeth Lampton herself, grasping the back of his neck with a bony hand. He had once seen a rabbit hanging limply in the jaws of a fox, and the memory flashed into his mind and filled him with shame that he should be as defenceless as a baby bunny. Yet, though he had been shocked at the time, he understood that the fox was just doing what a fox must do and that the young rabbit was somehow resigned to its fate. But to be treated roughly by an adult – and not just any adult, but his own flesh and blood – horrified him. The effortless way in which this glamorous woman could be so cruel filled him with dread and made him powerless to resist.

Lorabeth Lampton kept hold of Phil as she guided him through a doorway and into the cool interior of the building. She marched him along corridor after corridor, while Phil desperately tried to remember the sequence of left and right turns. Perhaps, he hoped, if he could escape he would be able to find his way back to the door and the outside world. He did not dare think what he would do then, alone in that immense heat, and he pushed from his mind the image of the four-metre perimeter fence and the pictures of the vast expanse of shimmering, empty desert they had driven through from a remote and seemingly disused airfield. The driver who had met them had been a young man, big and square like Bardolph and Frimley. Unlike those thugs who wore grim expressions on their faces, Phil had noticed a glimmer of a smile lighting up the man's eyes whenever Phil's glance had met his in the rear-view mirror. Now the man walked ahead of them with a slightly swaying gait. Perhaps, Phil thought, he could befriend this man with the smiling eyes.

They turned into a corridor that led only to a dead end and a closed steel door upon which a sign read:

🚫

Authorized
Personnel Only

Strictly No Admittance

'Open the door, Eddie,' said Lorabeth Lampton.

Eddie punched out a code on a control panel adjacent to the door, and it slid back.

218

Lorabeth Lampton pushed Phil into the room. 'I shall see you later for a little chat,' she said to him. To Eddie she said, 'Make sure he has what he needs,' and she turned away briskly and left them alone.

Phil stepped nervously into the room, rubbing the back of his neck where Lorabeth Lampton's nails had dug into his skin. It was less a room and more a prison cell. There was a bed against the opposite wall and in the corner a door stood open, revealing a small cubicle in which was a toilet and sink. The grey vinyl flooring reminded Phil of a hospital. There was no window but, glancing up at the ceiling in the small bathroom, Phil saw a grating providing access to the ventilation system, and his heart lifted a little. He turned towards Eddie, who was standing behind him, smiling from ear to ear.

'Cameras,' the man said, as if the word were the punchline to a joke. He pointed up at small boxes in two corners of the room near the ceiling. His finger continued to jab the air, pointing at the camera diagonally opposite the toilet as his shoulders shook with laughter. 'Better make sure you shut the door,' he spluttered. 'I don't get paid to watch you on the can,' and he exploded into loud guffaws.

Eddie turned to leave but as he stepped through the door he looked back at Phil. He was no longer laughing and now his eyes suggested only boredom and a cruel streak.

'Don't try anything stupid, OK?' were his parting words. The door slid closed and Phil noticed that there was no control panel for opening the door on the inside wall. He walked slowly to the bed and sat down carefully. He folded his arms across his stomach and tried to think what he should do.

19

Crossing the Desert

Kate looked around the sidecar where Harold, Barking and Fearless were asleep. Outside the window, Great-Aunt Elizabeth crouched determinedly over the engine of the Harley. Her face glistened with thick white cream from where she had applied two large palmfuls of sun block. Since crossing the state line, the winds had ceased raging and they were proceeding beneath clearer skies. They were driving on a straight road through barren red earth, littered with occasional cattle skulls and boulders. Ahead of them, a gigantic red sun was slowly meeting the horizon. At first there had been one or two birds flying overhead, but now, as far as Kate could see, there was no sign of life or habitation. They had not seen another vehicle for over an hour, apart from a burnt-out truck stranded on its axles, with black, gaping holes where its windows had been. Kate wondered where Phil could be in such a place and she closed her eyes tight. She tried hard to picture him, but the only image that came to mind was of him sitting on a bed, looking small and hunched over. Kate kept her eyes closed tight and willed him to be brave and to know that they were coming to get him.

When she opened her eyes again, Harold was staring at her. 'You're worrying about Phil, aren't you?'

Kate looked away out of the window, where even small rocks left long purple shadows.

'I feel he is right next to me if I close my eyes and think about him,' she said quietly.

Harold leant forwards and rested his elbows on his knees. He hung his head for a moment, then raised his chin so that he could look directly into Kate's eyes. 'Look,' he said carefully and turned his head to glance through the window at Great-Aunt Elizabeth's darkening profile, 'I probably shouldn't tell you this but ...' He broke off as Barking opened one eye and twitched his tail. 'Well, I think you've got a right to know some stuff, Kate,' he went on defiantly.

Barking opened both eyes and sat up. Kate stared at them and waited. It was Barking who spoke first and he addressed himself to Harold. 'She's been trying to protect you,' Barking snorted.

'OK, I know that,' Harold replied, dragging his hands through his hair.

'I know that Great-Aunt Elizabeth has been keeping things from me,' Kate said. 'She just tells me what suits her. What she thinks I ought to know.'

Harold sighed. 'When Lorabeth Lampton was Penelope Parton, she ran a business that traded in wild animals. When your mother realized how bad it was –

and it was really bad, Kate – she ran away and went to live with Aunt Elizabeth. You know that much?'

Kate nodded.

'Well, it was good for Aunt Elizabeth to have Charlotte with her as it made her stronger: the two heartstones and a common purpose. But you see, Kate, Penelope Parton, well, she had an ally too.'

'She did?' said Kate. 'Who?'

Harold tipped his head and looked Kate straight in the eye. 'Me,' he said sadly.

Kate frowned and began to shake her head, and Barking jumped from his seat on to Fearless's sprawled back. 'Wake up, will you?' he hissed into Fearless's ear.

Fearless staggered to push himself up on paws that slid away in front of him. 'What's going on?' he yawned, adding, 'I'm starving.'

'It's all my fault, Kate,' Harold continued. 'It's my fault your mum got kidnapped and it's my fault your dad nearly died, and it's my fault . . . because if it wasn't for me he would have a heartstone . . . it's my fault that she's managed to get Phil.'

'Oops – er, should he be telling her this?' Fearless asked, and his mouth hung open,

'Oh, you're a great help!' Barking replied, flinging himself at the glass, where he scrabbled furiously with his paws to get Great-Aunt Elizabeth's attention.

Great-Aunt Elizabeth glanced into the sidecar and promptly veered off the road. She brought the Harley to a stop and dismounted. As the domed glass roof rolled back, all the occupants could be heard speaking at once.

'Be quiet!' Great-Aunt Elizabeth shouted. 'Get out and tell me what this is all about!'

The animals jumped out and Kate, followed by Harold, stepped into the deep orange light of a desert sunset. Across the rough ground, their bodies threw lumpy shadows three or four times their height.

Harold turned to Great-Aunt Elizabeth and grimaced. 'I know you said not to say anything, but I feel so bad, Aunt E. If I could turn the clock back, I would.'

'I don't believe you did anything wrong,' Kate said in a small nervous voice.

Great-Aunt Elizabeth stretched out her hand and touched Kate's shoulder. 'Having done things you regret in your past is not the end of the world. Perhaps Harold should tell you what he did; but while you're listening to him, Kate, I want you to remember that Harold now makes an invaluable, superhuman contribution to the fight *against* evil!'

Kate looked down at her feet. 'I just want to be told what happened,' she said. 'I don't like the way you try to protect me all the time. I can't understand if you don't tell me.'

Great-Aunt Elizabeth sighed and looked affectionately at Harold. 'Are you sure this is necessary, my dear?' she asked.

Harold stared back at her. 'I've partially decoded the last files, Aunt E. I think she may be planning to re-activate the Humanitron.'

Great-Aunt Elizabeth's face seemed to crumple in the half-light. 'Are you sure?' she murmured.

Harold hung his head, gulped and nodded.

'OK, Harold, you had better tell her,' she said wearily, 'but get back in the sidecar, all of you, and let's go and find Phil.'

By now it was so dark inside the sidecar that Kate could barely see Harold's face. She sat still in the darkness, grateful to have Barking and Fearless beside her as she listened to Harold's voice.

'She wasn't Lorabeth Lampton then – I knew her as Penelope Parton,' he began, 'I won Young Scientist of the Year when I was eleven and she wrote to me and offered to sponsor my education. When I was twelve I went to work for her. She gave me my own laboratory – everything I wanted. She encouraged my inventions – helped me achieve the impossible. One day she came to me with an idea for a device that would alter nature, change what it meant to be human. It was amazing – nothing like it had even been dreamt of . . .' Harold's voice faltered and Kate shuddered and noticed that, now the sun had disappeared, it was rapidly getting cold.

'It was her idea, but I made it,' Harold continued after a pause. 'I was young, Kate, but I should have known better. I got carried away – I had to see if it was possible to transform people. I didn't think of the consequences until it was too late.' Harold's voice dropped to a low whisper. 'I invented the Humanitron.'

His words hung in the chill darkness of the sidecar as

225

the Harley came to a halt beside the perimeter fence of Lampton Cosmetics Research Laboratory, Nevada.

Phil had sat still for a long time, imagining his escape. At last he rose from the bed and felt a stiffness in his legs and back from lack of use. Telling himself not to glance up at the cameras, he walked into the toilet and closed the door. He looked up at the ceiling and the square wire grating. Taking a deep breath, he stepped on to the toilet seat and pushed the grating up with the tips of his fingers. It slid out of the way easily. Phil bent his knees slightly and jumped up to the opening. He propped his weight on his elbows and hauled his head and shoulders inside. The tunnel was narrower than the one he remembered in Washington. And darker. Phil was about to pull himself up when he heard the door to his cell sliding open. He dropped to the floor and quickly flushed the toilet, hoping the sound would prevent whoever it was outside opening the cubicle door. He ran his hands under the tap while glancing up at the gaping hole above his head. Drying his hands on his trousers, he opened the door into the other room and tried to look casual while closing it carefully behind him.

Eddie was putting a tray of food on the bed. ''Ere you go,' he said cheerfully. 'Ham and eggs for you.'

At these words and the sight of the food, Phil felt a rip of hunger rise through his gut and into his chest; he couldn't remember when he had last eaten. He went over to the bed, sat down, and lifted the tray on to his lap.

Eddie stood near the door and watched him. 'Right, I'm off. I hope you've got good table manners – don't want you putting me off me own dinner.'

Phil, his mouth full of food, glanced up as Eddie left the room. He had no idea where Eddie went to watch the cameras, but he hoped it would take the man a few minutes to get there. He quickly finished the meal then, turning his back on the cameras, he bundled the tray under his blanket. He put the knife in his pocket, then carefully balanced the plate on its side and held it in place with the bed cover. He folded his pillow lengthways and stuffed it under the blanket, below the plate. From where he stood it looked ridiculous, but maybe, he hoped, from the camera's angle it would look like he was in the bed.

Phil slipped into the toilet cubicle and shut the door. In a moment he had pulled himself up into the ventilation tunnel and replaced the grating.

Virtual Invisibility

The Harley circled the perimeter fence at a distance until Great-Aunt Elizabeth found a large boulder that she could park behind and be out of sight of the building's few windows. Kate peered from behind the boulder while Fearless dug underneath the fence and ran inside to see if he could find a way into the laboratory. Kate shivered in the cold night air and turned to watch Great-Aunt Elizabeth and Harold, who were setting about the sidecar with spanners and wrenches. Great-Aunt Elizabeth wore Robogloves, gloves with built-in intelligence that had been precisely wired with the finest microelectronics and programmed by Harold to do whatever job was required. Kate watched Great-Aunt Elizabeth's flying fingers as she rapidly attached leads and wires to a panel.

'What are you doing?' Kate asked, rubbing her hands together and glancing back for a glimpse through the fence at the laboratory.

'Harold has fitted the Harley with a missile launcher,' Great-Aunt Elizabeth said, and she smiled faintly at

Kate's stunned expression. 'Don't worry – no weapons! We're going to be the missile.'

Kate frowned. Was this information supposed to reassure her, she wondered.

Harold was screwing a large bolt into place with a spanner, and spoke in breathy grunts from his exertions.

'If – I – get – the trajectory right –' He dropped the spanner to the ground and reached for another, smaller one, 'then we should – land ten metres inside – the fence.' He stood up. 'There, that should do it.'

Fearless returned. 'We've got to be quick. There's a guy waiting by a limousine – my guess is he's taking someone out. The doorway is dark, so if they get in the right position Kate and Barking may be able to slip inside as the door opens.'

Great-Aunt Elizabeth frowned and began tapping her bottom lip with a finger. 'Are we ready, Harold?'

'Not quite. I need time to check the electronics.'

'We've got to go now!' Fearless exclaimed, turning tight circles and eager to be off.

Kate could see distress and confusion in her great-aunt and she did not like what she saw. She reached out and put her small hand on Great-Aunt Elizabeth's arm. 'Don't worry, I'll go through the tunnel – I'll be all right.'

Great-Aunt Elizabeth put her arms round Kate and crushed her against her stomach. Kate was overpowered by the scent of leather and chocolate.

'I know you can do it,' Great-Aunt Elizabeth said,

releasing Kate from her grip. 'Harold and I will be inside the fence when you get back.'

Harold stepped forwards and gave Kate an awkward hug. 'The sidecar has location deflectors; the dome will reflect the rocky terrain back at anyone who looks at it. It's perfect camouflage.' He added, 'Don't you worry, we'll guide you in.' He pushed a heavy strand of hair away from Kate's face. 'I'm so sorry for what I did, Kate, and I promise you I'll make it up to you – both of you. We'll get Phil out of there.'

Kate nodded at Harold and closed her eyes against his chest as she gave him one last hug. As she clung to his thin frame, she remembered the sorrow in his voice when he had told her about the Humanitron and the hundreds of children and thousands of animals who would have suffered if it had not been destroyed.

Fearless, who had been watching the building, turned to hurry them along. 'Quickly now, Kate,' he said, 'someone's coming out. Follow me,' and he disappeared into his tunnel under the wire fence.

Kate thrust her head into the hole and hauled herself through the dirt after Fearless. She emerged on the other side and crouched in the darkness, flicking the red dust and grit from her eyes and hair. Barking appeared behind her, and they ran to the building and sank down low against the wall where there was most shadow and least chance of being seen.

Silently they slithered forwards on their stomachs and, keeping close to the base of the wall, turned the corner and cautiously approached the area where the limousine was waiting near large but unwelcoming reception doors. Kate felt her heartstone roar with a sudden burst of energy and she caught it up in her fingers and dropped it down inside her sweatshirt.

Just then, from inside the building, they overheard Lorabeth Lampton's icy voice cut through the cold night air. 'Eddie, do you have a still from the video camera?'

The man who had been waiting beside the car jumped and flicked his cigarette into the darkness. 'Yes, Mrs Lampton.'

'What's he doing?'

'Sitting on the bed looking miserable, Mrs Lampton.'

'Perfect. Drive me to the motel.'

Barking crept along the ground, belly-crawling close to the wall, where he lurked in the shadows beside the door. As Lorabeth Lampton stepped out into the night, he darted silently behind her. Skimming the hem of her fur coat, he was inside just as the door swung shut. Kate pulled herself against the wall and held her breath. The young man held the car door open as Lorabeth Lampton took the first long stride towards the limousine.

Suddenly she stopped and turned her head. Kate felt a roar of warmth from her heartstone as she tried to shrink into the ground.

'Everything all right, Mrs Lampton?' the driver asked.

Kate heard Lorabeth Lampton's shoes scrape the ground as the woman turned towards her. She kept her face averted, knowing that to look up would risk reflecting light in her eyes and so giving herself away. Kate felt her heart pounding, and she willed it to slow down as if that wildly jumping muscle was actually visible and might betray her. She heard and felt Lorabeth Lampton step closer.

'Shall I call security, Mrs Lampton? Is there a problem?'

Kate thought hard about the grains of red dust that had clung to her after she had crawled through the gap under the fence. She imagined that she was a piece of grit: minute, inconsequential, virtually invisible. She concentrated on being so small and so still that no one would be able to see her even if they were looking straight at her, just as you can hunt forever for a pin that you know has been dropped but which proves impossible to find.

'A heartstone,' Lorabeth Lampton murmured softly, and Kate's heart jumped and began to race once more.

'I beg your pardon, Mrs Lampton?' the driver asked, abandoning the door and walking towards his employer.

'Stay calm, stay cool,' Kate repeated over and over in her mind, and she felt that she was addressing her heartstone as much as herself, fearing that it would flare up once more with a surge of red glowing energy and give her away.

Fearless must have feared the same thing, for he suddenly growled softly and ran off into the shadows.

The driver jumped back towards the car. 'Flippin' heck, what was that?' he cried.

Lorabeth Lampton turned and walked past him. 'Call security,' she said. 'I want the fence checked – every last inch of it,' and she strode off and climbed into the car.

As the car pulled away into the night, Kate crouched beside the wall and waited. She waited so long that she began to fear that Barking was in trouble. Perhaps he was neither big enough nor strong enough to be able to operate the door mechanism. Kate began to look around for another way in. Craning her neck, she could see there was another door, several metres behind her. She began to slide her body down the wall towards it when suddenly it opened and Barking's back swung out, hanging on to the emergency push-bar mechanism by his front paws.

'Quick!' he hissed, and Kate scuttled at a low crouch along the wall and slipped inside the door.

Ahead of them, a long corridor stretched into the distance with nowhere to hide, should someone turn into it from the far end. Kate looked up and saw a grating that led into the ventilation system. She looked around for something to climb on, as it was far too high.

Barking looked up while walking round her in a circle. 'We've got to get up there,' he said and jumped into her arms and put his front paws on Kate's shoulders.

Quivering slightly before launching himself at the ceiling, Barking jumped from her head and glanced off the grating. He dislodged it a fraction before falling awkwardly, but landing neatly, on his feet. Kate watched the corridor as Barking sprang up her back for a second attempt. He leapt upwards and pushed his paws against the grating, and it slid away as he fell back to the floor.

Kate and Barking surveyed the gap he had made.

Suddenly, a military-sounding announcement was broadcast through the corridor: *'Will all security personnel proceed to check the grounds and the perimeter fence.'*

'Oh no,' said Kate. 'I hope they're OK out there.'

'We have to get out of sight. I think I'll get through there this time,' Barking said and he turned to take a run up. Kate braced herself as Barking sprinted along the corridor, ran up her back and sprang from the top of her head. She looked up in time to see his tail juddering out of sight into the hole.

Kate stood below the narrow opening, wondering how on earth she would follow him.

The grating was dragged away and Barking's head appeared, his yellow eyes peering down at her. 'Undo the straps on your rucksack and throw it up to me,' he said. 'I'll tie one end to something up here and lower it back down to you – it might just be long enough.'

Kate did as she was told, then stood nervously in the corridor and waited. Suddenly her bag dropped down and the strap swung like a pendulum just above her head. She reached up and took hold of it.

Barking's face reappeared above her. 'You can do it, Kate,' he said, sensing her self-doubt. 'You must be positive, imagine succeeding before you attempt it. Your heartstone will help you.'

Kate breathed deeply and thought about being strong and weightless and gliding effortlessly into the air. She eyed the corridor one last time as she bent her legs and hauled herself upwards with all her might. With clenched teeth she worked her way, hand over hand, up the webbing strap until, first her left hand, then her right elbow were inside the ventilation tunnel.

She pulled herself on her stomach through the gap and exhaled.

Barking patted her face with his paw. 'Well done!' he said. 'Now move away while I put the grating back.'

The tunnel was lower and narrower than the previous one they had been through. Kate could not crawl properly on all fours and had to drag her body forwards on her elbows. It was dark and cramped and a pungent chemical smell irritated the back of her throat. Kate kept her eyes on Barking and her mind on Phil. The sense she had that he was near by gave her hope and made the discomfort bearable.

They soon came to a junction where the tunnel divided into three. Barking went straight across but then turned to face Kate so that she surveyed him and the shafts that angled away to the left and the right of their original tunnel.

Kate pulled the architect's plans from her rucksack and placed her finger over the room Harold had suggested as being the most likely place where Phil would be kept: a square, windowless room with an adjacent toilet cubicle, deep within the building. But these plans did not show all the ventilation ducting and they would have to decide which shaft would take them there.

'Any ideas?' Barking asked.

Kate stretched out her hands and placed one of them in each tunnel and closed her eyes. Her left hand felt warmer.

'This way,' she said. 'It feels warmer this way.'

Barking curled past her and stepped into the tunnel.

'It *is* warmer,' he said. 'There's probably a heating pipe running alongside it.'

Kate blushed in the gloom.

'OK, which way do you think we should go?' she asked.

Barking shrugged and shook his whiskers. 'We might as well try this way first.'

A tiny light on Kate's watch flashed. She raised her wrist to her ear and pressed a small button. It was Great-Aunt Elizabeth, her voice miniaturized and tinny-sounding in the metal tunnel.

'There are security guards checking the fence so we've removed ourselves to a safe distance. Fearless is with us. When they find his tunnel, they'll think a coyote dug it. Don't come out without checking in with us first. We'll let you know where to meet us.'

Kate whispered acknowledgement into the watch and proceeded to haul herself after Barking down the left-hand fork of the tunnel.

The Humanitron

Michael and Charlotte had been sitting silently on the end of each of the twin beds when they heard the car; they both jumped to their feet and made for the door. As the key turned in the lock, Michael grabbed the handle from the inside and yanked the door open. Eddie lurched into the room, instantly bracing himself and raising his fists.

Lorabeth's voice came from the dimly lit hallway behind him. 'Relax, Eddie. I'm sure these good people would rather invite us in than have a brawl in the doorway.'

Charlotte walked backwards and bumped into the bed as Lorabeth Lampton stepped into the room beside Eddie.

Michael stared at her through narrowed eyes. 'If you have anything to do with our imprisonment here or if you've done anything to harm my family . . .'

He did not end the threat as Lorabeth Lampton raised a slender, long-fingered hand in his face then walked across the room to stand in front of the television set, where she turned to face them. Eddie closed the door

237

and stood guard in front of it, his arms folded across his chest.

Lorabeth Lampton gazed down at Charlotte, who sat, ashen-faced, on the bed exactly where she had stumbled into it.

'Where is your heartstone?' the newcomer demanded, her left eye flickering slightly with the smallest of twitches. 'I have been waiting years for your heartstone to become active again. Where is it?'

Michael pushed his way between his wife and the tall intruder. 'She's not telling you anything – who the hell are you?'

Lorabeth Lampton blinked languorously then slowly turned her head to look directly at Michael. She frowned slightly, then leant quizzically towards his face.

'I know you,' she said, carefully studying his face.

Charlotte jumped up from the bed and tried to stand between them.

'It *is* you!' said Lorabeth Lampton to Michael. She then turned to face Charlotte. 'Well, Gina, I had no idea.'

'Stop it,' Charlotte interrupted her. 'He doesn't remember anything, and that's not my name. I'm called Charlotte now.'

Michael looked from one to the other, his expression veering between anger and confusion.

'Come now, Gi– . . . *Charlotte*, surely the poor man has a right to know his mother-in-law?'

Lorabeth Lampton smiled as Michael wavered un-steadily on his feet and looked aghast at Charlotte.

'Would you care to sit down?' asked Lorabeth Lampton as if they were guests at a tea party.

'Stop it!' Charlotte repeated. 'Michael doesn't remember anything – he can't help you.'

'Yes, and you won't, I suppose? I am very sorry, Charlotte, but in finding you I hoped to get my heartstone back. Now, I see there is a possibility of my getting the keystone as well. It really is too good an opportunity to miss.'

Charlotte's dark eyes glared defiantly. 'It never was *your* heartstone, and anyway, I don't know where it is and Michael doesn't remember anything. We can't help you.'

Lorabeth Lampton took a compact mirror from her purse and, flicking it open, surveyed her face in it. Her voice, when she spoke was casual. 'Eddie, pass them that little souvenir snapshot you've got there in your pocket, will you?'

Eddie reached inside his jacket and handed a brown envelope to Charlotte. She took it and, anticipating a shock of some kind, allowed herself to slowly sit down on the bed. Michael sat beside her and they both gasped as she pulled from the envelope a photograph of Phil sitting, forlorn and alone, in a strange, bleak little room. The picture was black-and-white and grainy and taken from above, clearly a still from a closed-circuit camera. In the top right-hand corner a digital recording of the date and time showed that the picture had been taken less than three hours ago.

'Now, let's see, shall we?' said Lorabeth Lampton,

snapping the mirror shut. 'I have something – oops, I mean some*one* – that you want, and you have something that I want. Perhaps we should come to an arrangement.' She tilted her head slightly and smiled at them, 'What do you say?'

A moment's silence was interrupted by a piercing electronic tune, which crescendoed as Eddie removed his mobile phone from his pocket.

'It's my dad, Mrs Lampton, ma'am. He and Frimley have just arrived in Reno and he says to tell you the old lady never showed up.'

Lorabeth Lampton took a deep breath and drew herself up before exhaling slowly. 'So, I did sense the presence of a heartstone at the laboratory. Come on, Eddie, we're going back. We'll take these two with us.'

She looked gloatingly at Charlotte and Michael as she turned towards the door. Then she began to laugh. 'This is turning into quite a family reunion.'

Phil lay flat on his tummy, laid his head on his forearms and closed his eyes. He had been in the tunnel for more than an hour and had not found anywhere that looked like a good place to jump down. Some time ago there had been a security alert, so he knew that his escape had been discovered. If he did manage to get out, he feared the fence would be guarded. In any case, he was no longer sure if he was heading further into the building or making his way towards the outside. All the gratings he had peered down from were over corridors and so high up from the floor that, once down, he would never get up again. He kept his eyes closed tight, afraid that he was in terrible trouble. He tried imagining he was Spider-Man and he stretched out his fingers, ready to throw a web with which to haul himself through the tunnel, but after a second or two he opened his eyes and looked at his hand, his ordinary, normal, useless hand, and his vision blurred until at last hot tears ran from his eyes and soaked his sleeve.

The tunnel Kate and Barking had chosen arched ahead of them in a shallow curve and so, since they could never see where they were going, it seemed endless.

'This is the wrong way,' Kate said at last.

Barking stopped and turned to look back at her, one front paw left hanging in the air. 'We'll go on for another five minutes, then we'll turn back, OK?'

Kate nodded and shuffled forwards behind Barking who, after he had taken only a few more steps, stopped and looked back over his shoulder again.

This time he spoke with enthusiasm. 'There's a grating coming up – maybe this will be it.'

They reached the grating and peered down into a tiny room with a toilet and a sink. Kate lifted the grating and pulled it out of the way.

'This is the room that Harold suggested we try, I'm sure of it!'

Barking sprang down and Kate climbed down after him, stepping from the cistern to the toilet seat. Once on the ground, she bent and stretched her legs a few times and raised her arms over her head before reaching for the door handle.

Suddenly her heartstone glowed warm and red at her throat and she hesitated. She glanced down at Barking and smiled. 'Phil's here,' she said, almost laughing, and pushed open the door.

For a moment it seemed as though the room was empty, but then they saw the small lumpen shape in the bed.

'Hang on, Kate, this doesn't feel right,' said Barking, who lingered in the doorway of the bathroom and was sniffing the air suspiciously.

'Phil!' Kate cried, rushing forwards. Before she had taken more than two steps, the sliding door to the room began to open. Kate had no time to do anything but turn in the direction of the door. Barking was quicker to react and darted back into the toilet cubicle, snatched up Kate's rucksack in his mouth and sprang from the floor to the cistern and disappeared into the ventilation system.

Kate stood, rooted to the spot, while in front of her, her eyebrows raised high on her forehead, stood Lorabeth Lampton.

'Well, well, well!' she said as Charlotte and Michael were ushered round the door by Eddie. The sight of her parents softened the rigid muscles in Kate's back and neck, and she fell towards them as they rushed to her and flung their arms round her.

'This reminds me of Shakespeare,' said Lorabeth

Lampton. 'I thought I had the brother, but it seems I have the sister.' She smiled at Kate, who glowered up at her from her parents' arms. 'And you're wearing your mother's heartstone – how thoughtful of you.'

'Where's Phil?' Michael asked Kate in a whisper, but Lorabeth Lampton heard him.

'Oh, do tell!' she said. 'It will make Eddie's job so much easier.'

She turned away abruptly and spoke to Eddie as she passed him in the doorway.

'Bring the child to my office and alert security that the boy is on the loose somewhere.' As she stepped from the room she called back over her shoulder, 'Oh, and Eddie, you had better take her watch from her.'

Overhead, Barking crouched near the grating and listened. As Lorabeth Lampton left, he padded softly back and forth in agitation. He wanted to go back down, to speak to Charlotte and see that Michael was all right; but he knew he would then risk being caught himself. He put his mind to guessing what to expect from the security team. He decided to get away from the area where the investigation into Phil's disappearance was likely to start, and he resolved to find Phil before any-one else did. A search party would be sure to try the ventilation system, but what if they found the grating sealed? If he could secure the grating, it would slow them down and give him time to find Phil.

Moments later, with one of his claws bleeding from

being torn on a screw and his ears lying flat against his head, he struggled into the straps of Kate's bag and shortened them by yanking on them with his teeth. It was far from ideal and the bag dragged behind him awkwardly as he hurried through the tunnel, his yellow eyes fierce and determined in the darkness. After he had put a distance of some minutes between himself and the room that now imprisoned Charlotte and Michael, he activated the two-way radio in his collar. In a few breathless sentences Barking told the occupants of the sidecar that Charlotte and Michael were locked in a cell and that Lorabeth Lampton had taken Kate away for questioning.

'No wonder there's been no response from Lottie and Michael in New York,' Harold murmured. 'I've been trying the hotel every day.'

'And Phil? Where's he?' Great-Aunt Elizabeth wailed.

'I'm still looking for him, I've carried on down the tunnel – he must have come this way or we would have seen him already,' said Barking.

There was a sound of rustling on Barking's device, then he heard Fearless's gravelly voice. 'If Phil is in the tunnel you should be able to track him.'

'OK, tell me how to do that!' Barking hissed.

'Sniff around the tunnel and work out which of the smells is Phil. It isn't difficult.'

'Not for you, perhaps. You're a dog.'

'You can do it, though. Once you've got the scent, you just follow your nose.'

Barking lowered his face gingerly to the floor of the tunnel and sniffed at the cold metal. There was still a pungent chemical smell in the air, but suddenly Barking got an unmistakable whiff of boy.

'I've got it!' he cried.

Great-Aunt Elizabeth interrupted him. 'Harold says we must stop communicating as they may intercept the signal and locate us. Listen to me, Barking: we are coming inside. I cannot leave Charlotte, Michael and the children alone. Fearless will stay outside the fence. We may need him later on.'

Barking bounded through the tunnel until he came to a junction. After pausing to sniff carefully at the inter-section, he picked up the scent once more and hurried on. Some four hundred metres along this last offshoot, he stopped beside a tiny pool of water. He tasted it carefully with the tip of his rough tongue. It was salty. Walking now, Barking rounded the next bend in the tunnel and came face to face with Phil who was coming back towards him.

'Phil!' Barking said and leapt on him, purring loudly in his ear.

Phil collapsed and hid his face in Barking's fur as tears overwhelmed him again.

'It's OK, Phil,' Barking said, nudging his small, furry face against Phil's damp cheek. 'I'll get you out of here.'

Phil lifted his head and pressed his tears roughly away. 'We can't leave, Barking, there's something terrible up there.' He jerked his head over his shoulder behind him. 'We've got to help them – we can't just leave them.'

Barking's face furrowed into a quizzical frown. 'Who? What are you talking about?'

Phil turned awkwardly in the confined space and began a hunched but purposeful crawl through the tunnel. Barking watched him for a moment, but he could see that Phil was set on going back and so he trotted behind, wondering if he dared risk radio contact with the sidecar.

Phil led him through a maze of tunnels to a grating through which a strong shaft of unnatural light was beaming. Phil pulled the grating away and rolled on to his side, edging close to the wall of the tunnel so that Barking could crouch beside him. They peered down into a large room full of cage after cage of wild and domestic animals. Directly beneath them, a row of forlorn monkeys stared dolefully through wire mesh. Some had pushed their fingers through into the next cage and linked shiny knuckles with a neighbour. On the far wall, a stack of cages, eight high and running the length of the room, housed birds: silent, staring crows, eagles and kestrels standing on perches and making small, barely perceptible movements as they stared across the room. Facing the birds, behind the central rows of apes and monkeys, were cages housing cats, rabbits and dogs.

'We have to let them out,' Phil said, and he glanced sideways at Barking, who did not respond.

The cat's head was low, his chin touching the floor of the shaft, his brow scrunched low over his eyes. He stared intently at the far end of the room. 'Oh no,' he whispered.

Phil lowered his face and craned his neck round to follow Barking's gaze. Raised on a low circular podium stood a large metal-and-glass box that stood four metres high. On both sides were familiar revolving glass doors, just like the Dried-and-dressed, but round the outside a webbed network of electrical cabling ran, and cylindrical steel tubing spiralled across the roof of the box.

'What is it?' Phil whispered. 'Is it bad?'

'It's a Humanitron,' Barking said, 'and yes, it's very bad indeed.'

22

Forever Young

Eddie squashed Kate's twisted hand as he wrestled her watch from her wrist. Outraged, she dragged the back of her hand down the side of her jeans in an attempt to remove the sensation of his touch. He had tried to guide her along the corridor, but she had yanked her arm away from him and turned her head so that she would not have to look at him. For his part, he watched her out of the corner of his eye and kept his distance.

They reached a small lobby that, unlike the rest of the building, was carpeted. Eddie nudged her into a chair and knocked at the arresting oak-panelled door, incongruous among so much steel.

They heard Lorabeth Lampton command them to enter and Eddie kicked the leg of Kate's chair, his signal that she should stand up. She scowled at him, and he smirked back. He opened the door for her but did not go in. Instead, he stood in the doorway so that Kate had to pass horribly close to him in order to get inside.

'The young lady to see you, Mrs Lampton,' he announced, and Kate riled at his tone of voice – so smug and mocking.

She pushed past him into the room and stood in front of a raised desk where Lorabeth Lampton sat, preoccupied with the screen of a laptop computer.

Without looking up, she spoke to Eddie. 'Take the girl's watch to Carter and see if she can locate the transmitter.' She raised her eyes to look at Kate before continuing, 'And when she has identified the location, tell security that, even if all they find is an old lady on a motorbike, they should arrest her immediately.'

Eddie nodded and left the room and Kate turned, partly to watch him go and partly to hide her reddening face from Lorabeth Lampton. So, she knew that Great-Aunt Elizabeth was near by. Kate suddenly felt hot and stifled, as if she were still in the ventilation shaft. Lorabeth Lampton reached into her desk and pulled out a bottle of Legacy perfume, which she sprayed into the air between them.

At last, she addressed Kate. 'I am a very powerful person. You know that, don't you? I get what I want.'

Kate glanced round the room and took her time answering. 'Actually, from what I've heard, Great-Aunt Elizabeth usually puts a stop to your plans.' Kate hated the way her voice sounded, unusually high and thin.

Lorabeth Lampton smiled wryly up at the ceiling and slowly raised her hand to her eyes in a gesture of mock despair. 'Oh! I have déjà vu. It is like dealing with your mother all over again.' She stared directly at Kate before continuing, 'Believe me, I *will* get what I want. Elizabeth

249

has had the irritating habit of getting in my way – but not this time.'

Lorabeth Lampton rose from the desk and walked over to a drinks cabinet where she poured herself a glass of a ruby-coloured spirit. 'Once upon a time, your Great-Aunt Elizabeth may have been a force to be reckoned with – but now she is a has-been. She is old, forgetful, bossy and no longer "at one" with her heartstone.'

Kate, who had been trailing her eyes round the room, taking in the shelves of books, the panelling, the leather sofa and armchairs, jumped in surprise.

'I see you've noticed,' Lorabeth Lampton said, smirking with pleasure. 'She is past it, my dear. She poses no threat to me whatsoever ... which leaves you. And you've had your mother's heartstone for – how long is it?' She studied Kate through narrowed eyes before hazarding a guess. 'A month? Six weeks?'

She could tell from Kate's uncertain eyes and the flush that spread from her cheeks and crept down her neck that she was right, and she let out a small, shrill laugh.

'That hardly makes you proficient, does it?'

'I don't care. I'll never help you. Never.'

'Listen to me, child. I need the power of one more heartstone to help me achieve my goal. And you have a heartstone that you have not yet begun to understand the potential of. I'll make a deal with you: you help me and I'll show you what you are capable of.'

'Never!'

'Wouldn't you like to hear what my plans are first?'

250

'I don't care what your plans are.' Kate had raised her voice and was feeling bold and righteous. 'I will never help an evil old hag like you. Never!'

Lorabeth Lampton blinked slowly. 'It would be such a pity if something were to happen to your family.' She spoke in a dreamy voice as if to herself. Then, looking directly at Kate once more, she continued, 'Are you fond of your parents, Kate? Only your mother doesn't seem particularly fond of me and I thought perhaps it runs in the family.'

Kate felt her throat closing up and a hot, prickling sensation attack the back of her eyes. She was repulsed and wanted to shout, 'You are not part of my family,' but she feared her voice would break and so she stayed silent.

Lorabeth Lampton reached across her desk and took a rosebud from a vase. It was just opening and its white petals had begun to unfurl, revealing the softest of pink edges.

She held it out for Kate to see. 'Beautiful, isn't it? But sadly nature will have it wither and die. It doesn't have to be like that, Kate. Once everyone is using Lampton Cosmetics and making regular visits to Lampton Life Spas, no one need ever look old or ugly again.'

Kate stared through her tears at the blurring face in front of her and pressed her quivering lips tightly together.

Lorabeth Lampton brought the rosebud to her nose while her eyes remained trained on Kate's face. Kate sniffed and said nothing.

'But human beings are never satisfied with their lot. It is not enough to look young, or it won't be for long, not once people get used to it. What people really want is to *be* young.' Her eyes began to shine with a cruel enthusiasm as she continued, 'My latest discovery is the most amazing of all. I have discovered the ability to slow down the ageing process. After one brief treatment, a person will age only one year for every seven years that they live.'

She leant across the desk and fixed Kate's eyes with her gaze. Kate felt her heartstone glowing and she fought to resist the eyes that held hers.

'Now, you tell a young, beautiful twenty-year-old that she can spend the next fifty years doing whatever she pleases and at the end of it she will still look younger than thirty, and you will be making her an offer too good to resist.'

Kate blinked hard and two tears fell on to her cheeks. The feeling of defiance was fading inside her and she battled to recover it and give it a voice. When at last she spoke, her words were loud and angry. 'In the meantime, the world is falling apart. There are earthquakes and tornadoes and ice storms – no one wants to live on a planet that's dying just so they can be young and beautiful!'

Lorabeth Lampton's response was equally violent. Her eyes narrowed and her own heartstone glowed fiercely at her throat. 'Well, that's where you're wrong, you poor, naive child. Human beings care for nothing but themselves. Given an opportunity to look beautiful and live longer, they'll take it, no matter what the cost.'

Lorabeth Lampton stood up and walked round her desk until she towered over Kate. 'You will help me,' she whispered, placing her cold hands on Kate's shoulders and gripping them firmly, 'you have no choice.'

Kate gazed up at her, unable to look away. She felt as if she were shrinking under Lorabeth Lampton's grip and would gradually disappear into nothing if she did not find a way to resist.

At last, Lorabeth Lampton released her and Kate began to tremble. 'Can I go back to my parents now?' she asked quietly.

'Not yet,' Lorabeth Lampton replied. 'There is some-one I want you to meet first.'

The woman gestured towards the door and Kate allowed herself to be guided through the corridors of Lampton Laboratories. She listened to the clicking of Lorabeth Lampton's heels and tried to still the fear that had alighted in her stomach and threatened to grow and spread through her body.

Kate was led to a large laboratory and when the doors first slid open she saw in front of her what she took to be a large version of her Dried-and-dressed, and she was startled. A young woman in a white coat emerged from behind the machine. She had a pale, fragile face and listless eyes; on a chain at her throat she wore a tiny heartstone.

'This is Carter,' said Lorabeth Lampton, smiling. 'She is helping me with my technological advancements.'

Lorabeth Lampton touched the glass revolving door. 'How are you getting on?'

Kate heard Carter respond in a dull monotone that she had still not been able to harness enough power; but her attention was elsewhere. To her right, the laboratory extended in a seemingly endless room and, stretching out before her eyes and disappearing into the distance, Kate saw rows of caged animals and birds. A volatile mixture of fury and disgust welled up in her and she turned an angry, accusing face towards Lorabeth Lampton and Carter. 'What are you doing?' she cried. 'Why are you keeping all those animals in cages?'

Lorabeth Lampton reached out her long arms and placed one hand on Kate's back and the other on Carter's shoulder. Carter immediately seemed calm and she smiled obediently up at her employer – but for a fraction of a second she had looked confused by Kate's outburst, and Kate saw doubt flash across her eyes. But now Lorabeth Lampton had them in her grip and Kate felt her heartstone glowing, and she saw Carter's glow too.

As Lorabeth Lampton spoke, Kate felt her will dissipate and her indignation fade. 'Carter was reluctant to help me at first, weren't you, Carter?' Lorabeth Lampton's voice was syrupy and indulgent.

Kate saw Carter smile and shrug modestly. Her eyes were glassy and her manner was one of acquiescent, lifeless obedience. Kate glanced back at the rows of cages and met the gaze of a large falcon that seemed to be staring directly at her. Lorabeth Lampton is more powerful than I am, Kate thought, and I will not be able to resist her; she will use me like she is using this woman, and like she used Harold.

Lorabeth Lampton tightened her grip on Kate's arm.

'If you won't help me, then I shall have to find your father's heartstone. I understand he has a poor memory, but I am sure he can be persuaded. No doubt I can think of ways to help him remember.'

Kate suddenly felt weary, as if she had been carrying a great weight for far too long. She looked into Lorabeth Lampton's eyes and felt herself relax. It was such a relief to let go and give in. 'What do you want me to do?' she asked simply.

Over the Fence

Harold checked the sidecar's launching device one more time and climbed inside, strapping himself in beside Great-Aunt Elizabeth.

Fearless had recognized Bardolph and Frimley as they arrived through the main gate by taxi and since losing radio contact with Barking, Great-Aunt Elizabeth's anxiety had been increasing. She decided that they must go over the fence without any further delay and had hurried and harassed Harold, before getting herself into the flight position. Fearless looked on sympathetically as Great-Aunt Elizabeth continued to badger Harold in a loud whisper.

Harold patted Fearless's large curly head one last time and took his place beside the enormous woman, whose dark presence loomed beside him.

'Come along, Harold,' Great-Aunt Elizabeth said. 'Let's see if we can bump into those two bodyguard cronies of my sister's. I shall demand that they take us right to her.'

Harold cracked his knuckles and flexed his long fingers before reaching for the switch. He had not subjected this invention to as rigorous a testing as he would have liked, but the mechanics and engineering were straightforward enough. Exhaling sharply, he pressed the button, and the response was immediate. With a force that drew the skin tautly from their eyes and mouths, and pressed them into their seats, the sidecar hurtled up into the starry sky and sailed over the perimeter fence with ease. The sensation of falling was so fast and brief, they became aware of curious and previously unfelt sensations in their internal organs. The impact, arriving before they had had time to consider and dread the force of it, embedded the sidecar some thirty centimetres into the ground and Harold's right molars deep into the soft flesh of his cheek.

'Harold, dear, the design could do with a little revision,' Great-Aunt Elizabeth said, undoing her safety belt and hauling her large bag on to her shoulder as she stepped out of the sidecar.

Harold held his chin and rocked backwards and forwards, before groaning and mopping his mouth with a handkerchief. As he climbed out of the sidecar he saw Great-Aunt Elizabeth striding towards the two stocky men who had been about to enter the building. Perhaps they had been stunned by the sound of the sidecar landing nearby, but now they stood where they had halted in their tracks and stared in disbelief.

'Right, you two,' said Great-Aunt Elizabeth as Harold, still holding the handkerchief to his mouth, trotted to catch up behind her. 'Well, don't just stand there gaping gormlessly. Take us to Mrs Lampton immediately.'

Bardolph was the first to move. He reached for Great-Aunt Elizabeth's arm with one hand, while swatting the still gawping and immobile Frimley round the side of the head with the other. 'Grab that fella, Frimley – hurry up before he gets away.'

'We're not going anywhere until we have spoken to Lorabeth Lampton,' said Great-Aunt Elizabeth. 'I can assure you of that.'

From a vantage point beyond the fence, Fearless watched as Great-Aunt Elizabeth and Harold allowed themselves to be led inside the laboratory. He lowered himself to the ground, rested his chin on his paws and sighed.

Inside the laboratory, Charlotte and Michael sat on the narrow bed, the same bed where Phil had sat some hours earlier, and they waited. Charlotte made several attempts to talk to Michael, but he sat in a daze, as if lost in a day-dream. He could not – or, worse, would not – hear her. Eddie had brought them a tray of the same fare he had brought Phil. It sat, untouched, on the floor by the bed, the bacon glued to the plate by a bonding of grey-white fat, and the eggs, once sunny side up and glistening, now sunken and wrinkled.

Wearily, Charlotte got up from the bed and went to splash cold water on her face. As she closed the cubicle door behind her and stood before the sink, she was startled to hear Barking's voice whisper her name. Glancing up, she saw first Barking and then Phil's tear-stained face pressed against the grating.

'Mum,' Phil sobbed softly.

'Oh, Phil!' Charlotte cried and reached up to touch the grating with her fingertips. She glanced over her shoulder to check that the door was properly closed.

'Can you open it from inside?' Charlotte whispered.

'Yes, but listen, Lottie,' said Barking, 'Phil has found the main laboratory and there's a Humanitron there – and cages full of animals.'

'Oh no, no, not that!' Charlotte gasped and her arms dropped to her sides. 'Are you sure?'

They were interrupted by a noise from the room outside, and Charlotte signalled to Barking and Phil that they should move back out of sight. Charlotte quickly composed herself and returned to the cell. Two wide, stocky men stood by the open doors, barring the way to the corridor, while dominating the small room, a red-faced and indignant Great-Aunt Elizabeth blustered and ranted.

'I told you to take me to Mrs Lampton! Do you know who I am?'

Michael sat quietly on the bed. He was staring at the two men as if trying to puzzle something out.

Great-Aunt Elizabeth reached her hand out towards Charlotte and said, 'Good, you're safe – but how did you get here? Never mind, you can tell me later. Where is Phil?'

Charlotte hesitated, shocked by her aunt's tired face, and, before she could answer, Michael was on his feet and had grabbed Great-Aunt Elizabeth by the shoulders. 'Don't you dare ask where Phil is. He's supposed to be with you!'

'Michael, I'm sorry, I . . .'

But Michael's anger was over in a flash, and Great-Aunt Elizabeth's apology trailed away as he slumped back down on the bed and hid his face in his hands.

Harold stepped out unsteadily from behind Great-Aunt Elizabeth and moved towards Charlotte. He pointed beyond her and asked quietly if the door she was standing in front of was a bathroom. Charlotte took his arm and frowned questioningly at the bloodstained handkerchief he was holding to his face.

'In here,' she said, opening the door, and she followed him inside.

Great-Aunt Elizabeth raised her chin and returned her attention to the two men who were barring her way to the corridor. There was no room to pace about, but she stamped her foot several times and punched her thigh with a fist to emphasize her words as she demanded angrily that the men tell her their names.

'Right, Bardolph and Frimley, when my sister, Lorabeth Lampton –' They looked shocked. 'Yes that's right, my *sister* – when she hears how you have treated us, your lives won't be worth living.'

Frimley looked as though he already thought his life wasn't. Bardolph backed out of the room, pulling Frimley with him. The two men held a murmured discussion while glancing furtively back into the cell.

'Right,' Bardolph said at last, 'you'd better come with us.'

He reached inside and made as if to take hold of Great-Aunt Elizabeth's arm, but she shook him off and strode out into the corridor and both men hurriedly fell in beside her in an attempt to look as though they were escorting her. As the door slid closed behind her, Great-Aunt Elizabeth had time to call out, 'Do not fret, Michael – I shall insist upon the safe return of the children!'

Charlotte checked the room and saw that the men and Great-Aunt Elizabeth had left and that Michael was now lying on his back on the bed, one forearm across his eyes. She hesitated a moment before turning back to Harold. He leant over the sink while running the handkerchief under the cold tap and patting his face with it.

'What's happened to Aunt Elizabeth?' Charlotte asked, 'She looks . . . terrible.'

'You think sho?' Harold replied, holding his swollen cheek. 'I guessh shomething'sh not right – she'sh been a bit shtrange . . .' He swilled his mouth under the tap and spat blood into the sink.

Charlotte touched his arm and raised her eyes to the ceiling.

'Philbert!' Harold cried, looking up. He listened carefully as Barking told him about the Humanitron.

'What ish she up to?' Harold wondered.

'I was hoping you would know that,' Barking replied.

'I decoded the document you shtole in Washington about an hour ago – it'sh the Humanitron all right, but

261

she's adapting it shomehow.' He interlaced his fingers and placed them on top of his head as he gazed upwards. 'I have to get to this lab,' he said.

'The tunnel's small,' said Phil. 'You're too big.'

Harold's face crumpled in anguish and he clasped two great fistfuls of his unruly afro as if he meant to yank it out. 'Will you go back and find out everything you can? I've got to stop her.'

'Be careful,' Charlotte warned as cat and boy moved off and crawled away.

Bardolph and Frimley were breathing heavily as they marched through the corridors beside Great-Aunt Elizabeth. They arrived at Lorabeth Lampton's private offices and ordered the old woman to sit down, but she was defiant and strode towards the door and rapped on it herself. There was no reply.

'You'd better sit down and wait,' Bardolph growled. 'You say you're her sister, well, trust me, lady, she ain't that fond of you.' He stuffed a fat finger inside his collar where the stiff fabric chafed his neck.

Frimley gaped at him as he waited to be told what they were going to do next.

Bardolph took out his phone and rang his son. 'Eddie, where the hell is Mrs Lampton?' He grimaced and rubbed at his chin, nodding and rolling his eyes as he listened to Eddie on the phone. Having finished the call, he snarled at Great-Aunt Elizabeth, 'Right you, sit down.'

Great-Aunt Elizabeth drew back her shoulders and glared down at him.

'Sit dahn, you old cow,' Bardolph said, 'and I'll go and tell Mrs Lampton that you're 'ere.'

Great-Aunt Elizabeth looked at the chair. 'I will wait standing up,' she replied curtly.

Bardolph's face turned dark and thunderous. While members of her family were noticing a decline in her, to Bardolph and Frimley Great-Aunt Elizabeth was a formidable presence.

'Damn it, woman!' he spat, and turned to go.

'Where are you going?' Frimley whined, his bruised and crumpled face grimy and bloated from lack of sleep and hours of travelling.

'Just stay here and watch she don't do nothing,' Bardolph said angrily and he walked off.

Great-Aunt Elizabeth took a chocolate out of her pocket and unwrapped it slowly before putting it in her mouth. Frimley stood awkwardly beside her and rolled his shoulders inside his shiny suit. He decided not to look at her in case she spoke to him.

Bardolph found Eddie at the door of the laboratory.

'She in there, son?'

Eddie looked aghast at his father. The older man's face was puffy and bruised. A black crust of congealed blood lay across his left temple and a day's growth of beard darkened his chin with a blue shadow. His eyes were bloodshot and swollen.

'What's happened to you?' Eddie inquired, shocked.

'Well might you ask. While you've been here, getting all the credit for being boy wonder, your uncle and I've been doing all Lady Muck's dirty work.'

'Where's Frimley now?' Eddie asked, unable to take his eyes off his father's ravaged face.

'I've left him guarding a prisoner – bloody great giant of a woman, dressed in motorcycle leathers and with wild grey hair like a gorgon. Horrible-looking thing she is. Mrs Lampton said she might come snooping about, but she claims she's Mrs Lampton's sister. Found her and some gawky-looking guy inside the fence. Hurry and open that door now, Eddie, your uncle Frimley's a jibbering wreck – he'll mess his pants if she so much as says boo to him.'

Eddie pressed the code for the door to the lab and cleared his throat as it slid open. 'Mrs Lampton, my dad's here, looks like he's found your intruder. She says she's your sister.'

Lorabeth Lampton turned angrily towards him. She had been standing beside the large glass-and-metal chamber and had her hands on Kate's shoulders as if about to guide her through the revolving doors. Beside her stood the young scientist, Carter, who Eddie used to think pretty but who now looked like a washed-out rag doll.

'You wait there, Eddie. Bardolph, you come with me,' Lorabeth Lampton said, recovering her composure. To Kate she said, 'Stay here with Carter. I'll be back soon.'

As the door closed, Kate sighed and noticed that she

was able to breathe more easily, as if suddenly there was more air in the room; as Lorabeth Lampton's perfume faded, so Kate's mind cleared. She stood for a while and watched Carter, who had removed what appeared to be a drawer from the base of the chamber. Kate peered over Carter's shoulder as she carried the metal box to a laboratory bench. Inside the drawer were six glass valves filled with a yellowish, oily substance, and these were connected by wires to two small heartstones that nestled in ceramic sockets. Beside them, a further, larger ceramic socket remained empty.

'What are you doing?' Kate asked.

Carter glanced up, surprised, as if she had forgotten she was not alone. She squinted through her glasses and hesitated for a moment, confusion showing in small furrows on her pale brow. 'I'm trying to boost the power supply from these two heartstones. There isn't enough energy to make a transformation at the moment.'

'What sort of transformation?' Kate asked.

Carter hesitated again.

'I think I must be very tired,' she said at last. A wisp of blonde hair hung over one eye, but she did not push it away. 'What did you say again?'

Kate felt that she had an opportunity to do something that might stop Lorabeth Lampton's evil plans and so she tried to remain calm and casual. 'What does it do, this machine?'

'Well,' Carter replied, 'it's an old machine actually. I'm adapting it. The idea is, you go into the chamber through the revolving door on the left-hand side and when you come out on the other side, you will be transformed.'

'Transformed how?' Kate asked as nonchalantly as she could.

Carter looked quizzically at her. 'You are going to help Lorabeth Lampton, aren't you? That's what she said.'

'Oh yes,' Kate replied. 'I shall help if I can.'

Just then the caged falcon screamed and Kate jumped and, looking up, found its penetrating eyes staring straight at her.

Crouching at the grid in the tunnel overhead, Phil and Barking watched and flinched as they heard Kate promising to help Lorabeth Lampton.

Lampton's Legacy

Lorabeth Lampton, her head held high, glided through the corridor on her long legs. Bardolph trailed behind her. Tired and bruised, he did not bother running to keep up and allowed the gap between them to widen. When he turned the corner to the private office, he found Frimley sitting in the chair and saw Lorabeth Lampton disappear inside her office behind the tall intruder.

'Now what?' Frimley asked, getting to his feet.

'How should I know?' Bardolph replied angrily.

Inside the room, Lorabeth Lampton and Great-Aunt Elizabeth faced each other. Great-Aunt Elizabeth was the first to speak. 'You are not to harm the children, Margot. You can deal with me.'

Lorabeth shook her head slowly and began to laugh. 'I have no intention of harming the children. The girl, Kate, tried to resist my will but she has succumbed. But as for you, Elizabeth, why, you are of no use to me at all.'

Great-Aunt Elizabeth raised her hand angrily and made to reach for Lorabeth's long neck. Lorabeth Lampton gazed back at her and for a moment the heart-stones at both women's throats flared up. But while

267

Lorabeth Lampton's heartstone blazed violently and threw a sinister reflection into her cruel eyes, Great-Aunt Elizabeth's flickered and died away. The mighty leather arm was slowly lowered, and Great-Aunt Elizabeth's face looked grey and defeated.

'You've lost it, Elizabeth. Once upon a time you could interfere in my life and boss me around, but not any more. I have weakened your heartstone and you haven't even had enough wit about you to notice.'

Great-Aunt Elizabeth's eyes widened and she clutched desperately at her throat. 'My heart–' she gasped.

Lorabeth Lampton threw back her head and laughed shrilly.

'Please, Margot,' Great-Aunt Elizabeth whispered, 'just think of the consequences of what you are doing. You must stop before you do irreparable damage.'

Lorabeth Lampton laughed again, but softly this time. 'Damage to what? To whom? Do you think I care about this godforsaken planet? Do you think I care about people?'

Great-Aunt Elizabeth lowered the heavy bag from her shoulder and let it drop to the floor. She pushed a lank grey curl away from her eyes and spoke quietly. 'Our grandmother and mother taught us to care for others, Margot. Everything we were brought up to believe in – combating evil, taking care of those less fortunate. You have to remember that, Margot. It is our legacy.'

Lorabeth Lampton spat her reply. 'No, Elizabeth, you're wrong. It may have been everything *you* were brought up to believe in, but I was never included in Mother's plans, never! And as for Grandma – you were always her favourite. Caring for those less fortunate? What about those ignorant peasants who killed our mother? She was murdered because of their primitive and petty prejudices. I don't care one bit about them or anyone else – not you, not Charlotte, not her precious children.'

She snatched up a bottle of perfume and waved it in Great-Aunt Elizabeth's face. 'This is the only legacy I care about. "Lampton's Legacy" – my blissfully youthful, powerful, eternal existence!'

Great-Aunt Elizabeth fumbled in her pocket for a chocolate and struggled to unwrap it. 'Beaks and tails, Margot!' she muttered as the chocolate slipped from its wrapper and fell to the floor. 'This is madness. You always were reckless and self-centred. What do you think you will achieve by destroying humankind and wrecking the planet?'

'You just don't get it, do you, Elizabeth? Here, is this simple enough for you? – *I don't care!*'

Great-Aunt Elizabeth stood motionless and stared at her sister. Lorabeth Lampton stretched her leg forwards, and with the tip of her shoe tapped at the fallen chocolate.

'Still addicted to that sickly stuff?' she asked. Suddenly, her eyes became fixed on the bag resting at Great-Aunt Elizabeth's feet. She leant forwards and grabbed it from the floor, easily beating Elizabeth, who snatched at thin air in a vain attempt to stop her.

Lorabeth Lampton opened the bag and gazed down at the Historograph nestling in its leather cloth. She pulled it out and began to laugh, quietly at first, then throwing her head back in a triumphant cackle. 'You have exceeded my wildest dreams, Elizabeth – I meant to weaken you, to prevent you from getting in my way. I never imagined you would actually help me.' She hugged the Historograph to her bony frame and continued to laugh. 'How thoughtful of you to bring the Historograph. You must have thought you were so clever, giving Kate her mother's heartstone before I could get my hands on it. But why should I bother with that one when there is a far more powerful heartstone out there?' She smoothed an appreciative hand across the Historograph's cool surface. 'And this is just what I need to help Michael remember where the keystone is.'

Barking and Phil made their way back through the ventilation shaft and Phil carefully unscrewed the grating and climbed down into the bathroom. The door opened and Charlotte hugged him tight while Harold stood behind her in the doorway. Phil remembered the cameras and pulled himself away from his mum and stepped out of sight behind the door. Taking small, high steps, which made him appear all knees and elbows, Harold shuffled inside and closed the door.

'Where's Dad?' Phil asked, as Barking dropped from the ceiling into Harold's arms.

'He's asleep. I'll get him to come and see you in a

minute,' Charlotte said, pushing back Phil's hair. 'Are you all right, my darling?'

'I think so,' said Phil. 'Mum, there's animals locked in tiny cages and we have to let them go. We will, won't we?'

Harold stroked Barking's head. 'Did you manage to get a good look at the Humanitron? Does it look like it's working?'

Charlotte put her arm round Phil and pulled him close to her. He looked up at his mum and waited for Barking to tell them about the Humanitron and what they had heard Kate say about helping Lorabeth Lampton.

The small space was cramped, so Barking jumped from Harold's arms and landed in the sink, where he sat up tall and looked at Charlotte and Harold in turn as he briefed them. 'There's a young woman working on the Humanitron – seems to know what she's doing. We saw her take the power-housing out. It's not how I remember it, Harold.' He described the ceramic sockets with the heartstones in them and how the wiring appeared to be different and the liquid in the vials was yellow, not blue as he remembered.

'Yellow?' Harold echoed.

'Kate was with her,' Phil interrupted. 'Wasn't she, Barking?'

Charlotte looked down at him eagerly. 'Was she OK?'

Phil looked at Barking. The cat sighed. 'We heard her say that she was going to help Lorabeth Lampton. She looked kind of deflated, not like the Kate we know.'

'The scientist looks pretty weird, too,' said Phil. 'All

271

washed out and moving on autopilot like she's been hypnotized or something.'

Before Charlotte or Harold had a chance to ask further questions, Michael called out from the next-door room. 'Charlotte, where are you?'

Charlotte and Phil pressed themselves against the wall and Harold leant sideways and squeezed himself into the gap beside the sink while twisting round to open the door behind him.

'In here, Michael,' Charlotte called.

Michael put his head round the door and his eyes lit up when he saw Phil. He writhed himself into the room and, shutting the door, placed his hand on top of Phil's head and tousled his hair, before scooping him close and hugging him.

'Is everything all right?' Michael asked.

But no one could think how to answer him.

Bardolph and Frimley walked slowly towards the cell to carry out Lorabeth Lampton's latest bidding. Bardolph was in a foul mood, and he was becoming aware of more painful places on his body with each step he took. He muttered complaints out loud as they approached the steel doors, though more to himself than to Frimley. 'Do this! Do that! Never so much as a thank you. She's never satisfied, that woman.'

'I just wanna go to bed,' Frimley grumbled, scratching his unshaven chin. 'I never slept a wink on the flight.'

'Course you did,' Bardolph snapped as they reached the

cell. 'It was your blinkin' snorin' what kept me awake!'

The doors slid open and Bardolph and Frimley stared in horror at what appeared to be an empty room. It was one thing complaining about Lorabeth Lampton's unreasonable demands, but the brothers were terrified of getting into any more trouble with her. Frimley began anxiously chewing his fingernails, then fumbled to light a cigarette. Bardolph crossed the room and reached for the door handle to the bathroom. As he did so, the door opened and Michael, Charlotte and Harold tumbled out.

'What were you up to in there?' Bardolph asked, pushing past them to look behind the door. The bathroom was empty. He reached up and pressed his palm against the grid over the ventilation shaft, but it was fixed tight. In any case, he reasoned after studying it for a moment, no one, not even the kid, could fit through that hole.

He shrugged and closed the door behind him.

'Come on, mate,' he said, crossing the floor and slapping his fat, gnarled hand on Michael's back, 'Mrs Lampton wants to see you.'

Charlotte grabbed hold of Michael's arm and pulled him towards her, but Michael shook his arm free. 'It's all right, Charlotte.' Michael resisted the hand between his shoulder blades that was trying to force him forwards through the doorway where Frimley stood fidgeting. He reached out and touched his wife's cheek briefly. 'I am ready for this – I want to remember.'

'No! Michael, please, you don't understand how dangerous it is –'

But Charlotte got no further as Frimley stepped forwards, took hold of her arm and pushed her away from Michael and the door. Frimley then turned as quickly as his lumbering frame would allow and stepped through the closing doors behind Michael and Bardolph.

'Michael!' Charlotte cried as the doors closed.

Harold pulled at his hair and rocked from side to side in the doorway of the bathroom. 'Sorry, Lottie, I'm no help at all, I'm so sorry,' he mumbled, resting his hand on his swollen cheek.

Kate allowed Eddie to push her along the corridor while she stared down at her feet. Although she understood how her heartstone could help her, she did not think she could muster enough strength. Asserting herself and being positive were far too arduous tasks in the presence of Lorabeth Lampton. How could she resist, when first Harold and now Carter had not been able to? It was too difficult.

Michael walked between Frimley and Bardolph, who waddled beside him like squat bookends. As they turned the corridor they met Eddie, whose rough method of escorting Kate back from the laboratory made Michael react with lightning speed. He reached for his daughter, put his arm round her and hugged her to him.

'All right, that's enough,' said Eddie, pulling at Kate's elbow.

'And you, mate,' said Bardolph, tugging at Michael's sleeve, 'had best not keep Mrs Lampton waiting.'

'Yeah,' Frimley said, sniggering as he dragged on his cigarette, 'she might get nasty.'

Kate began to cry. This was worst of all. Her dad was in danger now, because of her. She had tried to trick Lorabeth Lampton into thinking that she was going to help her. But the terrible truth was, she had been weak and feeble and afraid, just as she had always been. Kate felt helplessness engulf her, and she twisted her fingers into Michael's jacket.

Bardolph rolled his eyes and began to tug more vigorously on Michael's arm as Eddie tried to prise Kate's fingers free.

'Dad! Don't go! Please, Dad!' Kate sobbed. 'Please, Daddy, please don't leave me, I'm sorry. Daddeeeee!'

In the second before they were finally wrenched apart, Michael bent towards Kate and whispered in her ear. 'Don't cry, be brave – remember the winged messenger.'

Eddie had his muscular arm across Kate's throat and shoulders as he peeled her away from her father. She slumped, sobbing, in his grasp and watched through her tears as Bardolph and Frimley wrestled Michael towards Mrs Lampton's office.

Tear-stained and shaking, Kate was ushered into the cell by a smiling Eddie, who placed a large brown paper bag of groceries on the small table beside the bed.

'Mrs Lampton says you're to make yourselves comfort- able,' he said, chuckling to himself as he left.

Kate collapsed on the bed and, as Charlotte took her

in her arms, Kate leant her head against her mother's shoulder and the racking sobs began once more.

Charlotte rocked her daughter and mumbled 'Hush' and 'There now' as she had when Kate was a baby.

It was some minutes before Kate's crying eased and she could speak. 'She's going to talk to Dad and make him remember what she did to him,' she said quietly, her eyes filling with tears once more.

Charlotte smoothed her daughter's hair and began to shush her, but again Kate gave away to the tears that had been choking her throat. Her sobs came in great howls that filled the room.

Harold sat on the floor beside the bathroom door and grimaced as he watched until, unable to bear it any longer, he lowered his forehead to his knees and wrapped his arms round his head.

In time Kate's tears were spent and she was able to tell them, in a small wavering voice, what had happened. 'She wanted me to help her. I tried not to listen to her, but it was so hard. She makes you feel as though you can't resist doing what she says.'

Charlotte trailed her fingers gently across her daughter's brow and murmured soothingly as she listened. 'It's all right, darling. She is impossible to resist.'

'You did it, Mum, you got away from her,' Kate said, tears running freely down her cheeks. A new thought overwhelmed her and she struggled to breathe as another great wave of crying consumed her. 'And I don't know where Phil is,' she sobbed.

Charlotte squeezed Kate's hand and gave a slight nod towards the bathroom. Kate looked over at Harold, whose head was raised to meet her gaze. He smiled and glanced briefly at the bathroom door.

Kate understood, and she felt a space begin to open in her tight chest. 'Is Barking with him?' she whispered.

'Yes, darling, they're together.'

Kate began to dry her eyes and nose on her sleeve. 'Lorabeth Lampton said that Great-Aunt Elizabeth's heartstone wasn't working.'

'She must have tampered with it,' said Harold, sitting up sharply from where he had been slumped against the wall. 'Did you find out anything else, Kate? Do you know what she's planning to do with the Humanitron?'

Kate told them all about Lorabeth Lampton's plan for eternal youth. 'Carter, she's the scientist working on it, she says the machine will transform metabolic rates and . . .' Kate frowned as she tried to remember Carter's exact words, 'and . . . genetically assimilate the fourth dimension in order to . . . metamorphose the duration of human ageing.'

'Of course!' Harold said, scrambling awkwardly to his feet. 'She can make a direct reversal of the main side effect last time.'

'What exactly did happen last time?' Kate asked. 'Can't you tell me now?'

Harold sighed. 'I guess so. Great-Aunt Elizabeth was going to show you – she brought the Historograph with her from the Harley.' He suddenly lurched up straight and slapped the heel of his palm against his brow. 'That's it! That's when it happened!'

'What happened?' Kate and Charlotte asked together.

'In order to charge it with memories, Great-Aunt Elizabeth had to remove her heartstone and place it in the Historograph. She did it the night of the break-in. That will be when Lorabeth Lampton tampered with her heartstone. She couldn't have done it if Aunt E. was wearing it.'

Charlotte had been sitting quietly, contemplating something. 'I have just had a horrible thought,' she said softly. Harold and Kate looked at her troubled face. 'If Lorabeth Lampton gets hold of the Historograph, she'll use it to show Michael.'

Harold tapped his fingers against his mouth and rocked backwards on to his heels. 'And she will find his heartstone,' he said fearfully.

Kate did not fully understand why both adults were so worried. 'Maybe Dad will be able to resist her. I know I couldn't, but he's really strong-minded.'

Charlotte took both of Kate's hands in hers. 'She won't need him to cooperate with her, Kate. It has been lost and inactive for so long now, if she gets her hands on the keystone first, it will be hers to do with as she pleases. That's why she couldn't just take yours from you – once a heartstone is held by a compatible person, the bond is instant.'

Charlotte stood up from the bed and walked slowly round the room. Seeing the bag on the table, she went

over to it and looked inside. 'We should all eat something,' she said, lifting an apple from the top of the bag,
then to Kate she added, 'and then we'll tell you about
Penelope Parton's Pet Emporium.'

25

Michael Remembers

Michael entered Lorabeth Lampton's office and walked towards the desk where she sat, gazing at him.

'Leave us alone, please,' she said, and she waited for Bardolph to close the door behind him. On the desk in front of her stood the Historograph, and she tapped nonchalantly at one edge of it with her long, painted nails. 'Do you remember anything about the last time we met?' she asked.

Michael lifted his gaze briefly from the silvered plate where the seventeen embedded heartstones were humming softly. 'Some,' he said, his eyes returning to the extraordinary object.

'I think it's time you remembered all of it, don't you?'

Lorabeth Lampton got up from her chair and walked round the desk to stand beside Michael. She reached forwards and hooked a long finger over the rim of the Historograph, pulling it carefully towards them.

'Look at it,' she commanded.

Michael felt strange, as if the room had suddenly shrunk and the walls had closed in on them. He held the edge of the desk with his hands and gazed down into the plate. He saw his reflection and that of the woman beside him. He felt her place her hand on his back and press him forwards. Heat surged through his back and he was suddenly gripped by a pain in his chest that spread to his head. He felt as if he was falling and his knuckles whitened on the desk's edge. He watched, wide-eyed, as above the throbbing heartstones a thick mist hung and began to rotate, slowly at first, then faster, until it was spinning and swirling before him. He felt himself fall towards the plate, then the strange fog suddenly became recognizable as clouds which thinned as he hurtled downwards until trees, then roofs, then metal, then concrete came rushing up to meet him.

At first the scene was blurred, but he became aware of three figures and he flinched at the sensation that he was about to collide with them. They were children – two of similar ages to his own and a little one who was clearly afraid and clung to the boy nearest him. Michael continued to swoop down on them and wanted to shout out to warn them or throw his body to one side, but he could neither move nor speak. At the last moment, as he braced himself for the impact, the tallest boy looked up and into his eyes. With a shock of acknowledgement, Michael recognized himself in the pinched, worried face of the lanky, dark-haired boy. There was a piercing cry that seemed to Michael to begin inside his head, threatening to split his skull open in order to get out. He felt his whole body jolt in spasm, as if from an electric shock, and this was followed by a searing pain that ran down his arms and legs as if his blood were on fire. He screwed his eyes shut.

Suddenly, the violent sensations disappeared and Michael opened his eyes. He knew immediately that, somehow, the two Michaels – the boy he once was and the man he had become – were as one. Michael was not just seeing his past, he was about to re-live it.

On either side of him, the two smaller boys held his hands. The one closer to him in height and age he now knew to be his brother, Billy. Billy stared about him fearfully, his quick eyes alert to danger. The smallest boy, Frank, pressed himself closer to his eldest brother. Michael was holding their hands loosely, despite his desperate desire to squeeze them tight and hold them close to him. But no matter how much he yearned to communicate twenty years of love and grief, the young Michael's body did not respond. He was inside the head of his former self, yet he was unable to do anything other than think his own thoughts.

Gradually he became aware of his surroundings. They were in a laboratory, and in front of them stood a vast metal kiosk, flanked on either side by revolving doors. On the floor, beside the left-hand door, stood three cages. In one, a small black kitten lay curled, asleep. In another, a fat golden retriever puppy gazed with innocent contentment through the bars, his tail slowly wagging as he watched the approaching boys. The third cage was empty, for the creature that had occupied it was perched on the outstretched arm of Penelope Parton. The creature stared at them with magnificent yellow eyes.

'Come along. Eldest first, I think. Michael,' Penelope Parton said, her own eyes cruel and unblinking.

Michael saw his young hand, still holding Frank's, tremble. For a second Michael felt himself hesitate and he hoped it might be possible to defy the command. But the steady gaze from the two pairs of eyes intensified and Michael felt himself let go his brothers' hands and step forwards towards the revolving door of the Humanitron.

In the cell, Harold and Charlotte quietly watched Kate as she gradually came to understand the full horror of the Penelope Parton Pet Emporium.

'What was the point of turning children into animals?' Kate asked incredulously, shaking her head in disbelief. 'And how did she get away with it?'

Charlotte thought for a moment before answering. 'She made a fortune selling them to foreign governments. The animals were used for espionage. Security forces spend days scouring presidential offices for bugging devices, but they don't think about removing a cat from the president's lap when he discusses military plans with his generals. But I think she did it mainly because she could.'

'Didn't anyone miss the children?'

'She took children from refugee camps and orphanages – desperate places where it was easy for her to deceive carers and trick the system. When Aunt Elizabeth and

I got inside the laboratory, we found several hundred children, sitting like waiting evacuees, and row upon row of caged animals. Thankfully, she had transformed only a very few, Barking and Fearless among them, before we managed to stop her.'

Harold spoke quietly from his side of the room. 'I had lost my mind. I was having nightmares in which animals were speaking to me – even ones that hadn't been transformed yet. I didn't deliberately sabotage the Humanitron – I wouldn't have dared – but I couldn't make it work properly.' He paused for a moment and shuddered at the memory. 'I had removed the largest heartstone – the keystone – from the power supply and was working on it one night in the laboratory of the Pet Emporium. The lab also served as an observatory, and the glass dome above the telescope was open to the sky. Suddenly, a large falcon flew through the room. It swooped down on the bench where I was working and snatched up the keystone in its feathered claws. It was ... he was ...' Harold stopped and looked to Charlotte for help with the story.

'The bird was your dad, Kate.'

Kate was astounded as she thought of her dad, the parent who seemed most cautious and concerned for their safety, doing something so bold and amazing. She felt a sensation of pride as her mother continued.

'Michael was the first to be transformed, but Penelope Parton had not anticipated the consequences of combining your father's intelligence and morality with the falcon's defiant free spirit. She could not tame him. He stole the keystone the night before two hundred and thirty children were due to be transformed into cats, dogs and birds. He saved them, Kate.'

Kate shuddered. Her small face was grubby and smeared with tears.

'Go and wash your face, darling. You'll feel better then,' Charlotte said gently.

Kate slipped into the bathroom where Phil had jumped down from the shaft to stretch his legs, and brother and sister exchanged a rare and brief hug.

'Did you hear that?' Kate whispered, and Phil nodded. 'Our dad is a hero.'

'I knew you weren't really going to help Lorabeth Lampton,' said Phil.

Kate averted her eyes from Phil's and shrugged.

'You would have found a way to stop her, Kate. You're so good at stealth and fitness and knowing what to do and stuff,' Phil continued.

Kate looked at him and smiled. 'Thanks. But I'm no match for her, Phil.'

Phil shook his head and became agitated. 'No, don't say that, Kate. You're going to have to help me. We have to let those animals out. You saw them – stuffed in tiny cages. You saw how sad they were. We can't give in and do nothing, Kate, can we?'

Kate looked into Phil's eyes and saw a look she had not seen in a long time; it was the expression of someone who knows that their big sister will sort out life's problems, from being tall enough to reach the biscuit tin to standing up to the school bully. For a moment Kate felt ashamed, then she felt angry. Phil was right, they couldn't give in. Suddenly, she had an idea, and as she nodded and smiled at her brother her heartstone surged, a brilliant crimson.

'You're right, Phil,' she said. 'We mustn't let her get away with this, or everything that happened last time will all be for nothing. I'll come through the tunnel to the laboratory with you and we'll smash the Humanitron to pieces and let out all the animals.'

Phil grinned at his sister and, peering down from the shaft above their heads, Barking purred loudly.

There was a noise from inside the cell and Phil hurriedly scrambled up into the shaft.

Kate waited until he had hauled his feet out of sight before opening the door. She was shocked by what she saw. Charlotte and Harold were helping Great-Aunt Elizabeth over to the bed, where she collapsed, her face turned to the wall. At first she did not respond to Charlotte's gentle questions, but at last she was able to confirm that Lorabeth Lampton had indeed taken the Historograph. She looked tired and old. While they whispered at her side, she kept her face turned away from them, silent apart from the occasional sniff.

Kate took her mother's arm and pulled her back to the bathroom. 'Mum, Phil and I are going to stop her.' She beckoned through the open door to Harold and whispered to him as he approached. 'Tell me more about the Humanitron. Phil and I can go in there and sabotage it.'

286

Great-Aunt Elizabeth struggled to sit up on the narrow bed. Her sallow face was deeply lined and her hair, though as untidy as ever, no longer had its former wild vigour but lay in flat and lank curls about her face and shoulders.

'You are a good girl, Kate,' she said, 'but destroying this Humanitron will only delay her. She will make another. We have to get to the lost keystone first. She is desperate and will do anything to get her hands on it.' Great-Aunt Elizabeth's voice became thin as she ran out of breath and she collapsed once more on to the bed.

Charlotte moved over to the bed and knelt beside it. She took Great-Aunt Elizabeth's large hand in both of hers. 'We don't know where to look – and even if we did, we're a bit stuck at the moment,' she said, looking at the cell door.

Great-Aunt Elizabeth gazed at Charlotte with tired, blood-shot eyes; as she spoke, her heartstone fizzed and flickered faintly.

Kate came to her bedside and leant close to Great-Aunt Elizabeth, whose voice came in rasping breaths.

'Michael . . . flew to . . . New York . . . When he . . . was . . . brought . . . down . . . by Grand Central Station . . .' She broke off and took a long wheezing intake of breath before continuing, 'he no longer had the keystone . . . when . . . we . . . got . . . to him.' She gasped the last four words out and sank into the pillow. Perspiration beaded her top lip and her eyes rolled up in their sockets, before closing. Charlotte stroked her palm across her aunt's forehead, but Great-Aunt Elizabeth had fallen unconscious and did not stir.

'We must try to get a message to Fearless,' Charlotte said. 'If he could get to New York before Lorabeth Lampton, he might be able to intercept her.'

Kate felt light-headed. Her heartstone had begun to glow brightly. As her throat was warmed, she felt first her collarbone, then the bones in her arms and fingers begin to tingle. She frowned and tried to think what to do. Her instinct told her that there was a solution and, as she racked her brains, the energy from her heartstone surged. She held it between her fingers. *What should she do?* The sight of Great-Aunt Elizabeth looking so frail and feeble made Kate more determined. It was down to her now. She turned away from the others and began pacing the floor between the bed and the doorway where Harold hovered. *There had to be a solution, but what was it?* Kate took quicker steps as thoughts hurtled through her mind like images glimpsed from the window of a speeding train. Her dad had been transformed into a falcon and as a falcon had taken the keystone and hidden it. *What, what, what should she do?* And then it came to her, accompanied by a sudden electrifying sensation. Her heartstone flared between her fingers and every nerve and muscle in her body tingled with energy. She spun round and knelt beside her mother at Great-Aunt Elizabeth's bedside.

'Mum! I know what to do!'

Kate remembered the falcon's penetrating stare and

the way it had screamed at her in the laboratory, as if it were calling out to her. She glanced behind her at Harold.

'Is it possible to turn the machine back into a Humanitron?'

'No, Kate!' Charlotte interrupted her as this vaguest of details began to kindle the possibilities of her daughter's plan. 'Not the Humanitron – it is far too dangerous.'

Kate looked at her mother's face and then at Great-Aunt Elizabeth's. She was awake now and straining to lift her head from the pillow. Kate saw the concern in her mother's eyes, but in Great-Aunt Elizabeth's she saw a glimmer of hope. It was the most reassuring sight she had seen in days.

'Well, Harold?' she asked, turning her head to look at him out of the corner of her eye.

'It is possible.' He carefully avoided Charlotte and looked down at Great-Aunt Elizabeth where she lay on the bed. 'I would need your heartstone, Aunt E.,' he said simply.

Kate exhaled with relief, and her glowing heartstone lit her face. She turned confidently to face her mother and spoke in a hurried whisper. 'I shall go to the laboratory and get transformed. There is a falcon there; I saw it. If Lorabeth Lampton makes Dad remember, then –'

Kate stopped and her eyes widened as she remembered her dad's words.

'Dad wants me to do it. That's what he was trying to tell me.' Kate's eyes shone and she stared round the room at them. 'Winged messenger', that's what he had whispered in her ear. *Be brave. Winged messenger.*

Charlotte took hold of her daughter's hand. 'Kate, you may have to stay a falcon – be like that forever. It nearly killed Daddy. The procedure for transforming him back was so dangerous that we did not dare try with the others. We had to leave Billy and Frank –'

'Billy and Frank?' Kate repeated.

'Dad's younger brothers were transformed with him and have had to live their lives as animals.' The corners of Charlotte's mouth lifted into a small, sad smile. 'Barking and Fearless are your uncles.'

Harold stepped forwards. 'Actually, Lottie, I know a lot more now. I think I can make it reversible.'

Kate squeezed her mother's hand, then let go of it. 'I am meant to do this, Mum. There is no other way. And if I can't change back –' Kate forced herself to quell the feelings of horror and fear that flared up as she spoke, 'then I shall have Barking and Fearless to help me.'

Great-Aunt Elizabeth reached out a large wavering hand to Kate and nodded her head in encouragement. 'We . . . must . . . hurry,' she whispered.

Kate stared intently into her mother's eyes. 'Lorabeth Lampton said that people only care about themselves. But that isn't true. It isn't true, Mum, is it?'

Charlotte's eyes filled with tears and she pulled Kate into her arms and held her tight. 'No, my darling, it isn't true.'

Kate walked into the bathroom and, looking up at the

ventilation shaft, saw Phil and Barking's eyes peering down. Phil removed the knife from his pocket and began loosening the screws that held the grid in place. He had never been more happy to see his older sister nor more proud of her in his life.

Harold followed them into the bathroom and closed the door. As Barking and he talked about the Humanitron and how best to restore it, Kate hauled herself up into the shaft and talked to her brother. She lay close to the opening, ready to jump back down if her mother gave a warning knock from the next room.

'Are you scared?' Phil asked after Kate had hugged his head and one arm in an awkward horizontal embrace. Kate pulled a face. 'When I watched you talking to that woman, it was like you were her servant or something.'

'It's like being hypnotized. I didn't want to listen to her, but I couldn't help myself.'

'When you're transformed, it will be easier,' said Barking. 'Animals are more independent than people.'

'Do you think Lorabeth Lampton will be able to make Dad do what she wants?' Phil asked.

Kate considered for a moment before answering. 'I don't know,' she said. 'I hope not.'

An hour later, as Phil followed Barking through the tunnel back to the laboratory, he thought about their plan, and a thrill gripped his stomach. He was determined to do a good job, and he was soon daydreaming as he shuffled along in the dark. He couldn't help thinking of himself as a hero; perhaps Lorabeth Lampton would come in and surprise them and he would get his chance to test his martial arts skills on her.

As they reached the laboratory and the shaft of light from the room below was there to guide them, Phil knew what he was going to do. Once Kate was transformed, she would need to escape from the building. It would be up to him, Philip Reynolds, to protect his sister and cause a diversion. In any case, he could not bear the thought of all those imprisoned animals. A menagerie of cats, dogs, parakeets and howler monkeys cavorting about the building would cause plenty of confusion while Kate made her bid for freedom.

Persuading Carter

Outside the laboratory, the Nevada night was cold and Fearless's fur stood up from his body, making him look less like a dog and more like a large and shaggy bear. He had lain motionless for hours, watching the building for any sign of movement.

Several hours into his vigil, Fearless was rewarded for his patient observation. The main doors opened and the young driver who had taken Lorabeth Lampton out and who had returned with Charlotte and Michael strolled towards the car once again and unlocked it. Fearless raised his head and sniffed the black air. He recognized a familiar scent caught on the breeze that pinned a tumbleweed to the inside of the perimeter fence and gently ruffled his fur.

Then Michael stepped from the building at the side of Lorabeth Lampton. They appeared to be chatting in a leisurely fashion, and Fearless's brow furrowed in confusion. As Michael and Lorabeth Lampton climbed into the idling car and were driven away by Eddie, Fearless rose from his hiding place and watched them disappear into the distance. He could not imagine what had taken place inside the laboratory during the last few hours but, he reasoned, there was only one way to find out. He was going to have to go back under the fence and get inside.

As Phil, then Kate, dropped from the ceiling on to the lab bench next to the place where she was working, Emily Carter gave a small scream of surprise. Then she recognized Kate, and her expression turned from confusion to anger. 'What do you think you are doing?' she said, standing up from the high stool where she had been perched over an intricate circuit board. 'I shall have to call security.'

'I wouldn't do that if I were you,' Barking said, neatly landing on the bench in front of her.

Carter dropped the screwdriver she'd been holding and it clattered to the floor. While Kate bent down to retrieve it, Carter slowly lowered herself back on to her stool and moved her face carefully towards Barking, her eyes squinting behind her glasses.

'It's rude to stare like that,' Barking said, with a flick of his tail. He sat down and pushed the circuit board with his paw. 'What are you making?'

Emily Carter's mouth had dropped open but no words came out.

Kate reached for a nearby stool and dragged it over. Placing it beside Carter, she climbed on to it. 'The last time your boss used that thing,' Kate jerked her thumb over her shoulder towards the Humanitron, 'my friend

294

here was forced inside it. He was matched up with a little boy, and Lorabeth Lampton –'

'She called herself Penelope Parton back then,' Barking interrupted her.

'*She*,' Kate went on, 'transformed him. That little boy was my uncle, my dad's little brother. He has had to live his life as a talking "human" cat.'

'A side effect when I was transformed,' said Barking, 'meant that, while I have a predominantly human intelligence and the physical form of a cat, somehow the rate at which I age was reversed. A cat normally ages seven years for every one human year. With me it's the opposite. I was transformed twenty years ago but I am still a young cat.'

'Oh my,' Carter said softly and, removing her glasses, she placed them on the table and rubbed her eyes. She reached a cautious hand towards Barking. 'Can I touch you?' she asked.

'Under the chin's good,' Barking replied, raising his head.

As Carter stroked his throat with her finger, she began to smile. 'Yes, it makes sense – slow down ageing, that was my brief. That is what I am adapting the machine to do.'

'We need your help,' Kate said, leaning towards Carter.

Phil meanwhile had walked slowly down the aisles of cages and stared into the troubled eyes of every occupant. He now stood beside the cage of a large male gorilla whose eyes shone like black pebbles as he gazed steadily back at Phil.

'I'm going to help you. I'll get you out of here, I promise,' Phil mouthed to the gorilla before moving away to join Kate and Barking as they tried to convince Carter to help them.

Kate was admiring Carter's heartstone and she showed her her own. 'Lorabeth Lampton is using you; while you wear the heartstone, she can impose her will on you and prevent you trusting your own judgement.'

Carter held the tiny stone in her fingers. 'I don't know how to take it off . . . She did something when she gave it to me. She had something in her hand, but I couldn't see what it was. Now I don't seem able to undo it. I can't make the clasp work.'

Kate looked around on the bench and saw a soldering iron. 'She sealed it, but I can unseal it with this. When you've taken it off, you will be able to understand more clearly, I promise.'

'I don't know,' Carter said doubtfully, and she looked at Barking, who nodded encouragingly at her.

'Try it and see – you can always put it back on.'

Kate plugged the soldering iron into a socket on the bench and Carter stood stiffly as Kate raised the smouldering point of the iron towards the heartstone. There was a glow, and then the heartstone fell on to the bench. Carter stared at it for a moment and placed her hand beside it.

Kate told Carter about the hurricanes and earthquakes

296

that were racking the earth's continents. She told her how New York had been without electricity and how most of Europe was flooded.

'Lorabeth Lampton plans to make everyone dependent on Lampton Cosmetics. Her laboratories are stealing ozone to put in her face creams, and the spas she is building everywhere take magma from the centre of the earth and bring it to the surface to heat the springs.'

Emily Carter shook her head and placed her slender hands over her pale face. 'What have I done?' she whispered.

'It's all right,' Kate reassured her, 'but will you help us now?'

Carter adjusted her glasses and straightened her back. Already the dull, listless expression had left her face and she looked keenly from Kate to Barking. 'Tell me what you plan to do.'

Phil joined them at the bench and, putting his hand deep into his pocket, he carefully pulled out Great-Aunt Elizabeth's heartstone and placed it in front of Carter. She stared at it in amazement. Her own stone was small enough to sit on her thumbnail, whereas this stone was nearly as large as her fist.

'Where did you get this?' she asked.

Barking jumped down from the bench and ran over to the Humanitron. 'That heartstone belongs to Lorabeth Lampton's sister. She is a good woman and has always used her heartstone carefully. In the past she has been able to counteract Lorabeth Lampton's evil machinations, but her heartstone has been tampered with. Its energy is impaired.'

Carter picked up Great-Aunt Elizabeth's heartstone and followed Barking to the Humanitron.

'I did it,' she said. 'I made a device that reverses the energy flow.'

'Can you fix it?' Kate and Phil asked together.

'What we need to do,' Barking said, brushing the side of his face against Carter's legs, 'is restore the Humanitron. This heartstone, if you fix it, will give the machine more than enough power to make a transformation.'

Carter gazed down at the heartstone in her hands and nodded. 'I can restore it, but what do you intend to do with the Humanitron?'

Kate looked across the laboratory and saw the falcon's eyes staring straight at her.

When no one replied, Carter pressed them. 'Surely we should destroy the Humanitron, rather than make it work?'

They told her about the missing keystone and how Lorabeth Lampton was trying to find it. Kate thought of her dad and what he had been through and the danger he would be in if Lorabeth Lampton made him remember.

'I want you to fix the Humanitron and transform me with that falcon over there,' Kate said, shuddering involuntarily as she felt the yellow eyes boring into her skull. 'If Lorabeth Lampton gets her hands on the lost keystone first, we will never be able to stop her.'

Carter frowned as she considered Kate's proposal. Her

small nose wrinkled below her glasses and she scratched the side of her head with a delicate finger. At last she passed the heartstone to Kate and bent down to remove the drawer from the base of the Humanitron.

'OK,' she said, 'let's get to work.'

Carter glanced over to a stack of shelves in a corner and asked them to fetch bottles of chemicals, a box of tools and a roll of copper wire. Phil went to collect the materials and brought them to the bench where Carter had placed the power pack and was now busy scraping her hair back into a tighter ponytail. Kate passed her Great-Aunt Elizabeth's heartstone.

'Harold originally used a blue chemical in the valves,' Barking said. He had leapt back on to the bench and was now sitting tall beside Carter, who was removing the two small heartstones from their ceramic sockets.

'Harold?' Carter asked, glancing up.

'Harold Baker,' Phil said enthusiastically. 'He is a brilliant scientist and inventor.'

'He made the Humanitron,' Kate said.

'He has the best laboratory,' Phil added.

Carter smiled as she reached for the soldering iron and then cut a length of copper wire. 'I bet he has,' she said.

Behind Fearless, a mound of red earth was growing rapidly in the darkness when, suddenly, his claws scraped painfully against something hard. He scrabbled beneath the fence more gently to establish the extent of the boulder barring his way. He wriggled backwards out of the hole and sneezed the red grit from his encrusted nose, soil clinging to his fur. He glanced along the length of the fence to where two men stood guard over his original tunnel, then up at the sky where he saw the first sign of dawn in the thinning darkness on the horizon. With renewed energy he took several gulps of bracing air and thrust his head back into the hole and began to dig deeper.

Emily Carter placed Great-Aunt Elizabeth's heartstone in the large ceramic socket and attached a wire to the holding.

'OK,' she said, 'that should do it.'

Everyone turned and looked at Kate.

Kate sighed. Her body felt light and flimsy, as if it were made of fabric. The tingling sensation she had felt in her arms when she had first thought of the plan returned. But – and she held her head a little higher as the thought occurred to her – she did not feel afraid. 'I'm ready,' she said, and she walked purposefully towards the left-hand door of the Humanitron.

As Phil went over to the first cage in the row of birds and reached his hand up to slide the bolt, the falcon's head snapped round to stare at him. Wearing a leather gauntlet, Carter approached the cage, pausing at a small clinical fridge. Inside were racks of test tubes and pots of Look Lovely with Lampton cosmetics. She bent down to the bottom drawer and pulled a piece of raw meat out of a plastic bag. Kate grimaced when she saw it. How could she possibly ever want to eat that? Barking sat as still as stone in case his presence proved to be of interest to the bird of prey. He saw the dripping meat in Carter's hand and smacked his lips.

As Phil drew back the bolt and carefully opened the wire door, Carter raised her protected arm in front of her, offering the strip of meat with her other hand. Round the bird's leg was a leather cord and, as it swooped forwards and snatched at the meat, Carter took hold of the cord and held the bird fast, straining under the weight of the magnificent creature. Then, as she moved slowly towards the Humanitron, the falcon opened its wings and gripped at the gauntlet with its claws. The tip of one wing spread across to where Phil stood, a full metre away, while the other extended above and beyond Carter's head like a canopy.

Kate watched them advance towards her and she held her breath. She glanced at Phil's face. He had been watching the bird intently, but now his eyes swung to meet hers. Kate recognized the twinge of terror that curled his lip. The sight of it unnerved her and she looked away. She put her hand against the glass of the revolving door and leant against it. As Carter thrust the bird towards her, Kate felt herself fall against the moving door, and she let out a small cry of alarm. The bird shrieked and she became engulfed in scrabbling claws and frantically beating wings. Kate and the falcon disappeared inside.

Phil rushed forwards and yelled, 'Kate, are you all right?'

They could hear nothing from inside the Humanitron apart from soft gurgling and clicking sounds as chemicals began to flow through the pipes.

Carter dragged off the gauntlet, and she and Barking rushed to the other side of the Humanitron and waited for the door to revolve.

'How long will it take?' Carter asked as she scooped Barking up in her arms. 'Do you have any idea?'

'It may take anything up to half an hour,' Barking replied.

Phil stepped quietly away and slowly moved along the aisle of cages until he stood before the sombre gorilla. The animal sat, slumped forwards against the cage door, so that his slinky black hair hung in hexagonal tufts through the wire. Phil raised his hand to the bolt and whispered softly to the gorilla while staring deeply into the sad, glassy eyes. The bolt was stiff and unyielding and Phil jiggled it up and down, struggling to slide it back. All the time the gorilla was watching him passively. After one determined tug, the bolt suddenly slammed back – and at that moment the piercing sound of an alarm filled the room.

The Transformation

Fearless swore as the alarm klaxon screamed from concealed speakers over his head. He had thrown himself at the door three times before; on the fourth attempt the hinges popped and it caved in. He ran through the first corridor with his nose to the ground, trying to make sense of the smells that greeted him. Kate, Barking, Phil, Great-Aunt E., Charlotte and Michael – all their scents were there and he had to concentrate to decipher which was the most recent and in which direction they had been moving. Suddenly all the scents converged and, as he hurtled towards the next corner, he caught a new and fresh scent in the air. It was a mixture of stale sweat, garlic and tobacco, with a strident top note of pure unadulterated cowardice. Fearless had met this smell before, and after hours of inactivity he relished meeting it again. He took the corner at a spin, his paws flailing wildly on the polished surface of the floor, and came face to face with Frimley, who had just activated the sliding door to the cell.

Frimley and his brother had been sleeping in front of the surveillance cameras when the alarm went off, and

Frimley's eyes were still sticky with sleep. When Bardolph had slapped his head and ordered him to check the prisoners in the cell, he had begun to protest – until he realized that Bardolph was going to check on the laboratory. All those caged animals with their creepy, staring eyes gave him the willies. For once his brother had not given him the short straw. Or so he had thought.

Frimley's head jolted round at the sound of Fearless's approach. Despite the red dirt caked to his wild fur, Frimley immediately recognized the ferocious beast crouching in front of him as if ready to spring. This was the dog what bit his bum.

Inside the cell, Harold and Charlotte began helping Great-Aunt Elizabeth to her feet as Frimley let out a shrill and unearthly scream. Fearless had chosen that moment to pounce and he sailed through the air, placing his large paws high on Frimley's chest. The big man fell sprawling into the room and tried to protect his face with his hands. He continued to shriek and squeal while Fearless pinned him to the floor, baring his teeth terrifyingly close to the man's bulbous and much-broken nose. He growled at the others to leave the room and, with Harold and Charlotte supporting Great-Aunt Elizabeth on either side, the three of them managed to squeeze past Frimley's kicking, thrashing legs.

Once they were outside the cell, Fearless made one last savage snap in Frimley's fear-twisted face before bounding from the room.

Harold's long fingers flew to the control panel and

prised off the casing; yanking wires free, he caused a short circuit and the sliding door closed with a bang.

'Where're Barking and the children?' Fearless asked breathlessly, sniffing around for traces of their scents. Before they had time to answer, his tail was up and wagging, and his nose led him forwards along the corridor.

'They've gone to Lorabeth Lampton's laboratory,' Charlotte said, hurrying after him, while Harold explained about the Humanitron and Kate's plan. Fearless galloped ahead, glancing back occasionally at the slow, lumbering figure of Great-Aunt Elizabeth as she struggled to keep up at the rear.

Bardolph had been in no hurry to get to the laboratory. He knew Mrs Lampton had gone off with Eddie and that brat of a girl's father, and he thought it most likely that the escaped boy had triggered the alarm. He'd never liked children and he thought Mrs Lampton was mad, bringing a kid along. Everyone knew that kids couldn't be trusted and needed to be regularly beaten in order to keep them in check. As he strolled towards the laboratory, Bardolph cursed the wailing siren that blared overhead, and he recollected some of the thrashings he'd given Eddie when he was a boy. Twenty lashes with a leather belt had never done Eddie any harm.

As soon as he had punched in the code and the laboratory door had begun to move, he heard the commotion within and regretted not having Frimley with him. The sound that met his ears, a great cacophony of barks, mews, growls and squawks, made him recoil in alarm. It took a second for his mind to register the passing flash of fur and flit of wings. How the animals had escaped he had no idea, but the last thing he wanted was to be chasing them up and down corridors. He stepped quickly inside and closed the door behind him.

Running around on the floor were puppies, rabbits and guinea pigs, while, overhead, birds flew up and down the length of the room. All the cage doors had been flung open and, swinging from the doors or hanging from the sides, jibbering monkeys began jumping from cage to cage across the laboratory.

Suddenly, Bardolph caught sight of Emily Carter with a large black cat in her arms. Oddly, she appeared to be totally relaxed, as if she were casually waiting at a bus stop.

'What's going on,' Bardolph yelled. 'How did all this lot get out?'

Then, out of the corner of his eye, Bardolph saw Phil crouching down beside one of the lowest cages, undoing the bolt in order to release a large, flop-eared rabbit.

'Oi! Stop that!' Bardolph shouted, lurching forwards into a strained half-run, which was as much as his tight trousers would permit. Phil quickly darted round the back of the row of cages and made his way towards the front of the laboratory, where Carter and Barking were waiting for the transformation to be complete.

Bardolph turned awkwardly and struggled back towards the Humanitron, kicking out at any animal that got in his way. As he faced the Humanitron, he saw, through the thick curved glass of the revolving door, a shape moving within. He glanced at Carter and saw that the boy was now standing beside her.

'What you up to?' he growled at Carter. 'Mrs Lampton know you've got someone in there?' Going over to the Humanitron, he raised his fist and landed a powerful punch on the side panel.

Phil's first reaction when Bardolph made to grab him had been to run to Carter and Barking, but now he lost all sense of his own safety and rushed forwards, his face flushed with anger. 'Don't do that!' Phil shouted. Bardolph had moved to the revolving door at the entrance to the Humanitron and was pushing against the glass. Phil saw it straining as if it might give any moment.

'Hey, you in there, come out!' Bardolph shouted, hammering on the glass with his enormous fist. Peering round the Humanitron towards Carter, he berated her, 'You're gonna cop it, missy – look at all this mess!'

Phil reached Bardolph and grabbed at his sleeve, but the big man swung his arm violently and sent him sliding across the floor, where he lay next to a startled, panting rabbit. Bardolph banged on the Humanitron with both fists and Phil looked anxiously over at Carter and Barking. Carter was looking at her watch then back at the Humanitron, while Barking had jumped down from her arms and was circling round her legs impatiently. Carter glanced at Phil and he saw her eyes widen and her mouth open as if she were about to call out.

Phil turned round and saw what Carter had seen. Leaning forwards on far-apart knuckles, the silver-backed gorilla was moving slowly towards Bardolph.

'Who's in there?' Bardolph shouted, giving the door a hefty kick with his right leg. This time the door revolved thirty centimetres forwards and Bardolph forced his arm into the gap. Behind him, the gorilla rocked to and fro on his powerful arms. Bardolph was leaning into the Humanitron, one arm inside, straining to catch hold of whoever was in there.

'When I get hold of you, I'll –' he began to shout, but he got no further. After slowly leaning back on his haunches, the gorilla suddenly sprang at Bardolph and landed squarely on his back.

For a moment Bardolph's body was flattened against the curved door, his face squashed against the glass. The flesh of his jowls almost met in front of his broad nose. From his position, crouching on the floor, Phil heard a loud rasping sound as the air was forced from Bardolph's body and a series of sharp reports signalled his ribs cracking on impact. The gorilla, his stocky legs wrapped round the man's body, began drumming his fists on Bardolph's head. Suddenly there was a new cracking sound as the Humanitron door began to give way once more.

Phil leapt to his feet and rushed forwards. He flung his arms round the gorilla's waist, locked his fingers into the animal's fur, and tried to drag him off. Phil closed his eyes and pulled as hard as he could, while inside his head he had dreadful visions of what might happen to Kate if the transformation were interrupted: Kate with claws instead of hands . . . a gigantic falcon's head on Kate's body.

Behind him, the laboratory doors opened and Phil craned his head round to see Fearless and Harold – who was holding the short-circuited door control panel in his hand. They were closely followed by Charlotte and a panting Great-Aunt Elizabeth.

Phil felt the gorilla relax his hold on Bardolph, so he allowed himself to slide off the animal's back and into his mother's arms. Great-Aunt Elizabeth placed a large hand gently on the gorilla's shoulder and he turned his broad, flat face towards her. His black eyes gazed at Great-Aunt Elizabeth for a moment, then he looked beyond her through the open doors. The animal released his grip on Bardolph and hit the floor with a thud, before lumbering slowly round Great-Aunt Elizabeth and out of the laboratory.

For several moments Bardolph remained fixed to the Humanitron as a squashed fly will stay on a window, but slowly his body began to respond to gravity and he slid down the glass to the floor, where he lay, unconscious, his right arm still inside the revolving door and twisted awkwardly above his head.

'Who are all you people?' Emily Carter asked, staring around at them, her eyes at last settling on Harold, who had been trying to peer down the side of Bardolph's trapped arm and see inside the Humanitron.

As puppies, kittens and monkeys began to scamper out

through the open door, Phil pushed himself away from his mother and grabbed her and Harold by their arms and dragged them across the laboratory to meet Carter. Great-Aunt Elizabeth followed slowly, but planted herself wearily on a nearby bench and sighed deeply.

'Is Kate . . .?' Charlotte murmured, nodding her head towards the Humanitron.

'How long?' Harold asked.

Emily Carter looked at her watch before replying. 'Seventeen minutes and twenty-eight seconds.'

As she spoke, a soft hiss emanated from the Humanitron and the revolving door began to turn, emitting a shaft of bright light. After turning through one hundred and eighty degrees, the door stopped moving and the gathered party squinted into the open space. Several seconds passed before they were able to identify the silhouette of the falcon as it stepped forwards and cawed softly.

Charlotte went down on her knees and whispered, 'Kate?'

The bird opened its wings and made four flying leaps towards them, before alighting in front of Charlotte.

The beak opened and they watched as a pale pink tongue flicked forwards and the yellow eyes darted from face to face. The beak opened once more, and this time several soft guttural caws escaped before, at last, strangled and croaky yet clearly audible, the words 'Hi, Mum' were heard and they saw a heartstone glowing amid the ruffled feathers on the falcon's neck.

The Race Begins

Beyond the damaged doors where Fearless had forced his way in earlier, Kate could see the pale green and violet of a desert dawn. She fixed her sight on the space above the heads of the two guards, who stood with their backs to her. She opened her wings and the weight of them forced her forwards. In a few scrabbling strides, while she instinctively pulled and raised her great wings, she rose from the ground and flew towards the guards and freedom. Hearing her powerful wing-beat, the guards turned sharply and both ducked as her talons skimmed over their heads.

In the confined space of the corridors Kate had found flying cumbersome and awkward. But, in the three wing-beats it took Kate to shoot from the building and up into the Nevada sky, she experienced a hitherto unfelt sense of joy. She pulled her wings downwards and soared higher and higher. The air rushing past her body felt wonderful, and she opened her beak and screeched. She looked down at the building as it decreased in size below, circling the laboratory until she felt the sun on her right wing tip. Ahead of her lay New York, and she set her sights on a distant mountain range and pulled her wings through the air; after several beats she soon settled into a rhythm.

As she flew, Kate watched the shadows beneath her begin their retreat. Her attention was drawn to movement, and she quickly spotted lone trucks on the distant roads that traversed the terrain, and the dust balls that rose from the heels of a sprinting coyote. After several hours of the sun on her back, Kate felt a dryness grip her throat and descended towards a wide river that meandered slowly across the flood plain in the valley below. She leant forwards, folded back her wings and plummeted down towards the welcome water. She watched confidently as her horizon shortened and the ground rushed up to meet her. Fifteen metres above the river, she pulled back from her dive and opened her wings wide to slow down her approach. She skimmed across the surface of the river and lowered her talons, dragging them through the water and snapping at the spray with her beak. Refreshed, she raised her head and climbed again, continuously beating her wings as she drove upwards. She banked right towards another range of mountains and soared up through the low cloud that hung there. Wisps of white mist curled about her body until suddenly she was completely engulfed in dense, white cloud. For a moment, Kate felt a chill in her heart and beat her wings with renewed vigour. Then she broke through the cloud and was soaring once more in brilliant sunshine. Beneath her lay the rumpled surface of the cloud like a carpet of snow.

Emily Carter took the restored heartstone from the Humanitron while Great-Aunt Elizabeth slouched against the bench and watched, the dark circles beneath her dull eyes fading to yellow on her wax-like cheeks. As soon as Charlotte had placed it round her neck and resealed it, the heartstone flared with a powerful glow of energy, and colour and vitality immediately flooded into Great-Aunt Elizabeth's face. After five minutes, she dug two choco-lates out of her pocket and ate them in quick succession. Within ten minutes she was pacing the room, and by fifteen she was bossing Harold about, as he and Emily dismantled the main components of the Humanitron.

'Snail's teeth, Harold! There's two of you now, can't you do it any quicker?'

Once the vital components were stripped from the Humanitron, Fearless managed to drag Bardolph away to a corner of the laboratory, where Phil and Charlotte bound his ankles with his own shoelaces. Fearless and Great-Aunt Elizabeth led the way out into the corridor, followed by Charlotte and by Phil, who had slung Kate's rucksack across his back and who held the Insult Fermenter at the ready. With the others following behind, they made their way out of the building, dealing easily with any security guards who got in their way.

They arrived at the sidecar and stood between it and the perimeter fence so that anyone looking their way would see the deceptive location reflector behind which they were invisible. While Harold loaded the dismantled parts of the Humanitron, Emily peered into the sidecar and fired questions at him about interior expansion.

Great-Aunt Elizabeth placed a hand on Emily's arm. 'I must thank you, my dear, for helping us, but you must understand that you will have to come with us now; when my sister knows what you have done, she will kill you.'

Behind her glasses Emily's eyes looked frightened, but she nodded and managed a small smile at Great-Aunt Elizabeth. 'Thank you – I want to come with you. Harold tells me that he is going to reverse the Humanitron so that we can change Kate back – I'd like to help him do that, if I may.'

Beside her Harold nodded enthusiastically and grinned.

'Do we have enough fuel to run the super turbo-boost, Harold?' Great-Aunt Elizabeth asked.

'The two reserve tanks are full,' he replied.

'Right then, quick as you can, Harold!' Great-Aunt Elizabeth cried, and she slapped him hard on the back. 'Let's get this sidecar back over the fence and drive hell for leather after Kate.'

29

The Flight of the Falcon

Kate flew uptown towards 42nd Street, scanning the heads of shoppers and commuters. She swerved in order to cast her eye along Park Avenue and dipped her head and shoulders to plunge some twenty metres through the sky, and finally she swooped down to alight on the main entrance to Grand Central Station. Across the roof of the entrance a beautiful fifteen-metre-high pediment cradled an enormous clock. Kate was examining the statue of Hercules while two fidgety pigeons eyed her suspiciously, when she happened to glance down at the street, and suddenly she saw them.

Eddie was standing close to her dad, one hand on his shoulder as if guiding a blind man. Lorabeth Lampton, her head held high and haughty, walked behind them, oblivious to the people who turned to look at her as she passed.

Kate stepped forwards from her ledge, opening her wings as she fell, and flew in a wide circle until she noticed a woman gazing upwards and pointing. Lifting her head and drawing the air beneath her wings in three mighty beats, Kate rose and took cover, just as her father and his captors stepped inside Grand Central Terminal. She did not want to attract the attention of New York's ornithologists, but nor could she afford to lose sight of her dad. Kate spread her wings and then, tipping them to get just the right balance of air resistance and upthrust, she glided effortlessly into the station, where she perched on a window ledge and kept still, concentrating on being insignificant. She could see them striding across the concourse towards the information booth and the large square brass clock that hung above it.

Suddenly her dad glanced up and back. For the briefest of moments Kate felt him staring straight at her. Her heart jumped and she was thrown into confusion. She was her old self once again, the human Kate who wanted badly to be in her father's arms and away from all this. Her claws scratched against the stone tile of the ledge and she opened her wings involuntarily, suddenly as fearful of falling as she had always been. Had he seen her? Kate did not think so, but he had definitely looked her way and, as she gathered her wits and composed her ruffled feathers, she began to think more clearly about where her father could have hidden the keystone. He, too, had been a falcon and, like her, he would have had access to high and hidden places. She began to look around for likely niches. She sat still on her ledge, her head cocked to one side, and watched the three figures below standing by the information booth while around them commuters criss-crossed the station. Kate watched her dad closely. As he talked, his head tipped up and he shot a glance at the wide, curving arches of the ceiling. Was he giving her clues? Where was it likely to be? She followed his furtive glances upwards and scanned the ceiling space around her. Suddenly Kate remembered her dad's words. She could hear him as clearly as if he were whispering in her ear that very second: 'winged messenger'.

Her heart beating, Kate fell from the ledge and opened her wings. As she swooped in front of the first vast window in the concourse, she glided through a beam of dusty light and projected the shadow of a giant bird on the floor below. Everyone in the station looked up, and Kate saw the upturned faces of Lorabeth Lampton, Eddie and her dad. She lowered her head and aimed for the 42nd Street exit.

She soared out and up into the clear afternoon sky. She circled past the imposing glass tower of the adjacent building, catching sight of her reflection as it jumped from window to window. Beams of sunshine glanced off the brass clock above the entrance to Grand Central Terminal as Kate aimed for the enormous statue that crowned the great doorway. She stretched her feet forwards and landed on the shoulder of Hercules. Kate followed the gaze of the god's stone statue up to where Mercury, the messenger of the gods, stood poised above the clock face. Behind him, a gigantic stone bird of prey crouched, wings open, his proud head peering protectively from behind Mercury's chiselled knee.

Kate felt her heartstone glow as a breeze disturbed her neck feathers. She leapt skywards and landed on the stone bird's back. And then she saw it, nestled in the dip where the statue's wings met: in a shady crevasse beneath the god's billowing cloak lay a large black heartstone. Kate leant forwards and felt the air pushing against her opening wings. She reached out with both talons and plucked the keystone from the resting place where it had remained hidden for twenty years, guarded by Mercury, the winged messenger.

Beneath her, on the pavement, Lorabeth Lampton pointed up with a long arm while her other hand shook Eddie's shoulder. Eddie reached inside his jacket and took out a gun. Kate saw light flash from the silver barrel of the gun as she swooped down towards the street. She saw the alarm in her dad's face as Michael shouted her name, then she heard a sharp crack as Eddie took aim and fired at her.

Kate felt the bullet speed through the air beside her head and heard it ricochet off the statue. As she curved in a wide arc and flew down 42nd Street, she feared for her dad's safety and willed him to run away. She wanted to wheel round and go back for him, but she was afraid of losing her grip on the keystone. She could see it beneath her, clasped in her claws, mostly black but now beginning to glow a deep red at its centre. Beyond that, in the street below, she saw people running in various directions and heard sirens wailing across the city. Kate saw the trees of Central Park ahead of her and adjusted her path slightly, aiming for Great-Aunt Elizabeth's house.

Kate had just crossed Park Avenue when she saw the

Harley-Davidson and sidecar speeding towards her along the middle of the street. It was filthy, spattered with red dust and grime. Great-Aunt Elizabeth lay flat along the tank, her elbows sticking out as she held the throttle wide open. Her chin and nose were thrust forwards and extended well beyond the silver-rimmed headlight.

Kate opened her beak and flew screaming towards the bike. Behind Great-Aunt Elizabeth three motorcycle cops were weaving in pursuit through the heavy traffic.

Great-Aunt Elizabeth glanced up as Kate plunged out of the sky towards them. She turned her face to the passengers in the sidecar and pointed at the sky.

Just as Kate was about to draw level with the Harley, the dome slid open. Kate's falcon eye took aim and she opened her talons and released the keystone. Relieved of its weight, she rose up into the sky, while the keystone fell ten metres and landed in Phil's lap.

The Owner of the Keystone

The copper beech tree was waving in the wind when Kate landed on it. She clasped the narrow branch in her talons as it gave beneath her weight and plunged her down into the heart of the tree before restoring her, gently bobbing, to the top. Kate felt dizzy and her heart was beating so hard she could feel it banging against her ribs. The starlings that had been resident in the tree when she arrived, had flown in tight formation to a neighbouring tree and were now murmuring fearfully. Kate raised her head and eyed the sun. She took a couple of slow breaths then left the branch and flew gracefully back towards Grand Central Station in search of her father.

Kate glided above Park Avenue, where the traffic stood still, the sound of impatient car horns filling the air. Up ahead, the police had cordoned off the area immediately in front of Grand Central Station, and traffic was being diverted away from 42nd Street. Kate perched opposite the station entrance, in time to see two policemen guide a handcuffed Eddie into the back of a police car. Her eyes scanned the people down below, carefully scrutinizing each head, tracing a pattern that criss-crossed the scene.

At last she took flight and flew in widening circles as she gradually climbed higher. It was reassuring to see Eddie arrested, but losing sight of her dad and Lorabeth Lampton was deeply worrying. Then she remembered the last glimpse she had had of Great-Aunt Elizabeth, deftly steering the Harley at full speed through the narrowest of gaps. Great-Aunt Elizabeth was clearly her old self again, and she would know what to do. Kate banked and made her way back to the Central Park house.

Barking and Fearless had been sitting on the step outside the house, watching the sky. Fearless stood, his long tail wagging in slow sweeps, as Kate descended over the tops of the trees. She landed beside them and they moved closer to her, walking round her, brushing themselves gently against her feathers.

'Well done, Kate,' Barking said. 'That was fantastic.'

They moved inside the house and Kate's claws scraped and slid on the tiled floor. Her wings felt heavy and her tail dragged behind her. She felt awkward and clumsy; her body was not designed for walking. She was a flying machine and her powerful legs equipped her to drag prey from the ground.

As Charlotte came forwards to greet her, Kate realized that she was tired. She closed her eyes as her mother stroked her head.

'I am so proud of you!' Charlotte murmured into the feathers.

'I looked for Dad, but I couldn't find him,' Kate said in her soft, cawing voice.

'Don't worry. Now that you're here, Fearless will go and track him down,' Charlotte replied and then, as Kate began to sink down and her feathers puffed out, she added, 'Come up to your room, everyone's up there.'

Kate flew up the staircase and waited on the landing for Charlotte to catch up. In her room she saw Phil sitting by her pool, trailing his feet in the sparkling water. He jumped to his feet with a splash and punched the air with a whooping shout as she flew past him to land in the apple tree above her bed.

'Well done, well done, dear Kate!' Great-Aunt Elizabeth cried, reaching a hand up into the tree and holding up a chocolate. When Kate tilted her head to one side and then shook it, she popped it into her own mouth.

'Now I must go down to my desk and get the law enforcement agencies out to Lampton Laboratories World Wide. Emily has given us the plans of the ozone extractors and the magma drills, so we can get people out dismantling them – oh! and I'll get animal welfare out to Nevada to care for all those poor creatures.'

Kate watched Great-Aunt Elizabeth leave the room and saw that she was indeed fully recovered. She walked tall and looked strong now, and her face once again shone with light and energy.

Phil came over to the bed and stared up into the tree at Kate. She was nearly a metre tall; her legs were brilliant white and looked soft but ended in thick black tendons and razor-like claws. Phil peered closer to examine how her head feathers hung down in layers over her neck so that she appeared to be wearing a helmet. Narrowing his eyes, he continued to scrutinize her, wondering at the number of different colours in each feather. At first glance they were brown in appearance, but closer inspection showed they were in fact made up of tiny fragments of gold, orange and black.

'Will you stop staring at me like that – you're giving me the creeps.' The voice was metallic and came from the falcon's beak, but it was unmistakably Kate who spoke.

Phil grinned.

In the corner, Harold and Emily were busy converting Kate's Dried-and-dressed into a Humanitron. Emily waved at her and Harold called over, 'We shan't be long, Kate. We'll have the old you back in no time.'

The scent of apple blossom filled the room as Kate finally closed her eyes and fell into a deep sleep.

She awoke to see Great-Aunt Elizabeth's arms reaching out to her. 'We're ready for you now, dear,' she said.

Kate blinked across at her Dried-and-dressed. Several extra cables ran from it to a circuit board, at the centre of which the large keystone was fixed. Emily stood beside it, adding drops of blue liquid to a vial. Harold was typing at the keyboard where once Kate would have requested a T-shirt. He smiled up at her expectantly.

Kate flew over Great-Aunt Elizabeth's head and landed beside the revolving door. She turned her head and looked at each of them in turn before walking slowly forwards.

Twenty minutes passed slowly as they waited quietly for the makeshift Humanitron to make the transformation. Phil stood beside Charlotte and held her hand as he sucked on the chocolate Great-Aunt Elizabeth had unwrapped and popped into his mouth.

The keystone glowed a brilliant red and the vial of blue liquid bubbled gently and gradually evaporated. A soft hum came from inside the machine, and at last the revolving door began to turn. A bright light filled the room and turned the water of Kate's pool to a lake of shimmering gold. They all held their breath and stared at the opening door, straining to see into the glare. Gradually they made out a shadow moving towards them, and then they recognized Kate standing before them. She held her left arm out at her side and on it perched the falcon. As Kate grinned at them and moved forwards, the bird rose up and flew to the tree, where it began preening its feathers.

Kate ran to Charlotte and Phil, and clung to them both as the room filled with cheers and shouts. Harold rushed over to Emily and, lifting her off her feet, spun her round and round.

Kate stretched her arms and looked at her hands while she wriggled her fingers. She arched her back and could feel the ghost of her wings as she scrunched and rolled her shoulders.

'How do you feel?' Charlotte asked as she kissed her daughter's head.

'I'm fine,' she replied, then she let out a joyous squeal as she caught sight of two shadows stepping into the doorway of her room. 'Dad!'

Kate and Phil peeled themselves away from Charlotte and ran to Michael. Panting hard and grinning broadly, Fearless trotted happily into the room.

While the falcon flapped his wings and screeched overhead, Kate went round the room hugging everyone in turn. Barking curled his sleek black body round their legs until Michael stooped down and picked him up.

'So, Billy,' he said, 'are you going to change back too?'

The room fell quiet and everyone looked at Michael and Barking, who was rubbing his chin against Michael's chest.

'When did you find out?' Charlotte asked, moving to her husband and placing a hand on his arm.

'Things started coming back to me at the motel. I could see how difficult it was for you – I knew you were trying to protect me.' Michael allowed Barking to spill to the floor as he hugged Charlotte. 'You had said that my brothers had altered beyond all recognition, and when we got to the laboratory and I met those Bardolph and Frimley characters I thought it was going to be them.' He grimaced and shook his head. 'After meeting those two, discovering your brothers are a cat and a dog is one hell of a relief, I can tell you.'

Charlotte sighed as Michael moved away from her. No

325

more secrets, lies and half-truths. Michael had remembered everything, and he was safe. What's more, he had survived another encounter with her despicable mother.

Michael stooped down to ruffle Fearless's ears. 'Well, Frank, how about it? Are you going to change back? Is it possible, Harold?'

Everyone turned to look at Harold, who shot a questioning glance at Emily.

'We should be able to do it, with some more adjustments. A lot of time has passed since they were transformed.'

Barking jumped up on to Kate's bed. 'After all these years I think I'm too much of a cat to change back,' he said.

Fearless nodded. 'I think I'd miss chasing rabbits too much.'

'You could still chase rabbits,' Phil said happily. 'I'd help you.'

'As a twenty-nine-year-old man I think I might look a bit ridiculous chasing rabbits!' Fearless retorted.

Great-Aunt Elizabeth walked over to the Dried-and-dressed and removed the cable from the keystone. 'In that case,' she said, 'we won't be needing this any more.' She picked up the keystone and walked over to Phil and placed it in his hands. 'Here you are, my lad. This is your rightful inheritance.'

Phil gazed down at the keystone and watched as it began to glow in his hands. He felt the warmth from it spread through his fingers and tingle up his arms.

As Kate watched Phil, she felt her own heartstone glow at her throat and she recognized a nagging worry that was pushing to gain prominence in her thoughts. 'What about Lorabeth Lampton?' she asked, looking from Great-Aunt Elizabeth to her dad.

Michael shrugged. 'I don't know. There was a lot of confusion after the gun went off. One minute she was holding my arm like she was trying to snap the bone, next moment she had gone. Slipped off into the crowd, I guess.'

As Great-Aunt Elizabeth nodded she began pacing the room. 'We'll not see her for a while, I'll warrant. It is just like her to disappear. She'll be planning her comeback, though – you mark my words.'

Great-Aunt Elizabeth went over to where Phil was still staring into the keystone. It was glowing brightly now and Phil's face and his white T-shirt had a soft, red hue. He appeared to be oblivious to everyone in the room. To Kate and his parents it was the familiar sight of Phil lost in one of his daydreams.

'It is your turn to fulfil the legacy of the heartstones, Phil,' Great-Aunt Elizabeth said as she touched his shoulder. 'Like Kate, you will discover how your heartstone can extend your potential. Like Kate, you must learn to trust your instincts and let the keystone guide you.'

'What were you daydreaming about, Phil?' Kate asked.

Phil frowned down at his glowing heartstone. As he had watched the power surge through the keystone and felt the energy flow through his body, the voices in the room had faded in his ears.

At first there appeared to be nothing but blackness, until he became aware of stars twinkling around him. In the distance he could just make out the peaks of a mountain range against the night sky. He was overwhelmed by a feeling that there was a presence in the darkness and he watched as the incomprehensible sight of hundreds of children filed towards him on the mountain path. At the front of the line of children, as if leading them, Phil saw a wizened old woman. She was dressed completely in black and in her bony arms she carried a baby.

Phil bit his lip as the image faded from his mind and he became aware of everyone in the room staring at him.

'What did you see?' Great-Aunt Elizabeth asked. 'It could be important.'

Phil hesitated, before smiling weakly. He had made too many mistakes in the past, and now it was time to be cautious. Just because he saw things that appeared convincingly real to him, it did not necessarily mean that they were. What about Dr Sprake's boarding school? He had had his heartstone for less than five minutes and, like Kate, he would need time to understand what it was capable of. He smiled round the room, and as he did so his stomach rumbled loudly.

'I saw all of us sitting at King Arthur's Round Table while plates of chicken and roast potatoes came flying towards us on tiny silver train tracks.'

328

'You saw *what*?' Michael laughed.

'Come on, Dad, we'll show you!' Kate said, taking her father's hand and pulling him towards the door. To her brother she added, 'Nice one, Phil, I'm starving.'

As they descended noisily towards Great-Aunt Elizabeth's kitchen, Kate turned at the door and looked back to where the falcon was tearing blossom from her tree. She lingered there a moment or two, before racing off to join the others.

Afterword

The real Great-Aunt Elizabeth lived in Pittsburgh, Pennsylvania, nearly a century ago. I only know about her because her great-niece is a friend of mine. In March 1998, Annie (Baker) Graham and I met to discuss plans for a picture book that I would write and she would illustrate. Annie suggested that perhaps her Great-Aunt Elizabeth would be a good subject. For years, Annie has been entertaining her family – her sister Charlotte, brother Harold and nephew Phil(bert) – with her stories and drawings of Great-Aunt Elizabeth. So, I started writing, and Great-Aunt Elizabeth soon began to assert herself and she quickly grew too big for the short story we had planned.

The real Great-Aunt Elizabeth was a formidable and intrepid woman too; her husband was an eminent doctor, and if she thought her house guests were ailing she would follow up her unqualified diagnosis with a rummage through his medical bag, prescribing and administering whatever took her fancy. She had five white Scottie dogs that accompanied her everywhere, leashed together on a five-pronged lead. She was once asked to leave a train because she was mistaken for the animal trainer from the visiting circus and was accused of travelling without the proper papers. She was outraged by this and by the subsequent scandal – prompted by allegations in the press – that she, a pillar of the community, had shot and eaten venison out of season.

In real life, Annie's brother (Harry Baker), an accomplished electro-mechanical engineer, continues to conduct experiments to further his understanding of electricity. In particular, he feeds his fascination with the peculiarities of bolt, ball and bead lightning. His basement location in rural Pennsylvania is best kept a secret.

I would like to be able to tell you that Lorabeth Lampton is a figment of my imagination, but I am trying to keep on her good side. Oh, and I am sure you will be pleased to know that Fearless is alive and well and living in Wimbledon.

Acknowledgements

I am happily and gratefully indebted to my friend and mentor Damian Kelleher and to Helen Boyle at b3.

For their kind interest, advice, practical help and enthusiasm I wish to thank the following: Mary Gibson and my colleagues at Yerbury Primary School, the pupils of Yerbury, and specifically my Year Six classes. Also, Ruth and Anna Broadbent; Susan Everett; Anna Fairbank; Lyn Gander; Rebecca Kogan; Jack Pitkeathley; Kate Poynton; Leah Schmidt; Timothy Sowula and Helen Wright.

I am grateful to Ginny Clee for her friendship and her twenty-year conviction that I should write a book. You can stop nagging now, Gin.

Finally, I would like to thank everyone at Puffin, and especially my editor, Pippa Le Quesne.